The Last Judgment
Robert Steiner

Spuyten Duyvil

New York City

Library of Congress Cataloging-in-Publication Data

Names: Steiner, Robert, 1948- author.
Title: The last judgment / Robert Steiner.
Description: New York City : Spuyten Duyvil, 2023.
Identifiers: LCCN 2023029199 | ISBN 9781959556671 (paperback)
Subjects: LCSH: Lincoln, Abraham, 1809-1865--Assassination--Fiction. |
  United States--History--Civil War, 1861-1865--Fiction. |
  Presidents--United States--Fiction. | LCGFT: Historical fiction.
Classification: LCC PS3569.T376 L37 2023 | DDC 813/.54--dc23/
eng/20230816
LC record available at https://lccn.loc.gov/2023029199

***The Last Judgment* is a dark vision**, an apocalyptic fever dream, a panorama of chiaroscuro lit by the torched South at the end of the Civil War. In this, his final novel, Steiner recounts the aftermath of Lincoln's assassination and the defeat of the South in a style that is Proustian in detail, Jamesian in stateliness, and Faulknerian in its rhythms. It is a remarkable achievement.

    Vincent Czyz

Robert Steiner has given us an extraordinary work: a microscopic and kaleidoscopic vision of Lincoln's assassination, assimilating the dead president to the Biblical Abraham, and the war that surrounded him to the End of Days. This novel combines a marvelous ingenuity of concept with a vatic, thundering style that does the Old Testament prophets proud.

    Madison Smartt Bell

Fierce, blood-stained and breathtaking, *The Last Judgement* is a lamentation on America's original sin of slavery and its attempted expiation in the civil war. Focusing on the dying and unconscious Lincoln, the novel weaves its terrible and stylish magic around questions of guilt, atonement, shame and retribution. No comforting Zen bardo here, this is old testament history, where vengeance is the Lord's and redemption uncertain. This is a darkly brilliant book.

    Jeffrey DeShell

THE LAST JUDGMENT

I struck for my country and that alone
—J.W. Booth in his red notebook.

Then the seven, three of these physicians, the rest soldiers, lifted the figure from the carpet that last night of life while one loosed coagulate from the wound with a finger. Seven among soldiers and physicians carried the dying man down a staircase strewn with lonely corsets and bustiers, then down another of parasols and mushroom hats before a third emptied into the dark dirt street flawed by a day of storms. Along the rut path of mud and dung seven carried him who was gunshot to the head at the back, where the bone behind the left ear bedded it, and where just inside his hairline a hole had opened the size of a child's thumb that a tiny lead ball bore into, crossing the west of his brain to the east of it before resting under the deep soft dark pouch below his right eye, the balcony to the window of his sadness. From the onslaught the unconscious victim in torn shirt and undone trousers now and again groaned as if he were suffering in one or another of his nightmares, or wrestling to wake from it, or wrestling inside of it, one such groan of many he would groan that long hard night of dying whenever the wound's blood congealed to swell his brain against the broken skull. Seven among soldiers and physicians carried him into the cool air under a beclouded sky fragrant with sleeping blossoms, the aroma most almond where the day's rain still dripped from nearby trees. As for stars and a moon, there were none.

In the near distance horses cantered so as to spread the calamity, and to spread rumors of worse to come these same horses, and hundreds more, galloped till there could be heard, so said all, a constant clamor of metal on stone and on brick and on wood hour after hour of darkness lit by gas lamps as yellow as the missing moon and by the torches of a thousand soldiers and civilians roaming streets, alleys and avenues in search of invading rebels. In the farther distance rifles reported all hours of the night as did faint cries of warning and alarm. What with hobnail heels on the boots of soldiers running among dark byways and passages in search of roving killers, so many said, that many claimed to watch enter the city by its bridges and canals till every man expected to kill or to be killed before daylight, none could tell the sound of horse from soldier against cobbles and brick across the city in its deadly ordeal.

Then there is this, brethren, that from the officers' ball there gathered in the streets hundreds of men and women to serenade their leader, singing as they walked down one avenue to this and that street till these voices became a thousand before the theatre to celebrate the victory not only over rebel states, but over slavery and war itself, singing hymns their leader abominated, but soon these same thousand wept and prayed before the rooming house across the street where the victim, now and forever the victim, lay dying in his coma. One desolate and riddled by fate, whose hopes died before he died, mute and deaf at the horizon between dying and death, who knew thereby *what it is to live and to be dead*—this the murder victim's prized conviction of his prized aging and doomed King Lear since both of them existed weary of heart and broken day in day out and in dream after dream night after night of the violent end to come, as that violent end the war's leader had at last undergone without knowing he had undergone it. Alive only by his unconscious, dead to his conscious, as had been his poisoned mother and his consumptive true love when they lay dying, on this night in this city of death and despair, he did not know that his dreams of decades on and on foretold his end truly. The victim said of his dreams that till dawn's red rooster dissolved black night into cold gray mist on the other side of his window he dreamt dream after dream of a violent end to him and to his people.

He will lie unconscious for nine hours, brethren, while across the city bonfires light neighbor beside neighbor along street after street to endure the grief and to suffer the terror of imminent death by a raging rapacious defeated army, their last command to burn the capital city as theirs burnt, to rape and to pillage as ancient armies did so as to lay waste to both cultures and histories, and as if by murdering the dying leader smashing to bits for all time the cartouche symbolizing his acts and words. *Now that he dies how long before his name be forgotten?* one of the psalms of David asks that the dying man read daily during the war of atonement. Before yon house cavalry draw swords astride their horses signifying to a crowd that here, look, this is the assassin's hiding place, and down yet another street men aim rifles at an upstairs window where here, look, some claim they saw a man pointing a gun into the air, and yet again swordsmen and riflemen stand guard outside the house where the victim, not yet the murdered man, no, but the unconscious mortally wounded man, will remain to his last breath moments after the break of dawn.

Even before the death black draperies would hang from window sills and porches and doors in sweeping shows of mourning since one after another horseman pronounced the victim dead before he died, as had the victim's wife from their box in the theatre pronounced him—*They have killed my husband!* she shouted again and again before swooning into the arms of her guests, so said most, and by most was taken at her word till others claimed from the orchestra floor, so said many, that he lay dying, not yet dead, but hardly alive, alive in his unconscious only, no longer conscious, instead deep inside dream after dream of his violent end without dawn to dissolve such dreams one after another, and so damned to dream over and over without end till the very idea of *without end* ended. Death would be a blessing after dream over dream of imminent death and the dream of death itself again and again. Weary with fear and woe women and men would cling to each other in damp dark streets who had never before met, touched or spoke, but would come to embrace to weep for their fate and for the fate of the city that had never been peaceful for years and years, and of a sudden it seemed as if the anguish would never end, just as the dying man's anguish might never end since he could dream in one or another dream that he would or would not forever wake, or he could dream or could not dream that death was his only salvation, *anguish* of that ilk.

Such were gathered by that dread and rueful night as encamped soldiers beneath the monument to the first president that stood unfinished for the cost of war of atonement, and then freed slave families gathered to walk dazed and numb the same streets as the dying man walked nightly past bars and brothels, they with their children come before bonfires and preachers to pray and sing spirituals that they sang, but softer, before the dying man unbound them. And listen to this, brethren, never were churches so lit and filled at midnight, and then from midnight till dawn filled with worship and prayer and song, and with sickness too from grief, and

swooning too from the presence of God's will in the fall
of their leader, so many said among many who believed
it so, as if those who knew to see the victim's face as he
passed nightly down the streets past bars and brothels,
or touched his sleeve, or touched his hand as he passed
unguarded as far as a mile from the manse, knew the man
himself who greeted passersby and permitted them to
touch him who asked or did not ask. All of these among
bonfires and bridges and churches draped in black knew
then not the consolation of God's mercy, no, but God's
wrath that cursed the enslavement, as the dying man
addressed it in the war of atonement, speaking again
and again of the curse that only the spilling of blood
could dissolve, only the spilling of blood and only the
blood guilt to follow the spilling of blood, as among
ancients the dying man read day in day out during the
atonement, reading morning after morning of Hebrews
and Greeks who sinned, disobeyed and lay accursed,
and therefore warred to atone by blood and the blood
guilt that ensued.

Neither hundreds nor thousands, but more than
a million atoned by blood that flooded rivers, woods,
fields, meadows, and roads again and again here and
everywhere, there being Shiloh among them, being
Manassas too, and at Gettysburg fifty five thousand
atoned, so we say it to remember, as at Andersonville,
and at Atlanta burnt to atone for Andersonville, and
all venues and tributaries overrun with killing, as hills

and valleys up one side before down the other ran with blood and blood guilt as a consequence, no different to ancient curses older even and more malignant than those known by writing, prayer and sacrifice. When he named the ancient curse bleeding the landscape since before the country began being a country he spoke of it abominating a god he only believed as a god abominating his country for enslavement, whose god and which god where in what book of which language otherwise did not matter in the least. And so, to lesson you, as the seven men carried the unconscious leader from the box in the theatre he groaned his discomfort till Dr. Leale, battle sworn surgeon not yet twenty five years old, but a slicer of limbs and such, scorcher of stumps and such in battle ground tents, again and again retrieved coagulate from the mortal wound behind the victim's ear with his smallest finger. For hours he alone would dissolve coagulate from the mortal wound behind the left ear, with his fingernail gently easing encrusted blood away from the injury over and over when the dying man groaned till he no longer groaned, though yet lived if his breath and heart measured anything at all, living in the deepest of dreams out of which there could be no waking other than death.

Thou hast broken the teeth of the ungodly, broken with a rod of iron—of this psalm the frightful distemper of the dying man's dreams night after night haunted him across the war of atonement till he said again and again that he thought to break the teeth of slavers in his dreams as King David had done of Philistine teeth first in dreams and then by the light of day, breaking teeth wherever whenever till he had burnt Atlanta and won Gettysburg, the bloodiest battle anywhere in the world in the history of it, slaying slavers on the battlefield or hanging them from cottonwood trees even on their properties, as David before him slew every man with foreskin wherever he found such. From sunrise to sunset then blood flowed for years from valley to valley and meadow to meadow, sunrise and sunset being time reckoned by humans to measure blood, death and atonement day in day out since sun and moon fell after rising and rose after falling, the moon of night turning blood black everywhere there was blood, and it was everywhere year after year, and by dawn's light the carnage under the sun lit the ground redder than roses or as brown as bread. Across landscapes as far as the eye could see, vultures and varmints devoured innards and the skins shaping them till blood guilt flooded the mind with despair, the gift by an indwelling god older than time or thinking that thereby cursed the land with misery and mayhem. Where there is war, blood and atonement much is made of gods even by those who believe in none, as the dying leader believed in none but a god of blood and reckoning, as you know, the familiar god of his childhood who brought suffering and sudden death that were the curses of life. *I would wish not to be born,* the dying man said on the day of his election, *or at least to hang myself by that tree yonder,* the dying man said looking to the other side of his office window in the manse on the day he arrived in it for the first time.

Seven men carried the body into the street of a damp beclouded night whether in their arms, on a door or on a bench no one knows, though many lay claim, but most said, and continued to say for decades, that they carried him by their hands and arms, Dr. Leale holding the man's head fast whose eyes could have looked into the sky if he could have looked into the sky. Where this sky began, at the tops of trees, let us say, wind resounded like the faint march of distant armies, so many said, armies invading the city, so many said, borne on a damp night wind in search of dawn's light whereby blood would overrun the banks of this before that river or canal at the scene of battles to come so as to begin war again, and so as to burn the city to the ground as the south had burnt from one city after another in the last year of the war, as a consequence of which blood guilt would ensue as it always ensued wherever blood flowed in the *war of atonement,* as the dying leader named it so that it could not be mistook for any other war, neither of conquest nor of vengeance, no, but to end the curse that could only end by blood and would end only in blood guilt, as you know.

Begin the tragedy.

Street lamps burnt across the ruined city as the seven

carried the dying man limb by limb in their hands and arms, so most said, to the view of a gathered vigilant crowd drawn close and in step as they walked, though none touched the man or any of his bearers, restrained inward by solemnity and shock that quieted them unless some gasped at the sight of Abraham whose torn shirt revealed his chest hair and ribcage while his undone trousers memorialized the hair of his belly and groin. Dr. Leale held the head in his hands so as to retrieve with his fingernail the congealment at the wound whenever the victim groaned, as he did for hours, groaning so that Leale and Leale alone retrieved the coagulate till near dawn he ceased to groan, till instead his shallow breath spoke to the swollen darkened distortion of the right side of his face and head. Street lamps burnt then against the solitude of the gathered despite their gathering, alone each in their vigilance and already mourning though he yet lived, but they remained more mute than not as they watched and memorized, enrapt by inexpressible brooding that silenced them and stilled them though each walked in step with the bearers that began a sleepless night of stupor and dread since death had come for the godless and godly alike. Rain laid waste to the earth the city built on, waste that had begun already to flood the salt causeways and nameless savannahs at all compass points, all desolate waste at all compass points despite street lamps burning and torches smelling acrid from oil, grease and smoke, and bonfires roared across the city that were made from wet tree limbs downed by the day's hard storm—all this from darkness till dawn, brethren, when cold whispers crossed the gloaming that the man had at last passed.

Take watch as the seven almost lose him from their grasp where their boots skid on the muddy boards and so his frailty stiffens before suffering to turn as if he is unconscious from sleep only, who moves to free himself from this or that odious dream of a violent end to him and to his country or to disentangle from linens during such dreams driven by desolation of the spirit, or still worse, brethren, wrestling to shake himself from an irredeemable past of dead mothers, lovers and children— twists and turns of that ilk causing him almost to fall to the mud and dung of the dirt street. Take watch then, that though lamps burnt along the drear street from theatre to rooming house, the night was nothing that night had been before, no, but denser in its darkness, darker in its dangers and black to human eyes when the vigilant who gathered together reached out to it as the body passed or up into the sky of it in search of solace or understanding. Burning lamps drew shadows on walls and sunbursts on windows—specters, so many said, swooping from heaven out of chimney smoke, torch smoke and bonfires crackling in the wind while bats lured by heat, light and motion streaked across the sky.

Then too, take watch of this, that the time night measured seemed not to move either, that the boot steps of the seven across mud and dung measured time as did the silence of the gathered crowd, or by turns in this or that street the song or the prayer measured time that night, as the dancing shadows of lamp light, torches and bonfires from one end of the city to the other did, or the rumpus of horses galloping here before there before everywhere to guard bridges and close gates to the city to the sound of metal hoofs on brick and stone did, and as the night wore to its bone weary end the reports farther and farther distant of rifles fired at this or that imagined rebel during the longest night any of the gathered anywhere in the city had ever known did, and so call these signs and symbols of *the soul in despair* that time measured and what that night measured of time call *death in life.* It was time you could watch like a play on the stage, the slowest time any had ever so far measured, that of human souls too awed by tragedy to fathom it and too vexed by the awe of it, even though each of those gathering to suffer and grieve saw in one after another face the awe inside themselves that they must be wearing on their faces too. For thousands this would be the fathomless tragic awe that did not abate for years and years, if ever, so that whenever torches, bonfires or street lamps shivered in a spring wind warning of rain they stood or sat reminded of that sleepless night and its terror.

Of the wind before midnight there is this, so said most, that it sang across the city like a cry, not only portending another hard storm wherein of the sky nothing hung visible but angry clouds from tidal basin and river inland over marshes and savannahs already overwrought at their banks till canals began to overflow from one street to another while here and there a bridge washed out, leaving behind tales of drowned dogs and pigs and chickens, and this was a crying voice many would hear for years and years, just as the silence to follow frightened them till they heard it too for years and years. Consider the cry, the inward voice thereby, that many hear as they first wake in the morning and the voice of that cry the last sound before sleep as when they wake reminded by it of a recent dead beloved or suddenly cannot sleep at night since a recent dead beloved speaks into their ear in a whisper—such was the wind most remembered, and then such was the silence after, and so many tales regarding each recited for years and years, of floods and bonfires and winds that measured time during the longest night both white and black men and women had ever remembered living, and then from the high silent sky a darkness arrived that all who saw said it had a purpose to serve. Did others die? Others died. Were children born? Children were born, most named for the fallen leader, some by his first name, others by his last, by his first name mostly whites, by his last mostly blacks, but cheerless births, and deaths of less grief than deaths of the night before. Meditate on that, brethren.

The seven who carried him spoke of where to go

since he remained alive and they spoke of covering his face and chest from the gaze of the gathered because it was impossible not to stare so as to remember, and still others who did not carry him spoke of hiding his body under a blanket now that his flesh was as cold as the rain of the day's hard storm and already paler than death, and yet cradling him limb by limb over the mud and dung of the dirt street showed to all who gathered there the brute mystery and pall of the violent end he dreamt again and again night after night for decades. The city suffered such scenes of Friday Christians call Good that among some who watched their minds unhinged and their sleep knew trouble for months and months. The sight of him remained in the memory like sculpture, some said, or that the dying man's body half naked in the raw hands of his bearers reminded them of the dead Christ in the arms of his disciples on the way to his tomb. All who saw recited again and again what they saw to all who only listened that saw none of it, but those who saw nothing recited where they were and what they did among those with whom they did it when they heard of the shooting and went into the streets till they heard of the death from those among the gathered who bore actual witness. By this everyone became characters in the calamity so as to bridge the abyss between themselves and the man who was to die as the last martyr in the war of atonement, as so many said and more than many wrote, even as many below the jagged line of north and south stood or sat persuaded that his killer died the last martyr.

To scourge the godless owners of flesh, bone and muscle of millions of women and men of color, Abraham fought the war of atonement once the godless sought to deliver slavery to the territories west of the Mississippi River, and this not only to enslave millions more of black Africans or Haitians, as Samuel Houston delivered slavery to Texas, but to enslave red women and red men too, ten millions of them, twice therefore the measure of black women and black men in the southern states at that instant already conceived and determined thus for two hundred fifty years as a consequence of which the number since the onslaught of the slave states before they were states in a country that was not yet a country stood uncountable at many more millions than the five million at the onslaught of the war of atonement. *Thou hast rebuked the heathen at the gates of the daughters of Zion,* the dying man often recited in the light and shadow of King David's exhortations. *Thou hast destroyed the wicked and thou hast destroyed cities forever,* the dying man was fond of reminding the godly and ungodly alike as he exhorted the godly to unhorse and annihilate the ungodly. And they did.

Carrying Abraham uncovered to the elements whereby his face and hair misted and knew ash from a night air of torches that lit the way from theatre to rooming house, the seven men struggled with his dying weight so that the depth of their despair made visible the misery of his life that led to this violent dreamt end—that sight too, of the disciples bearing their burden. Some said who carried him that as they carried him he felt in their arms and hands to have been doomed to this moment from his birth, that therefore he spoke of this end often and more often as the war bled the country, atoning on and on day in day out so that he always remarked somewhere during his remarks regarding something else that his end was near, as if he had lived his life to these purposes of shedding the country's blood so that it would know blood guilt to its bones, and that it was his final purpose to atone for the blood that he had caused to be shed. Those among the gathered who saw his naked face and chest and belly, and who could have counted his ribs with their fingers, saw in the sight of him a naked life weary of its sadness, and not only that, but the horror that they would remember of his inward sure and true thought of a violent end to him, and before that violent end they would remember the despair that such thoughts created in him.

The faces of those riven by fear and mourning glowed in the shivering light of street lamps, torches and bonfires across the city that dreadful night, as you know to remember, so that as they lingered, prayed or walked step by step beside their fallen leader their skin changed colors, some to yellow or to orange, though some became red with blood rage while others looked as pale as the dying man, and the faces of freed slaves and their families, or fled slaves and their families, shone like plums or the hide of an eggplant in all these plays of all these lights from one end of the city to the other. As all these citizen mourners gathered or aimlessly walked from avenue to street they saw each other differently in these hard lights in the night that otherwise they did not see by, and so they spoke and heard each other differently too among hushed tones as if the air around and above them, like the earth below them, had translated itself while they watched and walked, becoming of a sudden a choking, austere and savage air, or an air, sky and ground as serious as wilderness or deep dense woods wherein only to know no hope, and to take for granted the utmost worst, as did the unconscious dying victim for years and years, was to know no fear.

Of these multitudes, look, they melt into one another in their grief and outrage and fear among the swaying and slithering lights of lamps, torches and fires in the streets, these *writhing* lights, let us say once and for all, that melted one face into another before yet another in an anguish of such depth and disturbance that it bound each citizen to every other around a desolation of spirit perfect in its purity, an insensate hopelessness almost holy to undergo, to even the blissful face of the tortured man or tortured woman appealing for transcendence to heaven. The despair at watching, listening and reciting the dying man's annihilation, and so to bear witness to the personal apocalypse inside his mortally wounded brain, bound citizen mourners each to each while Abraham traversed the unconscious that he had traversed for decades to overcome his direst thoughts and dreams so as to survive one further day of the world and the worst that the world meant to do that or any other day, never more than during the war of atonement, but before the war too, before everything that he could neither forgive nor forget from childhood on and on again and again.

And as the seven carried the dying man from theatre to rooming house his face too lit under street lamps and torches snapping in the wind so that such images as shadows cast across him became for the hundred who looked and saw their remembrance of him to their dying days, to their dying days bearing witness to his stricken face by lamp light and torch light as the seven carried him hands and arms from limb to limb on his last day having still to live. Beneath these street lamps marking the path and those torches dramatizing the wave of mourners, idlers and stragglers, grief incited dread till dread incited rage that incited cries for revenge whereby, so many said, the mourners could have mobbed up had there been something to burn to the ground nearby or someone to lynch by an oak limb, but since there was not any such place or person near to hand many spoke in bars and brothels of the need to burn every slave state to its last stick of wood and bale of cotton, hanging every slaver from every standing tree till there were none left alive other than black men and women and their babies to whom that scorched earth would therefore belong so as to cleanse and populate as they saw fit.

Those among the slave state dead already, from first day to last day of the war of atonement, deserved their violent ends, so thousands in the city that night said and for weeks and weeks said in thunder in bars and brothels or while carrying torches in the streets on their way to bonfires where men and women ranted and railed against showing the south mercy or pity since it would only rebel again and again for hundreds of years. *Howl, howl, howl! Oh men of stone!* Abraham intoned in the halls of Congress and at the War Department many times, crying as did Lear, from whom his despair drew strength, as it did from Macbeth, as it did from King Priam of Troy, quoting here and there plays, poems and attic oratory to exhort his allies to stiffen their spines and gird their viscera for the godly horror deepening from first salvo at Sumter to the final sword running through the last belly. Know this, brethren, that of the war of bleeding grasses, the war as wide as seas, of graveless war he intoned as always the book of Psalms, King David's exhortations to God to smite his enemies, the sweet singer of Israel who nonetheless slew Leviathan, *breaker of seas and maker of seagrass graves,* so the man not yet dead, yet like as dead as dead gets, intoned again and again to his advisers and to his cabinet, to newspapers and to foreign visitors, addressing the *sonority of ruin* that Whitman sang of, and of the howling emptiness whence he himself came (that too), and where he expected after life to go (there too), and of the just war of atonement that scourged the curse of slavery—all these he would speak of in his grave creaking tenor voice that in this time in this place he would bond together *the crack in everything made of God.*

The procession, brethren, that of hopes turned black, evoked now a dispirit for all who gathered to vigil, so many said, at the hell gate whereby the dead pass to their fate, as if death was the threshold to worse, that being the burden of a last judgment for the godly and ungodly alike, whether burdened to eternal damnation or eternal redemption, the time of that time, the space of those spaces. As for death *qua* death, the dying man feared none of it since he had witnessed it as a boy of nine—his mother's grueling noisome lingering death by poison, and he witnessed the grueling noisome lingering death of his true beloved, then too his young son's death by pneumonia, and then too his young son's death by typhus. Death held no personal dread for him, and yet he could not escape the ancient image of shades departing to the innards of the earth as phantoms with heads hung low at the loss of life and of heaven, shadows shuffling to their fates like prisoners of war chained at the ankles each to each inside the ether of an underworld entered hopeless and estranged among the silent majority of the once living who would suffer forever the memories of old defeats and black woes, murmuring to themselves in the sullen confusion of their deathly existence, of inmost secrets and naked truths.

Hardly shapes at all, yet mindful of their lives and their deaths, let us say they *writhed* in his imagination and dreams, mindful of eternity, of the irredeemable doom of nonexistence—all these the dying man had not dreaded before he lay dying in the hands and arms of the seven who carried him to his deathbed, and this is why he had not feared sending others to their doom since wherever he gazed at all compass points day in day out he saw a violent end for himself and for the country, confessing that the first moment of creation loosed into the world malignant thoughts and the deeds to realize them, and so he intoned in his grave creaking tenor voice to whomever listened wherever they gathered to listen that malign thoughts and their acts ground out death and ill to no purpose, heart or mind or will. In his grave creaking tenor voice he intoned, *Break the arms of the wicked, seek ye wretchedness till thou finds none, that the heathen are perished out of this land!* From therefore the book of Psalms that he daily read during the war of atonement he intoned to all and sundry gathered on the lawn of the manse below the window, *Raise high the horn*—by this to exhort patriots to annihilate the ungodly. And they did.

So said again and again the mortally wounded man

unconscious unto death inside dreams inside dreams and among the nightmares of nightmares thereby since he did not dream to sleep during his life, no, but to wake in a sweat to nausea, headache and a weeping he sensed from someone somewhere in the dark of the room who night after night proved to be himself. And then there is this, asked where he was going in such a fine suit on the day of his wedding he replied, *To hell.* He was never not going to hell, brethren, and so never dreaded dying since eternity was no more hopeful than existence as a consequence of which how he died to get to hell meant to him nothing at all, though he expected gunshot from the hour of his election as a consequence of war and the ravaged minds war left behind. Since he did not die on the instant, but lay carried to his deathbed by loyalists passing under street lamps and torch light before a bewildered silent gathering, he could have felt on his body the arms and hands that held him, and heard voices and deep unrepentant sobbing of strangers, and suffered in his long hours of coma this and that of the vigil bedside that entered or interrupted or reshaped one dream or nightmare into another, and so on over and over till the end of the end just after sunrise, as you know.

Trippers and askers surrounded the body as it crossed the street on its way to the rooming house where a man with a lantern in hand waved all on, congregants by then that Abraham had met or not, from old people and from women and their offspring taken soon out of their mothers' laps, till all who saw him pass saw him cradled by the seven with now and then a darkness of blood under the red roof of his mouth that now and then opened to the wind and droplets of rain from trees overhead under a moonless sky. That night in that pitiable city men and women alike knew one thing of the wreckage before them in spite of the dim sight day in day out year after year throughout their lives. The rolling thunder from marsh and river melted into the ruin filling the universal dread with the threat of nature and of nature's overwrought boom and jar as to why and for whom to what end did such tragedy occur, that another act drawn of the blood curse sweeping the landscape had made of the city a muddy pestilent rat-strewn necropolis in accord with the workings of a god of some ancient alphabet of some desert world.

The first to flee a crowd, drunkards and whores hid in alleys and doorways so as not to shame the tragedy with their existence, spending their dolor in shadows between one structure and another, squeezing together in despair as thick as the death to come, but they made for fearsome shapes when the vigil passed who followed the fallen leader still more terrified to see strangers lurking and ready to pounce. But these among the whores and drunkards of the city already knew how it was to be lost and hopeless, as well as to be inured to violent ends, and so all who passed them there saw eyes burning through the dark and heard sad voices deep and full of experience, knowing more than most the destiny shared with the dying victim whether in bed asleep or by yet another battle in another war, or by poison or consumption, or by pneumonia or typhus, and some by suicide, others by murder in the arms of lovers, and so as the limp unconscious body passed each in their way heard a quiet inward voice remind them that unlike the leader to whom they paid homage and respects for the last time, their lives would leave no trace, few would mourn their loss, let alone honor their memory, since most had done nothing to remember, and most lived forgettable lives unloved, disavowed and ill-used. To their ilk the dying murdered man often remarked in the streets before bars and brothels, *Beshalom,* explaining to them one by one that the word was King David's exhortation to God to give to each man peace. Bars and brothels, brethren.

Driven down to hell, he often recited from old blind Homer, *some god is angry,* he said old blind Homer said, *and with me since mine is an unhappy star good only for weapons of war,* so sang old blind Homer. From old blind Homer he recited that therefore, *Mine is no fruit other than dust.* When his head bowed all heads bowed with it in the street from theatre to rooming house, his black eyebrows bent toward the bridge of his nose, so many said, whether by pain or the twitch of a mindless nerve none knew to say. *Heaven's blood is shed,* he recited from old blind Homer when he read reports from battle at his desk nearby the sword standing in a corner like the soldier it was. And now strife, battle, bloody things, blood feasts still on and on in spite of his cry of *Beshalom* from a window of the manse to the crowd below, and now even after the peace evil followed evil like waves in the sea (that would be sung among the Psalms of King David). To rehearse the long funeral to come and thereby the long slow train homeward across the whole of the way to the middle west, the seven who carried him from theatre to rooming house under clouds of smoke and falling cinders remarked of him to each other that he was their commander by fire and water, and yet made of ice in his veins that ruined his mind and body, and yet now, only near death, did he look skin and bones that barely hung on him. To amaze all who saw it, and to stare at it to remember, Abraham's eyes briefly opened as if watching the sky pass by above him, tree limbs too that leaked rain from their leaves so that when and how his eyes opened those who saw him read there cognizance of his fate in them, as if he suffered a knowledge that here and this is how, where and when his life was to end. Weary of the fight in his flesh and bone, struck to death in the brain, eyes shining and black at the center, he saw nothing, so most said who saw, now and again opening his eyes by a mindless twitch that saw nothing, just as now and again he yawned as he would have yawned in his sleep whenever it was that he slept.

Came next, behind the seven who carried the unconscious leader from theatre to rooming house so as to die in his turn in his time, his wailing wife dressed for a dance, held now from mud and dung of the dirt street by her guests in the box, Henry Rathbone and his betrothed, Clara Harris, the same who was as well his half sister. Clara escorted the future widow from the theatre to the rooming house, wrapping her in her arms because Henry Rathbone had suffered the assassin's dagger that opened his arm from shoulder to elbow till he felt too as if to perish, leaving his blood on the carpet of the presidential box, and across its flags and draperies that overhung the railing to extol the event. The blood was not the dying man's blood, but Rathbone's blood since the dying man's blood had congealed at the small round hole behind his ear on the instant the bullet entered his brain, as you know, and then it was Rathbone's blood too that splattered the staircases down and up till out of the theatre, and his blood then that traced the path to the rooming house across the street, not the murdered man's blood, murdered and not yet dead, but nearly as dead as dead gets, or so Rathbone would recite to his two boys years and years later, narrating the shooting to them, and the stabbing to them, and his agony of the bloody walk whereby he memorized barking dogs and horses groaning against spurs that cracked the hide of their ribs, and he remembered to tell them that carts and carriages rumbled as fast as their wheels spun, and that horses galloped frothing and steaming from one end of the city to the other that damp night in the dread city of his past.

The wailing wife, not yet widow, kept from swooning only by the arms and hands of Clara Harris at her elbows and shoulders, the wife who had prepared with dread for years and years to outlive her husband by decades, an unmoored woman clinging to the sister wife and the sister wife's bleeding fiancé, all surrounded by frightening onlookers and idlers amid cries of murder under street lamps and torch lights that damp timeless night. And look there, in the box inside the theatre, across the blood of the wounded guest and the wounded dying victim, see there the derringer left on the carpet where the killer dropped it, the gun that stung the leader of fire and singer of poems. In the confusion of gun smoke, blood and wailing see there the weapon resting where the killer had dropped it, a souvenir even hours after the seven carrying the dying victim continued to choke on ashes driven by the wind, or so Rathbone would inform his two boys where they lived in Germany, sparing his daughter the gore, narrating to them who were too young to know why he was telling it, that he smelt that night the bitter odor of pitch and torchlight, and heard logs popping in bonfires, and smelt wet leaves stoking the flames that he remembered as he was driven by wagon or carriage or horse (he could not remember) first to home and then to hospital (he could not remember) so as to sew the skin and sinews of his arm back as they had been before that night.

Let us put to sacred seas on black sails over a sleepy, vapory, invisible dark surface, a surface like nothing, or of nothing and for nothing, and so thereby to face a low dense beclouded sky—what Abraham dying saw overhead or would have seen overhead if, when he opened his eyes, now and again, he saw or could have seen anything at all. Held by the hands and arms of the seven among soldiers and physicians, Abraham lay among them as if chained to each at the ankles and wrists arm to arm under the night sky on the rocking ship lapping the sea like bellies in bed, each diapered slave watched the sky for signs of salvation—so the dying man saw overhead when in his dreams he lay enslaved aboard ship, if he saw anything at all other than of his mind. Each diapered slave watched the sky for signs of salvation after a day of unscrupulous rain, each failing sleep, as he failed to sleep on the slave ship in his dream of the slave ship roiling at sea under a beclouded sky of great wind that pitched him and all his brethren from that to this side while going from far to near, far if you were him or any of his brethren, near if you were a citizen of the where that slaves, one after another in the millions, would live until dead, or freed, or both one and the same—*near* of that ilk. The dying leader thereby faced the sky for the final time of his life as the seven men, three physicians, the rest soldiers, carried him in their hands and arms from *there* to *here* where in its time (that would be the gloaming) in that space (that would be on a stranger's bed in a stranger's house) the murder came to an end. Of the ship's cradle, of its endless rocking, of the endlessness of an unforgiving sky, of endlessness as an ancient source of nausea that makes sick those who face it one time only, at death therefore, Abraham would have known only this, if he knew of anything, and that is too much everything in the inmost mind of him: sunsets, love, hate, loss, blood, desecration, and the descriptions thereof too much too, too much of all that issued from the dying man's dying.

The victim lay abed in his killing clothes opened to the begrimed hairy chest, such hair on his head fixed to his scalp and skull not only from blood, but from brain matter leaking onto it. Those in the room did not see so much as behold his barefoot body bedded at an angle for the furniture too short for it, the same room, bed and pillows that all there would later learn had been occupied often by his assassin during afternoon naps, when the bed was not too short, no, or occupied by the assassin and his conspirators, yes, conspiring even the week before in that same space in that house among the exact pillows. The owner's son invited the seven by waving a lantern and calling to them from his porch across the street, a gesture his father abominated, most said, since by inviting death into the house he frightened the boarders who fled in horror, whereupon even the son swore to hearing the ghost of the murdered man creak along the floorboards of the dying room from dead of night till the hour before sunrise for months after. And so he lay dying at an angle across the bed, exposed before physicians and soldiers, none of whom had seen him naked other than Dr. Leale, as you know, but who saw him naked now while seeking wounds and lesions and cuts to him till a coarse blanket came to cover and to warm him where he stretched from corner to corner but for the burly roofs of his feet that overhung the bed till he was dead. Then others entered, officials and surgeons, and then the wife entered unmoored and wailing before she left wailing and unmoored while thereafter the vigil gather began to memorize the face and hands and feet that never stirred in nine hours, though the groaning came and went when the brain pressed more and more against the skull till Leale, and only Leale, so most said, inserted his smallest finger to dislodge the congealment and bring the room to peace.

Observe this, that the dying man calmed his wife often when she wept and wailed for other causes than his murder since she locked herself away in her bedroom, sitting by a window already dressed as a widow, drugged by morphine or laudanum or tea mixed with cocaine, and then Abraham spoke through the door to remind her that she had been made sad by marrying him who was sadder even than she, speaking incessantly of his violent death and that of the country, and so to eat opium on a chaise by a window of the manse he expected of her, her head rigid, her lips barely open to receive the tea, daily tending inward toward her broken heart. No longer the young wife sleeping beside her young husband, but now as the city slept and the country slept, they did not sleep, neither together nor separate since they had become a tragic couple from the death of one child by typhus and the death of one child from pneumonia, and the bloody deaths of war and the blood guilt the bloody deaths of war imposed on them till he foresaw day in day out atonement of another ilk from the war of atonement, foresaw to her the last act of the war of atonement. It troubled his sleep and drove his wife to opium so as to swoon in a chaise in the afternoon of a sunny or rainy or snowy day, which did not matter in the least.

Holding her hand, he would calm his wife on the chaise by assuring her that everything had been set in its place, no less the war of atonement than the honeybee in the flower garden or the sun, whether they saw it or not, and so they were set in their places as they should be, their thoughts and deeds and feelings thought and done and felt as they should be, and that therefore Abraham and Mary had lived in their places as they should, and therefore would die in their places as they should—she by old age's infirmity and the fruit of her coming and going madness, he by violence for which he had prepared decades and decades. As wars have forever been won and lost with the same intention of mind and body among victors and vanquished, so is life lived and lost by the same intentions, he would remind his wife while brushing her hand with his lips, and so we live till life is no longer worth living and death instead is worth dying for among godly and ungodly alike, till even the coward desires one day to die to be rid of his cowardice. These words his wife said she remembered as he lay dying, their suasion for her that he had struggled with his thinking to soothe her for his violent end. *I suspect I shall feel no pain,* he often reminded her. As he continued therefore to die, all who saw him doing it remembered words and gestures and deeds that they had seen and heard before he lay dying, and wherever in the city citizens gathered to hear from horse soldiers or salesmen that he lay dying under a coarse blanket in a rooming house, they told tales of him that Good Friday night, by this already grieving and by this already extolling his life, some among them passing the timeless vigil reciting to each other this and that chance encounter on the street when he walked it near sunset past bars and brothels.

Of the tale telling from one end of the city to another there was this, that each tale and each teller spoke resigned to the world as they found it, to its flux and unfolding, to its relentless reshaping imbued always with the threat of extinction of all, if only even the smallest creature looked into the sky at midnight or at high noon, as it was rumored that Abraham had looked into the sky between theatre and rooming house. His dying long and hard hours gave to these tales of him the urgency to remind both tellers and told that he had been here and now he was leaving and soon he would be gone. So they doted on their memories, though he was not yet dead, no, but mortally wounded and mindless other than unconscious, the only form his remaining alive could assume, unless at an angle abed groaning now and again was another form of life to him. When he neither groaned nor moved he lay placid and needless, beyond desire and dread, so most said, his face more reconciled than any in the room had seen it since none in the room who was not his wife or son Robert had seen it before his first election, and before the war of atonement therefore, after which his face expressed to all who saw it day or night the burden of agonies public and private, those of his sins and the sins of the ungodly he had to sin against. This ravaged face Henry Rathbone remembered to describe to his sons, and that he witnessed soldiers in dress blues with drawn pistols and sabers, or swords and cutlasses that rattled at the quillon and branches in rings and scabbards hour after hour till they rang like bells over and over, just as church bells tolled over and over hour after hour from the darkness that had a reason to be till the grim gray rain stopped the silence that the sky had meant for prayer and sleep.

Abraham recited again and again to all who would listen abhorrent elementals of his dread and terrors, instances of real and imagined wounds and deaths, reading reports of battle when not narrating Trojan ones, comparing one to the other so as to frame the reports from the bloody fields of his own country, and he recited again and again to all who would listen the abominations that cursed his countrymen to violent retribution, atonement by blood and redemption by one or another god of one or another people of one or another language of one or another part of the world, among such recitations from *Psalms* that opened between his hands day in day out, as you know, or if not that book then his yellow copy of *Oedipus Rex* that caused listeners to flee the room, or if not that book of old blind Oedipus dying in the desert shunned by all manner of people then this of Macbeth's bloody hands, or that of King Claudius' rank and foul crimes, or of Richard Three Sticks murder of children and women—all these, and others, he recited to unhinge his audience whenever and where he gathered one that he might cause them to understand history, civil war, books, and the blood lust that nourished them, thereby perforating his listeners' dreams with his own. He spoke of dismembering and disemboweling warriors on Homeric beaches and in Jeffersonian forests so that everyone who heard him fled or fanned their faces or prepared to swoon, and even left alone he went on reading or reciting one gruesome crucible after another, whether of dispatches from battle, punishments inside Dante and Faust, or letters from mothers, wives and sisters did not matter in the least. *God is angry with the wicked every day,* he intoned through doors and walls of the manse whenever he overheard thunder.

Unconscious quieted the room around him, if not the demented part of him that dwelt on death and all its forms. Dying silenced his distemper on the issue of slaughter whereas living only enlivened it so that he again and again warned of mayhem and holy slaughter as the burden of his power that no one could understand as he understood it. He described the gruesomeness and the monsters to all who would listen because he abetted them, letting them loose into the cities and the countryside for year after year. Dying abed in an unconscious mind, that same orator who foresaw violent death and damnation appeared *delivered from the sword,* so the psalm pleaded, *delivered from the power of the dog,* so the psalm pleaded, *and from the lion's mouth delivered.* He lay barefoot and naked under a blanket as if beyond the reach of slaughter and its burdens, while rememberers gathered about the deathbed, and about the rooming house, and about the theatre, and in streets across the city where bonfires and torches burnt and mobs made to rule in bars and brothels. He looked reconciled and moored therefore whereas all gathered everywhere about him inside and outside raged with grief, each citizen seeing in each other raging grief and a dread they felt in their chests and bellies that each saw in each. Under a blanket, the matted hair of his head angled on a small square day pillow, the same pillow, brethren, that his killer had rested his head on one afternoon and then another over and over, from the calm of his expression Abraham might already have been walking the hills of Judea with a beautiful gentle god by his side when the large national flag arrived that would shroud him for the journey from the deathbed to the manse.

And then there was this, that the wailing unmoored wife in a drawing room at the farthest end of the rooming house clung to Clara Harris, half sister and later wife to Henry Rathbone, that same who lay collapsed near death on the floor just inside the door, as unconscious on the floor as the murdered man not yet dead on his deathbed, two unconscious victims of the end of the war of atonement, themselves atoning, if not redeemed by it. Where Rathbone lay bleeding from elbow to shoulder politicians, police, soldiers, and loyalists walked wearing boots that clobbered past the wounded man like horses' hooves in a stable, dozens heading to the second story back bedroom because the other unconscious man's death was to be more a death than Rathbone's death, so Rathbone reminded his sons to remember in their house in Germany years and years later, and to remind their sons in their time in their place that their mother tended the widow from gunshot to the dying man's deathbed till he himself (their father seated before them) lay near death, but less dead than the dying man because he was not meant to die, no, but was meant to be where he alone in all the world saw the world's most infamous killing, which he remembered even in his sleep all these years after, as he remembered laying hands on the assassin only to be ripped from shoulder to elbow by the madman's dagger that had a pearl handle at the end of it. He would roll a sleeve in the firelight to exhibit the proud pink flesh of his scar and the hard purple knot on the shoulder cup.

At the darkest hour of that timeless night rumors spread that other leaders had been murdered, and they had, and that other leaders were about to be murdered, and they were not, since rebellion had or had not begun again, the surrender undone and the war rewritten, and it was not, nor were slave state troops surrounding the city, but in the meanwhile gathered citizen mourners feared for their lives too, suffering throes of the heart against their ribs, as some who wrote of it wrote, so that all but the dying man who lay unconscious and the unconscious man who lay not dying lived in fear because they were not unconscious, no, instead they were conscious, that curse. Those who feared imminent death went on fearing it after the dying leader died, growing less fearful of it only when the assassin who fired the fatal shot died, and then growing less fearful when no renegade gray army invaded the city, and less and less fearful when each of the conspirators died, among these the first woman hanged in the country's brief history so that war, murder and execution were how the country atoned for the curse put on it for sinning one human against another day in day out for two hundred fifty years.

nourished by pigs' feet and sliced butt in sow gravy, that were my last meal to home, so that on the next rooster while the house yet slept I debouched to make war, so I remember, and so to see the elephant once for all, I remember, backward in my walking to eye the house and all in it, and on its front the porch at least, on that porch at least Pap's dog-bit rocker and the dog that bit it till it had no teeth, him resting under the seat of it, rocker and house and Pap and dog as old as old gets without being dead, nearly blind and legless knowing it were me leave taking of a sudden, one foreleg too useless to ambulate so that it smelt my going more than by another sense of it, which of these it yet owned inside who knows, his hair as gray as grandma's go to Sunday shawl now this, waked from tar paper tents to a clear nothing of sky that were like as no sun to say for to see the elephant, say a gloaming just gone, without light such as birds fly by or bullets fly by across this sky above till it were like as no sky at all, there, where the pointing goes, so that as soon as soon gets when you could see what there was to see coming it were a soft sun whereby at first I heard me nothing and felt inside the truth of a far away quiet like a church without a soul yet in it till I saw smoke at the edge of things and this smoke was the onslaught, as silent as boots on the inside against that sky that first of days to see the elephant since none of us knew what to name it the first time we saw an elephant, knowing the smell and sight of it on land where we didn't abide so it were to us one and all an empty thing of a sudden to be run over by thousands of strangers that didn't know it any better, and so not a one of us had ken of it till the place were for yelling and bleeding, for dying and death so to remember in us not to die, but the omens of the air knew the elephant, buzzards that learnt the below of things, turkey fowl so-called gathering already to circle lower by lower over the one after another hour till these disappeared to the ground nearby, and that were when the elephant stomped his foot till dawn cracked like thunder so that a tree trunk split and spavined, and that were when we heard the first man cry out and smelt for the first the stink of powder out of a big gun in the nearby, and since I saw and heard and smelt I knew I were not yet dead and that others were, them in their hollers and ditches dry or wet does not matter in the least, but all of them on their backsides watching the same heaven of the future out from where vultures swooped like we was jungle beasts netted by natives set to chuck spear to render our hides from our innards, and this so to devour heart and lungs of us, these beating faster and longer and stronger because of it in this holler here or in that ditch yonder, and all the other ditches and hollers and dugouts wherein the maimed and dying prayed to be salvaged   at this and that cry of dying where beak and talons met flesh and innards I said in my mind's voice Now he knows the underworld and I said in my mind's voice Not all birds be omens since there are them that sing, and so I thought as others in their hollers and ditches thought, by the drenching of the sun on their wounds or the moon's lit finger pointing to our maiming for marauders of the night that we and I searched out after the last light went, them that God sent on hoof and claw and paw to devour us, whether we kenned the dog's black eyes or the wolf's yellow or the fox's red looming looked at us one by one, whoever of us here if not there they or he or she caught first the stench of, even the stink of grief at the knowing of the loss forever of our beloveds, waiting for one or another of God's creatures to inhale the odor of our harms as if it be mercy to bite and claw one after another militia rent by cutlass or shrapnel or musket ball that could enter a cheek to come out a chest, or were you flat on your belly in tall grasses could enter the crown of you so as to leave out your bunghole, so ripping are the soft pellets no larger than a new bride's bud   I have seen the elephant I said inside myself in the cracked moonshine under a tree and hearing the same wind shake it since creation, but now the wind too of men in agony everywhere I turned an ear, there where the pointing goes, remembering that the onslaught were silent as were all that followed, and then there was sicking up and *stink whereat one by one we fell over dead to affront our enemies till after it the moaning and prayers and calls in the dark to beloveds, none of us undead as yet not learning by the next gloaming and the next look at this and that corpse that unblack and even bleached men darken by degrees in the heat where they desiccate or get devoured, and of the same or the next gloaming the maimed grovel in the nearby where them of us not maimed nor groveling see sunflowers as tall as ten year olds so that the unseen harmed and dying might as be invisible across crushed verdure and such, those who couldn't conversate no more, no, but lay emoting while and where they bled out   now they know the underworld I said inside myself day in day out waiting for it hunkered or marching or looking out for water as if for snipers in trees as silent as snakes till we got used to it one and all so that the dizzies and pukes we drew from nostalgia, being at home in the war therefore you could say till we saw our beloveds again in our minds, them dressed and them not— dizzies of that ilk*

By dawn of that last city battle that the south would lose rumor promised one or more millions of northers marching down to make an end to this war, and so churches cleared their flock after this and that hymn to a God that this and that church pastor or preacher never needed more to conjure, and then with singing come and gone those among the singers hurried home by hundreds before thousands so as to sell what in the streets they gathered across the story of their lives, selling all that they could lift to their lawns, walkways and streets for as little or as much as next to nothing. Chairs, tables, settees, Chinaware, bric-a-brac of porcelain and smooth wood, rare books too, and all manner of artifacts they peddled on the streets, families desperate for graybacks that were soon to be worthless, and who were the buyers of these goods, none but those neither fleeing nor fighting, those who would stay to watch the world as they know it end and yet gathering from neighbors of decades and lifetimes worldly goods among those set to flee. Condemned horses across the city died on the spot from bullets to their brains so as to be skinned, sliced, pounded, seared, and salted for road jerky, whether the one south or the one west did not matter in the least. Those thousands who fled formed a long parade of dying and maimed who preferred dying or cripple walking as far from the invasion as the eye could see so that in days and weeks going forward there would be roadside dead by hundreds without libation bearers bearing wine, oil or myrrh to hymn them to the grave or hospice in the grass or dirt that was their earth till now, the surface of it anyhow till they were dead when it was their earth the deep of.

Begin the tragedy.

The wrath begins, brethren, by documents gathered from one and another building to burn in this and that street before the victorious north marches by a hundred thousand to seize all that can be seized, and after the documents are set ablaze militias of other boulevards smash whiskey barrels by the ax, these thousands stored in this and that warehouse in one and another street so that the victorious north marching by thousands to seize all that can be seized cannot seize the tonnages of bourbon mash, and as this whiskey rushes out of this and that door into that and this street it runs in ribbons and gutters before and behind bordellos, bars and hotels, yes, so as to pool and puddle to meet these and those ignited documents gathered here and there, after which the bourbon, mash and moonshine encounter the massive burns here and there of paper histories, letters and memoranda, and then too these greet tobacco burnt out of their warehouses so as to prevent the marching thousands of the north from seizing millions of leaves of it since it intends to seize all that can be seized, as you know.

Now as a consequence of these fatal meetings on All Fools Day, that first of April, or on Communion Day, that first of April, the retreat becomes a chaos of fire awaiting only shifts in wind to enter this and that street of these and those munitions being moved, removed and sunk under waters since the north will want to seize ordnance when it seizes all that it can seize among documents, liquor and tobacco, or all that the slave states rely on to remain sovereign. Winds shift because that is what winds do, thereby setting off hours of deadly explosions among flights of blazing debris that engulf most of Richmond till we see the train terminal engulfed when its windows burst, its engines scorched or bursting like bombs therefore, and look there, the wharf is on fire where boats have departed that can no longer depart, and so we see boats afire along the wharf afire that citizens flee with none but the clothes they carry or wear. Eventually, and eventually always occurs, the retreat will end on pontoons and ass carts, inside canoes and carriages, though most of the exile happens by the bleeding feet of thousands who walk as fast as they can walk down pitted roads that head deeper south or pitted roads that head west as far as the sun lowering itself leads them.

Whether looking high or looking low, what has yet to flame is going to flame so that those who fear burning where they stand in their Sunday go to meeting clothes descend to chaos that strikes like the light and thunder of the city exploding inside their ears before blinding them by heat. The blessed by God in fear of God gather to them and to their familiars all that can gather in their arms, on horse or ass back, in wagons for driving sugar, flour and firewood till everything is here and now for them that abandon their homes and shops and histories so that what they do not carry or remember to carry remains behind as all of theirs that they left to burn. Of thousands none sees a shivering sky or roar of thunder that is not the devil's dream of bringing the city to its knees so as to bend its will or among other thousands here arrives disgrace that maps the divinity in their humiliation, those who suffer that losing all they know becomes God's sign of reckoning that they know in their innermost, how other than by losing all that they know themselves to be and to have in the here and the now that is either burnt or blown to pieces, or looted, or stolen, grants them redemption, God's grace, so many said and wrote and preached after the fiery fall of their city. Souls retreating by woodlands and rails and the river adjacent flee to settle farther south or head west to head farther west, those thousands done with the lower lands of their ancestors who have been always as poor as stink, bearing no more than a swayback nag for plowing or yanking stump or one child to carry by it, leaving as far from the bound south as far gets, going where the sun is going day after day for months till it gets there, and the millions with it.

The last act is going to be bloody, and it will burn. *Cry the Confederacy,* that furious place, so sing thousands of jonahs and leftovers marching north, not south, though not far north, to reckon a last battle for the last city fought after—*battle* of that ilk—while limbers bearing heavy ordnance hitch to mules and horses so as to disperse to all compass points between Petersburg and Richmond, thereby to stand fast to the last. These forty thousands, and in the surround these hundred thousands, and in the south entire these two hundred thousand fit to fight endure under the spell of impossible measures among hapless skirmishes hither and yon between Petersburg and Richmond, or if not under this spell then embracing the God of their bible spell who pronounces the south *promised soil* and enslavement a gift to all, and yet if neither this nor that spell that inspires these tens of thousands then theirs becomes the spell of their beloveds left deeper darkest loneliest south, or the spell of those already on the run westward by wagon, train or boat as far west as west gets before the blue ocean arrests them. But if none inspires these ill unfed ribcages to endure, then it is the shock spell of bereavement that moves them without yet knowing of what such bereavement consists since these thousands and hundred thousand own neither fields nor slaves, and their women do not recline prized or powdered, and after thunderstorms three days and nights long these last thousands of the million and more who have fought, died or gone lame endure ill, broken and feckless under the spell of a reckoning whereby these neither wholly alive nor wholly dead who cry the Confederacy cry from the thin seam between.

Theirs is the dirty grace of knowing too much and knowing not enough, not knowing that hogs prefer mud, or knowing it, and knowing that roosters prefer dust, or not, either way fouling the weft, warp and shuttle of victory in their grueling paths to all compass points between Petersburg and Richmond, inviting defeat therefore, to make of it victory in death, at the last inviting abjection therefore, enduring to march out of step one after another as long as forty miles night and day to make war a final time, enduring to become limping last conceits of a mournful decadent epic, *abjection* of that ilk. Who or whatever these thousands worship, him or it must desire the sight of death since he or it demands it of so many day in day out for as far as the eye can see. *When I was a soldier,* some say stumbling into deep ruts of dirt roads that after three days and nights of hard rain stiffen and gouge, burnt by unforgiving sun, and *Was it my dead mother's face I saw last night,* some ask of nobody nearby during the long march to nowhere and another nowhere, and this says nothing of the thousands persuaded that the shadows overhead are hawks at sundown, not buzzards at sundown till the wounded await darkness to hide their fear of the patient dark circle in the sky.

These thousands by the hundreds stumble before kneeling before rising again in perimeters thirty miles or more long, one or two miles wide between one hard road and the next that becomes like the longest line of the longest poem anyone could sit through, let alone sing. For those who flee that go down, and those who fight that come up past those who flee, there will be this, that all will go down at the end, whether south or west, and they know it, till more south and more west, and they know it, outmatched, outgunned and outnumbered at the last, five to one at all compass points, and all compass points shrinking hour by hour, if sun and stars mean anything at all. Till that flight from the million or more bluebellies invading them at their homes and their works, and those invading to invade their women's privacies thereby playing smash on the south's sacred soil, so God named it, these hundred thousand and two hundred thousand leftovers footslog stalking catastrophe, and they know it. Ulcerated and toothless, dropping roadside from thirst, hunger and disease, these jonahs and calhouns of the once white south, or now the white south (however it is or is not now the black south), not that it matters anymore in the least to any of these who owned nothing and nobody anyhow, but fought as if they each owned everything and everyone.

Those who move to flee pass those who move to fight, those moving south that pass those moving north who walk thereby with black frightened free people, those named contraband coloreds in the dying south so that walking nearly side by side to the same north and east compass points at the same speed they speak neither one to another nor look none in the face or eyes as each walks nonetheless nearby till of a sudden skin has become less color and become more hide, more the shell of the man wounded and killed than he flayed as runaway or insolent property. And so street free black women and men, and contraband coloreds, and threadbare teenaged ribcages move north white, pink necked and trembling, each move to their separate destinies, as of this day destinies at once undone and reversed so that the sensation walking downhill out of the city grows that the last shall be first and the first last. Among those last desperate graynecks are those who erect gabion walls of debris and tin, and those who form redans and redoubts at the skirts of the city by which to snipe the onslaught of thousands with what is left of muskets and small round balls, and those who spade earthworks to conceal themselves behind so as to fight to the last man, and those then making Quaker guns, so-called, that only resemble cannon muzzle, but rest as wooden and pointless as hope, all the time those thousands hear true cannon fire and true rifle fire nearing them hour by hour.

Now look there, see those who mount ordnance on limbers heading south, as if there is more war to make later and elsewhere, they sooner more than later overturn in ruts as hard and dry as the bones of butchered horses gathered roadside for forty miles the stretch—more horses the farther out, the farther out the more starvation, leaving to carrion nothing but bone and hide, or hide, bone and ordnance that nobody can eat or heft, or there is hide, ordnance, bone, and limbers that termites eat, and the ground eats if you watch and wait long enough. And there, look, where wagons and ass carts rend asunder in creeks and canals crisscrossing land that once met this small farm to that small farm, none now met or farmed, most burnt, nothing more for canals and creeks therefore than to carry cadavers downstream to nowhere till somewhere idlers and widows in their weeds cry mercy so as to draw one or another corpse by rake or tree limb to banks and to bulrushes either to bury or to recognize, or failing to recognize then letting such bloated remains drift farther down where other idlers and widows cry mercy to draw dead leftovers to recognize and to bury, or not.

From this morning's pulpits that ring bells from one end of the city to the other pastors recite the abiding faith God places in the south to succor the poor black upright arriving for centuries as if by magic, and that same God spares the half of them who do not die at sea, and so now these same preachers of sunrise service by noon cry from hilltops in the surround of the city on fire that the peaceable kingdom may be at hand since Satan's minions have come to walk the last mile uphill till the

Christ on his steed shall be sighted, a golden sword
delivered of his throat to smite the evil in their midst.
With fire behind and before them, all these among
slaves, slavers, preachers, preached, and the militia who
fight to the north of them, all keep to their deepest selves
an idea of purpose in a fallen world, one now of a sudden
delivered to fate that most never considered, and yet that
is how fate behaves. Thought through and reasoned fate
would not be fate, brethren, and so fate ignored is fate
embraced, and fate denied is fate assured. In these last
hours of a two hundred fifty year long sin, it is to some
apparent all about that few in the south knew well how
to read the meanings of signs that were placed between
one word and the next for thousands of years.

And there is this, brethren, that as the city burns
slavers hold their slaves enchained till this or that
ragtail or ribcage young militia orders these unlocked
by those who rant and wrestle against the thousands of
hours of human labor lost, and so the tens of thousands
of dollars of human beef left to roam, some chains as
long as fifty men held by this and that slaver trying to
board one or another train, or trying to buy a wagon out
from under others trying to buy a wagon, and so in the
midst of the firestorm retreat that would lay waste to the
last outpost of slavery there are some arguing still the
theory of it, its philosophy of kinship between man and
beast therefore, and thereby its religious conviction, the
spirit at the bottom of this barrel of good tidings. And

there will be spot arrests of free blacks among women and men both, these condemned to flogging and prison for being free and black on the same morning that the rebellion fails once and forever, but there is this too, that house slaves unsold by their owners selling all that they can sell walk away from yards and fences and homes where they have labored for free for decades, unless punishment is a reward, but these head north uncertain and of slow gait lest they be shot through their backs, not knowing of their way till they walk down the steep hill that none has walked before since this is the end of the city. These unfreed slaves stroll off down alleys and byways in silence, as quiet as the streets are loud with looters, drunks and half naked women dragged off behind trees and shrubbery. For many this is the way the world ends, and it feels, so many whites will write later, that whether God punished us or the world was born Godless we could not discern that Communion Sunday of All Fools.

No more shields to be found or formed, brethren, none left of artillery among combusting armories driving citizenry scared to death, and across the theatre of battle from Petersburg to Richmond webfeet soldiers spike cannons and sink landmines amid shrubs and grasses, but all these are as futile as uniforms dressing scarecrows strewing from bush and bulrush to woodlands. Even at the first hot breath that marks the fire moving to engulf all that it is not, some set the will to defend whatever wants defending against the end of the old new world, so-called, all brought down before their eyes, all burning so hot and bright that their eyes must look away or melt, and these defenders knowing little in the confusion other than not to be the last man to die for which hill whenever that will occur wherever that hill is going to be found before being lost, none wanting to peg out the instant before the truce, or surrender, or apocalypse, none to be the last dead by shrapnel in the last minute of the last battle, or the last mortally wounded by the last bullet so as to be borne away below ground by nature or devoured by creatures in nature that know nothing of war or slavery or race, but that have memorized the madness of the upright killing each other before them.

The death of all things shakes their minds among those who fight wearing starvation rags, bearing single bullet muskets in search of a single bullet to put into this or that breech that will, when time comes, not fire, or fire backward, or explode, this death among these thousands who march north before they flee south. For that is war, old blind Homer says, unless it is fleeing east before west, but there is only fleeing and not fleeing, and that is war sings old blind Homer into the innermost ears of these thousand hopeless who hope in spite of sores everywhere, and the flies everywhere who feed on them, these who do this do this on and on because the story had been foretold centuries before any of them were born. Their history that is their family's history from one end of the lower states to the other foretells the calamity public and private that will give burnt ruinations their odors and dying and death its taste till these thousands and the thousands bound to them in blood of one or another kind implore a God of their making to spare them death and the dread of waiting for it by firestorms, hangings and cannonade in the far and near, dreading the vengeful God who sends them to hell and to hell's tortures for the original southern sin that began as soon as the first colony began. Such are the breathing consequences of the war of atonement that of a sudden millions know the sin for a sin, so many said and wrote and preached soon after, but knowing this is the war's last betrayal of true believers who descend into the mud and blood of fruitless rage, hearing from neighbors of decades that enslavement always blasphemed and never knew the volition of anybody's God, and at the last hearing from neighbors that enslavement was the first lie told two hundred fifty years before, before the now where it has become the last lie told to those only born to believe lies, before this last firestorm that such lies breed.

Even as the northers arrive on foot and horse we hear the snap of tested wood as old as Indians, and the explosion of glass in banks, churches and from the homes of the hidden, and we see those in streets still seeking concealment for children and their neighbor's children, streets cramped by every sort of creature racing up and back against the onslaught of this or that wall of sprung flame driven by winds north before south when not east and west, and this means that we see here now dogs and cats catch fire, and squirrels up trees, and palm rats beside them, and horses breaking their stalls for the heat, smoke and flame, and then it is humans too catching fire, by ankles first, though up their dresses and breeches onto bare skins as fast as leaves on a shrub. So lean to this, brethren, that not long after night falls the city is vivid like noon, hailed on as if from heaven by stones, shells, bricks, bullets, hard hot musket balls, rocks as big as heads, all as if trapped inside a walled city made from the limbs of angry trees as vehement as the sun at noon, fire that fells trees from their roots to fall fifty and sixty feet to earth. A sow, so many remember, stands in the street till she stinks of burnt pork, and the cries of pain do not cease almost till the next dawn, the morning of the Second instant, so-called, of this exodus and destruction, this *infernum*, so many name it, the underworld lit hot.

By such comings and goings, and livings and dyings, foretelling and foreswearing the end of the end by distant lightning and distant thunder, the last grays resist though they cannot hold the day or night as they know less and less how many of the million blues come for them who have neither food nor water for a siege, or even for the battle to end all once and for all, and it is not yet summer even, not even today eighty under the sun. *War, Glaukos, war,* sang old blind Homer, whether to foretell or to forewarn does not now matter in the least to any of the actors of the burning south, those who flee to swamps of the Gulf coast as far as Texas, and who flee as far as canyons of the west or the arches that bind them to the sky. At all compass points where one or more million, some say, embrace exile as old as Egypt, the onslaught from treetops and high crags of crows in hundreds blackens the sky darker than moonless midnight, nor does the congregation depart, rest or light so long as the marchers march and the stragglers straggle. All that is lost fate took, so many say to becalm themselves among those who exile, but among those hundred thousand or two hundred thousand that are ribcages and webbed feet living to resist the last moments of the sacred soil, or among the thousands fleeing this fire that ends the war of atonement for once and all so that Richmond becomes Richmond ruined, the last burnt battlefield that undoes two hundred fifty years so that there is no south but on a map, for these and those uncountable souls there remains nothing to witness but bayou and desolation.

Their downfall deferred, the grays will flee south, and then more south, as they flee days in rain and then days on ground scorched by sun and cannon fire till the surface everywhere is pocked like drawings of the moon, so those flee slowly now and quiet in the sureness of defeat, walking less and slower out of harm's way if despair and God can be out of harm's way. And those north that fight one last fight in the surround of Petersburg and Richmond fight among high useless hills and cornless fields, and wheatless fields, and meadows of sheep and cows stripped clean, headless kine here or there strewn, but these soldiers flee south too when they flee the fall of Richmond, the last city to fall for the south to fall, and all after to fall with it, with thousands on thousands fleeing more south till there is little south left to flee to for the north to ignore them and their treason—to the Everglades some, or to the Keys of Florida, to Carolina islands others, crossing beaches by hundreds so to feel like Greeks fleeing Trojans on the shores at Troy, or who head west and will go on going west by thousands to meet and defeat red Indians, or west and west more until other than more red Indians they meet thousands and thousands of brown Mexicans, but hardly another white man or woman for a decade who does not know what it means to flee—*west* of that ilk.

Comes last the exodus that delivers the accursed out of a cursed land to be cleansed by fire, as you know, and the chaos of destruction from one end of the city to the other that is as violent and dark as that of creation till this redemption spreads from the first end of the lower states to the last end across what the ancients called, each in their turn each in their time, *sanguinary lands* of civil wars, blood smeared earth of internecine strife as old as speech among Hebrews and Greeks and Arabs, even though to these tribes two hundred fifty years of anything is not yet to disturb breakfast—*ancients* of that ilk. Among the accursed there are those who hear others among them speak of a vengeful God, though whose God confuses many, and on whom the vengeance is wrought confuses more, so that even the vengeful God is a righteous God among those who have lost all that is worth losing, for that is what it is to believe truly, and what now pastors and preachers must evangelize thousands to believe truly. In the void that opens for these thousands, and then millions, who have mistook the words of God for hundreds of years, and their forebears too who have mistook God for one thing that God was not, God was, is and will be something other from now on and on, more like Abraham has said of God than what he has not said.

How many hill crossings over and over do these thousands witness flowers blooming beauty, while for the leftovers among graybloods going this or that way, toward or from this and that skirmish, to say nothing of the citizenry too old and too young to be on the run who are however on the run—among all such how many bear witness to the natural beauty where they find nothing whatever to eat of it? How many fishless creeks and ponds do these thousands cross that are fished bare by those gathered nearby or by those on the run before these on the run, and what number of orchards stripped of fruit by those coming before these coming after, all and sundry starving, though those before starving less than these coming after, those fewer starving to death than these who do and will, and where is the well not poisoned by design, or the stream not poisoned by debris, among such bloated carcasses of dead men and horses that battled other dead men and horses left now to drift beside hogs and goats waiting to snag at fallen or blown tree boughs and rocks tumbled down by cannonade, whether errant or true does not now matter in the least? Unless you possess claws, paw pads or hooves, the carnage speaks for itself.

If there were deer left living in the nearby each of these thousands would on the spot become deer slayers, and were this the fall of Eden there would still be fruit, and if they fall elsewhere than where they fall they may see home, or they may see home if their homes are elsewhere, or if their homes are the homes of others that they see from roadways where they fall to die, or to be devoured before they die, dying stripped to the bone therefore. In the hot breath of defeat whether back or front north to south these thousands flee or fight till they fall crawling and dragging broken bodies to the promised shade nearby of peach, apple and cherry trees more blossom than young fruit, and so they see above them flowers, and the bees who suckle them, and above those in the dappling they see buzzards draw ponderous circles, patient turkey fowl in kettles of twenty or more gliding on winds so that at the last the dying do not march to nowhere for themselves or for their cause, but for the beloveds left behind in dread of the onslaught of a million among the blue army come down to deliver revenge at all compass points, these lands shrunk now to a patch of brown earth for each of every family whose two hundred fifty years durance is vanquished.

These thousands who flee look back after dark to watch the horizon quiver at the firing of their city, standing by hundreds in roads and fields so that in each beholder the eyes are ancient eyes, their gazes ancient, older than wisdom, and so the same eyes for thousands of years that have watched their pasts burn, and this gaze that mourns yearns also, *looks with longing,* as old blind Homer sings of it, always a gaze that reckons itself to the world it has found, or dies of its loss. God's believers will scatter roadside in wet ditches and weedy ravines to sleep till chiggers and dreams of deadly vipers wake them while on trains, on packet boats and pontoons crossing the James as if it were the Jordan, exhausted stinking bodies squeeze one to the other sick with hunger and thirst. These scenes sit as silent as prayer for all those heading south and more south, or west and more west, and for those who cannot resist turning again and again toward the past it takes much of the night, and all of their senses, to recognize so as to remember that whatever behind their flight not lit against their line of sight, it is seething ruin.

The last act is going to be bloody, and it will burn all that is not it. After one sunrise or another, and after one sunset or another day in day out, when the horizon is so far past that there is only the sky ahead and the mud below, thousands no longer flee but idle and straggle when they do not swoon from hunger and thirst, and when they are not by day buzzards rounding the exodus from the sky they are bats swooping to gather to them slow buzzless flies—the furthest of God's creatures—that have dwelt to rise from the swelled wounds of dying and dead souls in retreat. Funerals and burials run day and night for weeks so as to stage along the roadways the fading south's submission that is the end of the end of the war taking six hundred thousand lives, maiming six hundred thousand more who live limbless from one swath of brown south to the other. Those dying in the exodus who die clothed, buried and prayed over die in fortune, finished forever with the world of men who war, those exiles mourned by utter strangers collected together in dark thoughts of all that is lost, and why, and how. The last act that bloodies the invasion of Richmond after the invasion of Petersburg, and of the Points, and all environs at the compass circle, smells of exsanguination, gunpowder and fireballs that raze and level wooden riggings full of militias as young as ten, and so to the collapsion when wagon dog soldiers wave white shirts of surrender before the onslaught of blue troops still miles away.

Daylight takes no sides in this or that war so that the soldier's damp dirty hair spreads out about his shoulders like chickweed where the head of him lies face down on the ground as dead as the moon, and that soldier folded in two at the belly wound, or groin wound, or writhing over lost bollocks, and all those across one after another battlefield who are heard to wail, cry, pray, and whisper names to the sky above or to the earth below, or who lie silent to mock the noise of battle and commune with God, these breathless and resigned to have war done forever, each in his turn in his time trembles to discern what it is to live from what it is to die that he did not a moment before discern. Whether those still fit to die fighting or those fit only to die fleeing, the last lay-outs and leg cases among them too whether at the front or back, those more north than south, and the mirror of these heading south, and more south, all these dying and dead lie supplicant to a god who never arrives in time to save them, each whether dying or already dead already become an object in the natural world, the never again to be conscious.

Sunshine lights what darkness hides in dreams so that the soldier does not dream of killing till he has killed and so till he has killed he dreams of being killed whether by half moon to bowel or throat or by shrapnel that began a half mile distant fired by a nameless faceless gunner, which does not matter in the least. Wounded he falls, and fallen he crawls to cover like a dog as sick as a dying dog because the end will be bloody or it will not be. In the hard light of a last day thousands will end as near to nature as near gets. The stench of corpse, if you have not smelt it, undoes all other smells nearby and as far as the eye can see, whether of blossomed flowers or perfumes across the throats of ladies, or fresh new fruit sliced in the sunlight, so that nothing compares in nature to it since we are inborn to know at the first inhale that here there is something neither living nor ill present, and something not long dead either, such an inhuman odor that it must be humanity at the end of itself. To be dead in war is to stink up the landscape from one end to another where other men march, suffer and die till they too stink up the landscape—why sooner or later the stink hollers from one end of battle cry to the last. The dying and the dead know more intimate truck with varmints who feed on them than ever they have done with their beloveds left back and down and naked before their eyes—wives, sweethearts and whores alike. The soldier is nearest to nature in death, as unconscious as the tree beside him, and yet the stench of that resolution the living find unbearable so that it may be nonexistence the living cannot bear. For creatures that devour them beneath peach, apple and cherry trees the dead are the lowest hanging fruit in the orchard.

Those who flee battle at the end of the end or flee the city on fire at their own hands, these will find going south, and more south, mud gumbo swamps where snakes, lizards and gators flourish, and where disease and infection will kill or maim almost as many fighting lives as rifle shot, saber or cannon. And those who could not flee the city for the wall of fire circling them sit huddled in streets to watch building after building collapse, hiding their children's heads against hot and flaming debris that is all manner of matter flying as fast and hard as rain from the sky. Those therefore do not view the fire as a horizon where the past ends, but who inhabit the horizon for all others that have fled to view in the gathering darkness miles and miles at their backs. And there walk those to north, and more north, beyond those grays who stay to fight, beyond revetments, and redoubts, and gabions that skirt the city, free blacks by hundreds walking east, and more east, so as to alarm the blue shirts they meet of snipers and land mines, and of flames like the end of all things back there, where they point uphill for the miles that go up before the city opens.

Of that folly named the evacuation fire, it is the Trojan horse that Abraham cried aloud for day in day out from the side of the Potomac facing the other side every sunrise and sunset since he knew Richmond as a hill fortress implacable to scale, and he saw the river cleaving one country from another as if it were a roiling sea every day of those years of secession. *Where is my Trojan horse?* he would ask of his legions, as a consequence of which he would ask, *where is my Ulysses?*, as a consequence of which, *where is my Achilles?* he would ask of his legions over and over after reading to Grant or Sheridan or

Sherman from old blind Homer, or from Shakespeare's Henry kings, or from the Psalms by David the King of what he made from nothing into Israel: *Mine enemies would swallow me up/ Gather themselves/ Hide themselves/ Wait for my soul.*

On this morning of All Fools Sunday to some, that is Communion Sunday to others, the sun has hardly risen on either side of the river when the south's final retreat as a nation dividing a nation begins so that by mid day the city has set fire to itself, as some will say after, and this is the fire to end fire in the south that has already burnt at so many compass points from the river to the gulf that earth stretches black as far as the eye can see wherever you are standing. So the grays gift to themselves the Trojan horse they erect, so many will say after, ensuring that the rebellion fails, and that the new nation falls once but forever, so many will say after, while so many witness Davis board the Danville Line bound south and Lee bounds south by his stallion, both leaders abandoning the city for country south and more south. Some are to say in thunder that neither Davis nor Lee died for Richmond, neither did Hood or Jackson die for it, or Stuart, or Forrest, and Longstreet, or Pickett, these too did not succumb there, none there died for Richmond who saw the flames and heard explosions at their hindmost setting for home and hearth in the lower states after deserting the city no longer a city.

So place here the final retreat of front fighting

peckerwoods and leftovers, those ribcages fleeing revetments high and not so high that fail at all compass points to repel the invasion, whereby earthworks suffer breech under artillery and then by the hooves of horses riding hard shod over them, and so defiladed fields and trenches fall to cannonade, and so rifle pits and sentries empty as all manner of defense fails till none and nothing can spare the city its collapse. As if the last act is not bloody enough, in the spirit of gloom a gathering of drunk whites stage skits for All Fools, singing blackfaced at the sounds afar of artillery and rifle fire, naming themselves The Unbleached Citizens, and as if that is not bloody enough there will follow looting, drunkenness, rapine, and rape in view of all and sundry for hours while the fire to end fire courses one liquor ridden street to another, and in view of whoever wherever women of color and of no color bend across shrubs and chairs or hold their ankles by their hands to be penetrated however they are penetrable now that the world they know comes to pitiful finish. And as if the end is not bloody enough the judge and mayor and lord of Richmond orders whipped and salted the back of a free black woman and of a free black man lest they enjoy their freedom and the fall of the slave south.

No Mount of Solomon rises in the last battle that is barely a battle, but that rectifies the battle of three years back, the first battle for the heart of the south, as from the steps of the manse on the other side of the river the commander orated from David the King, and from Solomon the King, and from Macbeth of all kings, and Richard III of all kings, and Lear too—kings all, of curses and battles and treacheries thereby, surrendering to blood and to the blood guilt that ensues to save or spare who and where they can, but then falling to ground by the gravity that grounds it to spare none and that is the same gravity that at death drives blood to lower and lower limbs and venues of the body, and the body's organs, till blood, and all else with it, escapes into air, earth or water (if you are a drowned one) blood, feces, vomit, urine—the bloodpot whole and entire filled to the brim with the squeezed innards of corn crackers and butternuts who are the last grays to die in the last battle of the lost war.

Next of kin, you should know that beloveds bleed to death and are fed on by varmints of every foot, or none, eaten to the bones of them before these bones snap by jaws into twos and threes till your beloveds lay indecipherable of identity wherever those fields leave even a trace of human passage. And so by supper time those blue troops in thousands who look to correct the world do not see the faces they have waited to see, those who have retreated forever in trains, boats and horses heading south, and more south, saying goodbye to war therefore. Thousands of soldiers march the hill the two miles to the city greeted by freed slaves and street free black families without a white man or woman in sight. They smell smolder and char, and hear ordnance explode, and then see ordnance rising into the sky only to fall from it somewhere beyond the crest of the hill that enters the city. Behind these thousands Abraham in his stovepipe hat walks the two miles uprising for as long as it takes in the red crushed dust to greet street free blacks and freed slaves who touch his sleeve or offer prayers to him, and there walks to him the man who asks, *Am I really free?,* and leans in to hear the leader reply, *As the air.* When now and then a pistol fires, troops surround the commander since no one can discern by then whether a gray or blue fired it, or a looter, or a common drunk, or by then whether a suicide fired it. The man himself moves on determined to view by his own eyes the carnage done to the city so that word spreads among the inhabitants of his coming, and those who want to flee flee, and those who want to hide hide, but it is a deserted street in smoking ruin that he finds.

Now only the remains of remains of the south's families in Richmond stay back in their houses at the arrival of forces from across the river to fight the last fight and to incite the retreat south and more south in that flight into exile, and these thousands of armed northers come wary of the shivering curtain in a window, wary of the sudden move of children playing in one or another alley, soldiers with bayonets to the ready therefore wary even of those who stay rocking on their porches in silence to behold the catastrophe, to see how it all must end, anxious soldiers as foreign there in blue as Frenchmen, but who wary less of those who take to bed with cats, dogs and blankets over their heads, wary still less of those who cook lunch and dinner that can be smelt through open doors and windows, and this is to speak of those who do not die by fire, or flying ordnance, or hot debris flaying their skin from misfires and explosions one after another of ammo depots, and where along the James River dead powder monkeys no older than twelve float belly down from blown pontoons of gunpowder, or casements bursting whereby to send canisters of shrapnel into the hides of cows and horses a half mile far from the city. This day ends in the last and final victory against the secession, and against slavery even as it begins the last two weeks that the commander will breathe.

it must be true, and that is this, we massed this morning on that peak, where the pointing ends, at the sunrise so that the sun sets, and that is so to rest in its darkness till the blood letting again begins so that it ends, massed by thousands for as far as the eye could see, massed for nothing but not for something since never did we master the field before us, or to the sides of us, outsized by thousands more than our thousands, overawed by great guns fired from far redoubts over air shaggy with budding cotton thicker than flies so that all hours later, how many of them who knows, upon ravels of roots hard as knots we lay where the wounded lay, and the dying lay squirming and thrashing and howling like wolves beside the dead done howling and thrashing and squirming so that the living learnt from the dead what it is being as near death as near gets—all this I filled my eyes by and the hearing of filled my ears till I plugged my canals with my fingers and rocked on my hinders that I were not dying nor dead   these know now the underworld I thought in myself of the corpses in my surround, and these will know soon the underworld I thought in myself of the men on their backs or bellies cursing the day and the sky above them, and so I fled among the fleeing to the woods as if it were true that to be unseen is not to be dead, and it is the least true thing among the untruths of this war and these deaths and the fright of both, but I fled as far from the noises and stink of battle and of the men fallen by it till I heard nothing but the crackle and crush of leaves and twigs under my boot soles or the crackle and crush of other men's boot soles where other men fled that I couldn't see who couldn't see me back, and so finally, who knows when, it come to me that birds were perched in song whereby there was no more war to chase them as birds know first where and when the first shot will fire, if not why   I set myself to rest till sunset when the other man came from the yonder side of the same woods and set himself to rest, and to rest is to wait, and so we waited together with him in his bramble and I in my bush till each heard the other and knew his instinct as he knew his own, and this instinct was not to die since day and night hour after hour of waking and of bad dreams each of us in his turn in his time set himself to wait not to die   I bear witness now in my dying holler in my time to the worst of the worst other than the death of me in this wood thereafter where ghoul were a verb of grammar   I bear witness to the frangible brand of ball shot that I shot to that man across the bush from me, him who shot first whose pistol clicked first but clicked dead, so who knows with what shot in the breech he shot, if buck like candy as soft and round as caramel or hard as marble as mine were that day when it burnt his shirt above the mortal heart of him whereat he reached for his jaw coughing blood like from the sound itself since I did not know I hit him nor even that my gun fired and his failed to, and then he looked beyond me like another were standing there, but he looked surprised as a child looks for we saw there that he had bit away most of his tongue, and now that would be the pain I thought in my mind, till we saw one by one his tongue landing on an ant hill at his boot toes   I did not know if to help him or to hurt him after that, and since I did not know how to help I did not hurt either, no, but stood as we kenned the moment together the same way we had sat to wait not to die, him in his bramble and me in my bush, the both of us learning at the heart the dying at close range, and that is seeing into a man's eyes who knows he be dying once for all, this picture of him I could not tell him of, and yet had the instinct to say so he would know his face on the instant that a bubble like gum but of blood escaped his mouth before he keeled to a knee at the weight of his dying, at the earth's pull of him to

it, till he fell to his backside among fallen leaves that nature
yellowed   he is seeing the sky I thought inside myself, and
that is how the dead haunt the living I thought inside myself,
and maybe they whisper the living into death by talking of it
to them before they do it, and by remembering to the dying
the dying who came before their dying, remembering the
ease of it to some not fearful of God or silence and stillness,
that they who die soonest die best, without the mind's fearful
memory of the violent deaths on fields of great battles that
bag bones and pot stews one day far off that young boys will
read of so as to dream of being soldiers, if being is the word
his pistol did not sympathize with him, so the failure came
to be named, and therefore it misfired for something only
the dying man knew as he lay dying, in this here our holler
made by nature as a nest for us birdlings waiting a mother's
puked worm or bug to feed us by, and this is because I did
not move but for sitting as at his wake or funeral when the
shrapnel rent my boot like lightning—ours be a ditch of that
ilk, our dying ditch then, not only his   there be no good
since I smelt the wound I drew in the man dead at my feet
by my hand, him in his same holler I call mine till we are
boot to boot, me still thinking, as I do, me still paining, as I
do, with him heel to heel as gone as gone gets, there, where
the pointing is, that I murdered him, or the war did, or God
did—a mystery of that ilk that I searched in his eyes after I
shot till he learnt then there he was dying, and so his were
dying eyes before me till they one by one ceased to see me
or trees of the woods or the sky, eyes rolling back in the

skull of him so the darks disappeared under the lids with
the wonder of it, the body's dying, its shock, the surprise of
its dying to him in the mind, so the dying body signing to
the dying mind whereby at the end of the end white sightless
globes looked as if at something up as far as far goes to see
God or for God to see him who I shot and kilt without saying
a word or hearing a word from him I kilt   he had paper
written on it pinned to his chest, and that would be his name
and so his town and his family's town, his history of himself
and his beloveds therefore, all that ended when he came a
cropper in front of me, it that was done once for all without
him thinking on it, and so I were left to do the thinking on it
for him   those who hear of this hear angels I think on dying
in my holler, as if to be one at the end of the end, as if this
is something to believe, and so whatever you hear before
you, hear also me, and what you believe, believe in me also,
and in Satan's bones, as do I, those strewn among fields as
far as the eye can see, dead ones like weeds growing, crook-
backed and ragged or as burnt black as hog roast till all
in all estrange as estrange gets, estrange begetting estrange
across the ground among the unburied dead, devoured and
the dying of us like strange creatures not of nature or of God
rampant across the terrain till the land howls for us one and
all, there where the pointing goes

This point, here, on the line of history whereat five million slaves and their two million families slaved, or a fifth of the country, or a third of the south slaved, on this point in that history the atonement commenced till mustard heads and sheep dippers misruling millions of acres of cotton, fruit and whatsoever suffered that their inbred enrichment would be no more engorged by all that was delivered to them from bare men burnt in the sun and comely girls bent to ground this or that way fifteen hours day in day out for two hundred fifty years. When secessionists told the commander in an office of the manse that humans might be paid to labor, but never beasts, Abraham stood from his chair so as to walk to the nose of the speaker, whose tip he touched with a finger, before saying this, so many said, *When you on your bare chests grovel in dust to have lost all that you own and all that you love, know that I am he who did it to you.* They spoke of burdensome beasts stinking of sweat as black as an eclipse, and of wanton baby making night after night that even whipping could not prevent, and so the commander leaned into their midst in a room of the manse before saying this, so many said, *Bring my people from the depths of the sea that they foot dip in the blood of my enemies, and then the tongue of the dog dip the same. I will not be moved.*

This day those in that room who remembered the moment remembered that there the atonement began its onslaught whereby lands below the jagged line would cinder that did not flood with bellied up bottom dwellers profaning all that was holy till all who needed to die died, all that needed to burn burnt, all who needed to bleed bled, leaving before the last to free up their stock, when not cows and sheep and goats slaves by the millions, as you know, *stock* of that ilk, leaving slavers to starve or to drink tears, or to swallow their urine so as to drink what could be found to drink anywhere, and to eat weeds and poisoned berries everywhere anything to eat could be found. Scourge of God, and minister of wrath, think you not? Of ancient wars, of wars begun before time, think you not? He would have saved them if he could, even before he would have saved himself, think you not? In his merciless war of atonement against the worst sin that any there and then had been born to know at all compass points for hundreds of years, he killed and saw dead all manner of brethren fighting the unnatural life of bondage, killing and maiming the indrawn rife with disease as if the whole of the world they inhabited day in day out grew rooted in taboos older than words inside one long crippled bloodline.

A door of ancient ills and covenants since all who murder without God's command profane all that is holy since God alone gives life, and God alone takes it in its time in its place, whether by sound sleep or war and its ravages. The atonement became a sea of blood on earth of crimes against millions dead, dying and destroyed as if dead, none mistook among carcasses for the hides of deer and moose, for instance, or fox and goat, another, or any and all that are hoofed, but crimes against only the two-footed dead and dying under peach or apple or cherry trees in woods for thousands of miles to all compass points. And these stony dead that spread across fields of battle elicited in the doomed leader the image and force of the *golem,* the ancient Hebrew accursed created by men to do evil, who appear as men but inside are animals, and this because slaves were made to resemble animals but inside were men. The whole of the slave south he pronounced a nation of *golem,* of mindless men of stone, dead in heart and viscera, and their wives and children as afflicted as they, stony and lifeless, so that only their slaves and their livestock lived in innocence.

Abraham destroyed these accursed day after day for years and years till the engineless afflicted squirmed under peach, cherry and apple trees bursting or bleeding at their bellies, for instance, those gathering into their hands the long bleeding string of their innards while running to bridges that spanned rivers or canals to islets and deep dark woods, as those in old blind Homer gathered their innards too to replace them in their bellies and groins while running to ships at sea across sandy beaches. That he murdered again and again he confessed to all who would listen, confessing to all who would listen so as to suffer inside him the guilt of ringing down fate on millions of his afflicted countrymen who had profaned the holy promise of freedom for two hundred fifty years, before the country was a country, but even then an ungodly land, so he remarked over and over to all who would listen though he failed to picture of what a godly land consisted, just not enslavement, of God he knew that much. *I will not be moved!* he intoned in the well of Congress, *I will be song for my sorrows.* His biblical exhortations for battle after battle, those of King David to his God (*Give ear that strangers are risen against me*) punctuate the war of atonement like swords in the doomed leader's thoughts—this of God and his anointed as Abraham too had been anointed, neither anointed dissuaded from brutal means (*Swallow them up and fires devour them*) till each bore witness to the groveling of enemies on their bare bellies (*Their fruit destroy from the earth*), that those whose heads and faces were booted at the neck into the dust among dying and dead (*Gathered against me, they make the noises of a dog*) will forever foreswear the enslavement of men and women (*Consume them in wrath*), since had the enslaved been skinned white they would not have been enslaved (*Let them make the noises of dogs unto the ends of the earth*).

The first whom Mary Lincoln invited as guests to the theatre were General and Mrs. Grant, but they declined.

On that Friday it rained, but when did it not rain

during the warfight, unless it snew or unless a fierce sun hardened the ground after any and all walked against it, or fled across it, or barreled down it inciting the rebel yell till at the edge of doom by the very jag breaching slave from non slave thousands lay as dead as dead gets. Here bear witness to another cold pour gathered to ravage and flood one and another venue from the manse to Richmond, that smoldering, starving and deserted ruination whence most fled south, as you know, while some fled west, as you know, while a goodly number set themselves where they had taken root generations before hanging wash, boiling sweet potatoes, rocking in rockers whose legs had been chewed by generations of dogs, their owners creaking back and forth on porches so as to smoke tobacco bald-faced in the direction of soldier squads ever present front and back of every house, church and tavern in the city and its surround. Liquor was forbade, whorehouses too, gatherings too other than in churches by the hundred cramped with penitents and prayerful fearing the end of the world as they had found it. And it was.

Of the Good Friday forenoon, those royal hours before Vespers among local papists, bells everywhere of all beliefs called thousands to recite the same psalms of David that the commander recited day in day out through the war of atonement, and to hymn those hymns of centuries after David, singing one congregation after another to the end of morning without a sun to show for it, to afternoon of prayer and sermon and more prayer to the evening of the *epitaphios threnos*, lamenting thereto the dead Christ drawn down who bled on the rugged cross till he lay as dead as dead gets so as to rise as the bright unbearable reality of ages on and on. Those evangelists of the south by thousands, papists by fewer thousands, who worshipped and embraced enslavement no less than they embraced the broken bleeding feet of the martyr who had always already died for their sins no matter how great or dark, they prayed, sang and worshipped over and over from sunup till mourning midnight that proclaimed year in year out the Holy Saturday of Christ's entombment, the state of that death behind the rolled rock thereby touching the greater dark of cave-dwelling dead so as to rise in the high blue sky sooner rather than later of the Easter gloaming.

Let us pray, brethren, that God gathers and keeps those united by death in his one universal church. Amen.

The south bows down to the morning deluge as if the storm is God's judgment upon it till not only the surrender renders judgment upon it, and the sacking of cities at all compass points renders judgment, and fire as well as flood, but nature demands a reckoning and a sacrifice since of a sudden Eden is no more, and no song sung to invite it, instead now and forever only songs of failed rebellion bitter and twisted. And among those who bow down at the loss of all of heaven are these bent over so as to rut in a pasture as common as clouds in the sky, if those women were to look to the sky to see reflected there the last violation of their privacy, or in their shame looked rather to the grassed ground before their eyes, but they are bent or rode so as to spawn a generation of new rebels that sooner rather than later will war again and retrieve their two-legged property. Such dreams end in fire from one swath of the lower lands to the other, and so they end in looting, drunkenness, robbery, and rape at all compass points, those crimes that will invite children of generations on and on twisted and bitter and haunted, and these will be fat, derelict, mindless souls avenging losses after two hundred fifty years durance— slavers and their kin, and their kin's kin, and their kin's kin's kin on and on again and again—those *golem*. What any believed truly or would generations later believe truly their pastors and preachers told them to believe truly, that their bible believed it truly—the impenitent believers abandoned by God or who abandoned God centuries before.

Where was the preacher hanged by his spine who truly believed, twitching from leafy boughs till he swayed dead as dead gets, from which oak, or cypress, or cottonwood in which lower states could any be found flayed or burnt who for two hundred fifty years along a bloodline of preachers and pastors evangelized and brought the gospel's good news of enslavement? So to what or to whom and why did these lost souls pray and hymn that storm driven Good Friday from one mud washed town to another across thousands of acres as soaked by storms as soaked gets, and of soil therefore as barren as barren gets? For those who arrived centuries late to visit God, whether to pray for forgiveness or to succor the vastness of their tragedy, God befell them where they sat, knelt or stood, and those far west of the jag that was what the south left of itself, so far west that it was Texas where rebels went on killing, staging there a massacre of more than one hundred blue soldiers a full month after the surrender so that long after these white trash, nidderings and leg case washouts bragged of it, it was named the last battle of the war. Fought because there lay no farther west to flee, and fought because south stood the Mexico not yet stolen by slavers Houston and Austin, no, but there rested only desert below and only ocean on and on as far as the eye could see, and in that ocean were fishes that ate men, and in that desert south was nothing but Mexico and the Mexicans all over it talking in anything but American.

The second whom Mary Lincoln invited to the theatre were Congressman and future Vice-President Schuyler Colfax and his wife, but they declined.

We have arrived, brethren, at that infamous Friday in spring called Good, that day after Maundy Thursday, or the foot wash day, or incitements one after another to death and resurrection, the latter incited by Holy Saturday, as you know, or the sleep of all sleeps, or the dream of all dreams, or Christ's descent to the underworld reigned by the fallen angel, that closest to God at the onslaught of creation till his secession from heaven, and so none before Christ sat nearer to God than Satan. Here is that Friday therefore, and its mordant image of shivering cold rain as jagged as glass out of a sky darker than moonless night till dirt streets of sand, clay and straw ran rivers into pools of drowned creatures or swept along snakes and paddling vermin from one end of the city to the other. But there is this, that some of the morning passed in happy gunfire aimed at an invisible sun while drunken buglers bugled, and then the same whores who that same night would conceal their breasts, thigh and buttocks, by mid of the morning tended clients exercised at their loins to have been spared death and dismemberment across four years of war, so that instead they remained drunken in the royal hours of tolling bells and chorales overheard from windows thrown wide at any and all of hundreds of churches, drunken hour after hour to remember that they were neither dead nor dismembered by predators. The come to ring of Vespers gathered still more gospelers wrestling impassable streets by carriage, horse and boots as high as knees, those penitents drawn to this and that church, not drawn to this and that bar or bordello, but whose innermost ear leaned to the quiet jubilation thankful for peace, those for whom the warming sun of a sudden bespoke a finished drama in the heart of the southern surrender.

More whorehouses stood than hospitals nearby the manse, and yet since half a hundred hospitals stood a hundred and more whorehouses therefore stood, and thrice that many taverns from Goat Alley, where freed and runaway blacks abided, to Baptist Alley, that road behind the theatre where the seven who would carry the dying man carried him in their arms and hands across wood planks and slats and doors wrenched from their hinges that no less sank into mud, dung and silt three feet down, deep among long gone carcasses of dogs, piglets and rodentia as long as grown cats, or so Rathbone recited to his sons in the Germany of his exile, narrating all that he saw bearing the pain of his dead arm beside the dying body of his commander. Thousands of wounded soldiers lay treated and mistreated, Rathbone informed his sons before the fireplace, those moaning and sobbing all day and all night in the rattle and jag of wagons disturbing them from one to another bed whereby some should be recovered and others not, and so on the streets where they passed pressed together over and under troughs and peaks of dirt as hard as marble or as stuck as mud onlookers looked away and closed their ears to the dying and dead warriors, and looked away from Rathbone too for the blood and skin hanging off his arm. Those in their go to meeting best turned away at the sight of the passing dead who filled carts and wagons higher than their walls since now that these succumbed in the city they would enter shallow graves by thousands and could not in public view be massed together as they were in battlefields after battle, when carts and wagons gathered what was to gather for the swift burial of hundreds against heat, damp and critters of every ken.

Let us pray, brethren, for those who do not believe in Christ. Amen.

So the brothers and sisters in God's union observed the sun remember them that afternoon, quieting the angry sky of morning, and the floods thereby that loosened the shallow earth in the city and its surround so that, as one congregation after another mourned of a Friday that was to celebrate the Sunday of the rolled rock and the appearance of the risen messiah and so his ascension that craned the necks of all who saw his reach into heaven, in the here and now from days and days of cloudburst graves opened and shrouds unwound themselves till corpses as fresh as flowers surfaced to bob and float along canals, creeks and byways where rain drove all manner of sewage to hover. Many would say that day in day out after the rains dead soldiers in the penitent majesty of being undone from the earth commenced wandering to go and come first inside houses of worship, but then into streets, avenues and alleys till grievers and mourners everywhere recognized this and that neighbor or beloved who by hundreds walked upright and unbound in the sunlight after walking upright and unbound in the rain. Souls at once damned to war, that atoned for the blood of it, and those then redeemed by death in it so that those hundreds before thousands beholding the uprise of a nation of souls knelt, supplicated and submitted to the will of God or to ancient fate, and yet to their innermost despair or faith till bells tolled on and on for the day that ended the curse bedeviling the country from its birth.

Apparitions spoken for as relatives and lovers from one end of the city to the other as if they no longer lay dead or dismembered, but as if the onlookers could see their faces as clear as noon, though all feared touching their beloveds as they feared addressing them. And yet these were signs marking the great unknown that none knew who bore witness, or so Rathbone recited to his sons at their consular home in Germany years and years later, telling that those silent frightening souls roaming the city knew all of the mysteries of afterlife, such knowledge that terrified their beholders (their father among them, their father informed them when they held the ankles of his boots in their hands in fear), giving all who saw shakes of bewilderment that the warfighting dead on all sides could rise by thousands so as to be delivered to God in this way, among the living like the risen Christ. Those who saw, stunned and silent, described the sunset between heaven and earth as the gold of whiskey till dense fog overtook the city whereby none could discern anymore the play of air for lost souls and so of a sudden fewer human shapes formed, so many said (their father among them) before waxing like the horizon only to vanish on the spot. Those of the risen spirit army became for those hours nothing less than emissaries of the underworld who by thousands came and went in churches, shops, bars, and bordellos till all and sundry that saw them fell silent, prayed and trembled.

Some never ceased to witness the dead rise and walk, after the dead rose from the ground and floated or snagged or bobbed for days, whether at dawn's fog and dew or at midnight's moony shadows across walls and floors and doors inside and outside the intimate venues of people's private lives so that twilight, and all after, informed a hallowed sanctuary, that homes became meditative dungeons inviting memory after memory and vision after vision of timeless death to come for all till these ceased being comforting or godly visions, but foretold terror and death in the deepest mind of believers in the cloven hoofed rebel in heaven who fell before the invention of death. After centuries of blood curse and the blood guilt that ensued those who came to see what they saw suffered by thousands and thousands an irrefutable and eternal truth, and it was this, that on that Good Friday day death had opened the yawning gates of the huge nothing, the deepest darkness wherein dead and living roam alike indistinguishable one from the other in what had always been, and was now this day, eternal damnation.

Those who had become brothers to insensible dirt could be seen wandering the gloaming of dawn, so many said, and then again wandering at the fall of daylight, those green and young boys that nature had eaten by teeth as sharp as the sword, upright sullen dead now by thousands stalking true nowhere from one end of the war zone to the other at all compass points. These wandering souls counted real to all who saw them since memory said so on that dawn in the cruel month wherein the national blood-letting began to wash away clean by the morning that stormed and by the bondage unbound among enemy brethren of the same land, language and God who set down four years on and on the hounds that harrow hell till hell and its hounds dwelt everywhere for as far as the eye could see. For every mourner a dozen dead souls came before going, first in the rain that dimmed sight nearly to a void, but then by the sun that hardened the earth so as to snag by rock and limb one lost corpse after another for as far as the eye could see, and yet all the souls of all the corpses that walked walked one gait slow and heavy wherever they drifted till the city darkened into night and all who saw remarked each to each that the rain of the morning meant to garden the ground had laid waste to it and raised a crop of born dead.

Cry Havoc and let slip the dogs of war that this foul deed shall smell above the earth, and so this army claimed soldier for soldier the spoils from those they had killed among swords, daggers, shields, the rare golden tooth, and yet soldier for soldier victors from vanquished removed porcelain cameos of beloveds, and living lockets of beloveds, that became not only souvenirs of victory, but of the men they slew, that they were beloved, and fixed forever alive in death for those surviving them. Circling dead necks, so Rathbone told his sons years and years later, living lockets cased brown and gray portraits of wives, mothers and children, and some sweethearts no larger than a quarter, keepsakes for battle-dragged soldiers to look for the last time into eyes of innocence or passion or succor, any eyes not fixed on killing them, so Rathbone told his sons while he showed to them the locket of their mother he had worn around his neck during this and that battle that he had fought, and this or that keepsake portrait captured from a dead soldier that each man killed became then mementos of his own life and part of his family story delivered down to his beloveds for keeping and for holding generation to generation, thereby to say to all who looked, *Here is the family of the man I kilt, this is his bride, these his children.*

Now too, there were mourning lockets hung from the necks of beloveds left behind war lines, wherever these were drawn whenever they were, and these portraits as small as a quarter were of sons, husbands or brothers, or sometimes a betrothed marching as to war, so Rathbone told his sons as they sat wigwam at the toes of his boots, these portrait pictures that memorized the living smiling faces of men before they lay dead and buried or torn asunder such that beloveds among wives, and mothers, and children, and sisters studied even to their own deaths to persuade themselves that death could not end love, so Rathbone waxed to his sons, remarking to them that their mother had carried such a memento of their father before he became their father whenever he went to battle, and he went to battle thrice. After faces fixed in life there were those fixed in death among those bodies retrieved whole or in part from fields and woods where battle after battle raged, so Rathbone told his sons who wrapped their small fingers about the ankle of his boots that smelt of new polish, and of those fixed in life and in death some were wet-plated and varnished for printing on the spot by the same photo man traveling town to town before skirmish or battle and from town to town after skirmish or battle, seeking from horse carts filled with corpses faces neither mutilated nor blown off whether by gunshot or saber or varmint, or any other form of wildlife. Torn limbs did not matter in the least to the mourning portrait of Union and Confederate dead, and so some were legless and armless, and some in death were no less expressionless in the eyes and mouths that their faces might as well have been lost, faces therefore as dead as the *golem's* dead face, as stony, sullen and as meaningless to behold as bones in a desert, but to their mourners these dead died with lids made wide by the sight of God so that they possessed in their portraits no larger than a quarter the wise and comforting brown eyes of a familiar horse. And so believers and mourners who suffered the sight of bloated corpses floating, snagged or bobbing by all manner of disintegration in waters fast rushing to the river and from the river to the sea clasped close to their hands and hearts their lockets of the living and of the dead so as to feel the warm truth with their hands.

The third whom Mary Lincoln invited as a guest to the theatre was Noah Brooks, a journalist at the Sacramento Daily Union, but he declined.

As bugle, passing by, in the distance dies away, the vine decorates the ruin of the tree it embraces, so Abraham wrote in his youth of the life to come. *I'm living in the tomb,* so Abraham wrote in his youth of the life to come as a married man. He leaned always toward dreams and images of the guilty man, of the murderer and transgressor, relating thereby to the mental anguish of Oedipus, of Priam of Troy, of Macbeth, of Claudius the king, of Richard Three Sticks, that crippled king who hypnotized the commander by his eloquent mindful ugliness. But of David the king there was this, *he smote the Philistines from Gela till you come to Gazer,* and this, *he gat him a name when he returned from smiting the Syrians in the valley of salt, being eighteen thousand,* and there was this for him to learn at heart so as to speak it, *he slew the men of seven hundred chariots and forty thousand horsemen, and smote Shobach, the captain of their host.* All these, and tens more of such verse he memorized so as to say of the carnage about the land, and the desolation that lingered as thick as ashes in the air, and that all was no less in its place because of it. Whereas armies ravaged and besieged, he sat in the manse in his walnut rocking chair hundreds of miles from the dyings, deaths and the curdling cries of battle. He asked hour after hour how his generals fared, how his troops, and how the battles did. By the measures of ruin and rapine, thus numbering the dead and the miles scorched, and the desolation thereby as thick as ashes, he knew that the war of atonement would never leave the house of his mind as surely as his sword stood in a corner of the room to save him from murder.

His valet said to him, *Look, a crowd has gathered to hear you speak,* but the doomed man had little in his brain then to say to an audience, but no less, look, see where he strides to the portico below another beclouded spring sky after another day of hard rain, and commences to tell those few dozen out from under umbrellas and parasols that it has come to his thinking in a vision, though visions are fearsome events, how he yearns now for the day when he casts his vote standing beside a former slave casting his vote. We cannot see for bobbing heads and craned necks of the crowd, but among the stragglers and idlers overhearing are the future assassin, his conspirators and there, where I am pointing, brethren, the ubiquitous Dr. Leale, who will pass nine

hours three days hence scraping coagulate from the hole
in the dying man's skull, that man addressing him not
twenty feet distant, and whom Leale sees for the first
time, and that man's killer not thirty, whom Leale would
never see, whom Rathbone would see, as you know. After
this last brief note of a speech there could be no turning
to left or to right from his meaning, and so as he was a
dead man talking while he talked, when he disappeared
he became the disappearing man as dead as dead gets.

*Let us pray, brethren, for the Jewish people, the first to
hear the word of God. Amen.*

Foreseen and forewarned by dreams and books and
threats that he received in thousands from the instant
of his election, the man already dying who would not
have known it other than that he had always known it,
translated the story of himself across years of readings
in holy Hebrew scripture and the rhapsodies of ancient
Greeks who sang and acted curses, wars, murders, and
betrayals by and for those gods true and false, but in all
cases pitiless gods blowing men into the mercy of their
winds when not doom at the songs of their sirens, and
then he foresaw and foretold his end in the warnings
and visions of Shakespeare's cursed villains, rapacious,
brooding, traitorous noblemen who drew blood upstage
before drawing it downstage till corpses strewed before
foot candles that flickered against the dark of the crowd.

Forebear the gods, the dying man said before he lay
dying on the carpet of the box of the theatre. *We have*

earned their curses, he would conclude his conviction among all who would listen, more often than not ornamenting his conclusion by embracing its darkest inspiration, that gods overhear men and whisper into their inmost ears by which those they would destroy they first make mad, and he thought himself mad with despair not only since he despaired, but since despair strengthened him. He would lean toward the madness inside himself, envying therefore the deranged man who knew nothing whatever of his derangement, but was mercifully demented, blessed by gods thereby such that the lover mad with love might resurrect his dead beloved's bones out of her coffin to lie beside what was left of her and to taste her death. Romantic madness he envied, or so he said, read and wrote across decades and decades, and not the madness inside himself since he had to go on killing rather than coveting and desiring, rather too than summoning the courage of the romantic madman to hang his long neck from a tree never far from his line of sight in the manse.

He suffered the reason to war, that curse of the anointed, so as to crush all before him whether at Shiloh or Manassas, battles of biblical names, as David had crushed his enemies there thousands of years before, and he gave the order to burn Atlanta to ash and to dust that reckoned the deaths of twelve thousand captured near the close of atonement at Andersonville prison. He ordered this madness till all who opposed him fled, bled or groveled, but it was his curse, he remarked day in day out, to be God's wrath whether by fire, flood, famine, or cannon, all these weapons that were to him like King David's sword and shield. For him time had come to an end to explain further, or to explain again, or to exhort, or to quote this and that to accompany the onslaught of his madness that stood and delivered death to all who opposed him, to observe to all who would listen that forces deployed against him completed him, and now that he lay dying he left no time to examine what in him it was that even he did not know the name of, this that willed him to war against his southern countrymen and their families with a ferocity of mind unseen for thousands of years.

From this madness none could be saved by anybody whether by deed or by thought, even to the assassin who would shoot Abraham not from the front, but from behind, and so could not look at the face of the man to murder, or his eyes, nor did he shoot his heart or his mouth, but spoke of striking the name from memory, the name and his image everywhere they hung, of erasing everywhere they could be read the goat songs he recited that slit the throats of pharaohs and *golems* alike ear to ear. The assassin could save neither his cause nor himself, as the dying leader could save neither patriots nor himself, and neither of these saved the half million and more dead of the atonement, and none of the half million and more of the atonement could have saved the six million and more of the enslaved among twenty millions and more across two hundred fifty years of sinning against nature and reason and God. Thousands of years of blood curses, and the shedding of blood to expiate them, and images and words to dramatize and to recite them—these the doomed man in the box in the theatre embraced for the will to war and to be warred against, thereby to kill and to be killed in return since if he had hoped to be spared a violent end he told no one.

The fourth whom Mary Lincoln invited as a guest to the theatre was their son Robert, but he declined.

In the box were four, but then five (the assassin), then Dr. Leale (six), who cut open the victim's clothes down the middle with a pen knife, as if cleaning a fish, and this he did to seek stab wounds since blood spattered the carpet whereon the doctor placed Abraham unconscious, and blood spattered walls and flags too, and spattered drapes and banners and all manner of festoonery to welcome the commander of the peace, so Rathbone told his sons. And it was their father's blood, their father told them, that filled the infamous space in the infamous theatre. The seventh witness, actress Laura Keene, arrived to lap Abraham's head in her hoop skirt, and so it was because of blood dotting the lace cuff of her sleeve that Dr. Leale ran his fingers through the dying man's hair, finding there the hole where the lead ball smaller than a child's marble had broken skull bone, traversed the brain west to east so as to lodge under the right eye that would swell as the forehead swelled, as the jaw, sinus and cheek swelled till the right face entire distended and blackened, the eye engorged, white and rheumy till it resembled the eye of a horse.

Now more men came, physicians and soldiers most of them, who watched Dr. Leale bring a dead man to life after his pulse had passed, and after he had died on the spot, and so all who saw saw this, that the man lay naked in his clothes rent asunder, his head cradled in the lap of an actress who sat wigwam on the carpet to still it while Leale pounded Abraham's chest with a fist and breathed into Abraham's mouth with his mouth, and then massaged the chest wherein the stopped heart sat till the dying man sighed before inhaling loudly and deeply, and so for the first time groaned till Leale felt into the wound to scrape the caked blood from it that caused the brain to press the cracked skull, as you know, so Rathbone narrated to his sons who held the ankles of his shining riding boots as he did. The seven among soldiers and physicians lifted him now that he breathed and lived enough to groan to carry him by their hands and arms from the theatre to the rooming house, and they carried him before a gathered crowd that wept openly and without shame by hundreds, as you know, since the murder that had been threatened even before his election, and threatened day in day out every day for what was left of his existence, and threatened only three days before in bars and bordellos by drunken southers, had been threatened so many times across so many years that even Abraham began to doubt it would happen.

Now as he lay dying in a stranger's bed in a stranger's house he never in grown life had a place to come home inside that gave him peace where he might rest his head on the bosom or belly of a beloved as he did on those that were his mother's belly and bosom, and then those of his only true love, the one dead by poison, as you know, the second by consumption, as you know, whom he said he buried with his *heart in her coffin*, even though he may as well have buried his mother with his heart in her coffin since his heart then began to harden, by the writings he left as a child, so that he could fight the war of atonement heartless, repeating these intimacies of himself to all who would listen even to the end of his existence, reciting as if his was the tale of an idiot since he could feel even today the dip of Ann's back, and the curves of Ann's buttocks, and the cleft between so that he lived haunted by the dread his syphilis had killed her, if he suffered syphilis, and he believed that he did, as he feared it too since his wife across years and years had grown strange and addled in the mind till only drugs brought her solace. And she had birthed two weak children after the one strong one, and these little boys had gone young from pneumonia, as you know, and from typhus, as you know, so that he lay claim to killing them too by his disease that he earned in the sheets with a carnival high-wire walker whose name he could never remember.

He confessed to all who would listen that his only fear of death lay in living burial that he read of in sleepless nights, or being torn by dogs on distant beaches that he read of in sleepless nights, dreading too midnight pacts with demons from hell so as to wage war inside wood, hollow and bracken, confessing to dreading the spirits of dead women damned to roam the world for their murderous lovers—irritable night readings, *sleepless nights* of that ilk before he lay dying in a stranger's bed in a stranger's house dreaming hour after hour from midnight till dawn of what only his gods would know, and they spoke only to madmen they would destroy, as you know, and as he remarked to all who would listen. His tall muscular melancholy incited him to smite the *golems* and pharaohs of the slave states, and their kin, and their kin's kin that set him at the end in the door slab between here and nowhere, before the teeth and throat that form the huge maw of nonexistence while on the other side of the near window rain sobered the sky. On his deathbed all who saw him there gave witness that his face looked more peaceable than they had ever seen it.

The fifth whom Mary Lincoln invited as a guest to the theatre was the Marquis Adolphe de Chambrun, a diplomat with whom she conversed in French, but he declined.

Above the deathbed, dawn sought one object after another across the room to waken from the dark dread night, if only to appear to mourners and to idlers no less a drear venue than when the walls were black with the shadows of those who witnessed the smells that signed the onslaught of a death odor so that the window was thrown open in spite of the drizzle blowing in and in spite of the ropes of smoke from chimneys and bonfires blowing in that had ended the Friday so-called Good hours before. There then came death on horseback, all said who looked to the thundering sky before looking at the dying man to see if he roused to behold before him the huge nothing that would swallow him forever as it opened at the foot of the bed. Of a sudden not only death entered the room, brethren, not only death that had ridden all night across the sky to gather to it their fallen leader, but now a comforting sadness at the end of this action, an exhaustion addressing this final scene on this stage, of this his language come to an end, this that said to those in the room, *Watch here and now* the immemorial passage that undertakes all and everyone, but that desires nothing and everything, that dreams all and nothing as one and the same, that sleeps and dies one and the same, inexistence to inexistence—that is what they witnessed kneeling before the deathbed in prayer, that all else between this and that amid benevolence and ill would come to mean nothing without looking into each other's eyes to remember till their own eternities took them too.

Let us pray, brethren, that God may heal the sick,

From one end of the city to the other at all compass points silent mourners walked as if they too had died till there remained nothing in them but souls rent from bodies so that in the gloaming that was darker than gloaming they could be seen no more human than the wandering souls lifted by flood from their graves as far as the eye could see, moving then like the multitudes that were as shadows chained foot to foot in the mud, muck and dung three feet down. Deep eyeless inventions of despair, and despair's dream of redemption, the mourners joined therefore the lost souls up and down hither and yon in the new thunderous storm pacing the dolent city at the end of the dying man's dying. And so from the first sight of the risen dead, so many said still years and years later, it should have foretold to all who saw them there, and who of a sudden said what they saw, that these apparitions evoked ancient woes and dark defeats in shadows among shadows, phantoms beheld there that once were men while in the death scene of the rooming house all grew still and silent for Abraham to join them. But for the shiver of light that rose and fell from one or another window, and candles in one and another room of the rooming house that blew out as if by unknown breath, all grew still and silent till Abraham's soul left the corpse, so many said who said they watched while it did, and those that wrote that they watched while it did.

Those who bathed the corpse bathed little of it, remarking that he rarely bathed so as to stay in his health, but bathing rarely he suffered one or another skin ills on his body so that those who bathed what little they bathed saw till a few questioned that he should be entombed this day or night lest a disease let loose among those now who knelt to pray or walked the room to think, or not to think. Though no sun was seen to rise, as you know, but in the gloaming and without thunder a quiet rainful day dawned so that through the nearby window of the death scene a pall passed across the dying man's face that lay as dour as ever in its sleep. Those in his surround studied the face and the naked chest from moment to moment, staring down the dead lest his cadaver quicken to breathe, shiver or rattle at the throat when mourners turned in tears, bowed their heads or lidded their eyes, and of those who stared transfixed by the horror they waited to see him raise up to his elbows, and to speak, and to look around him at the room and its inhabitants.

Cats and monkeys! Witches' kitchens! Death's cloven hoof to the scene, attended by ravens too—the whole and entire history of God's curse rose against the backbone of the dying man's neck till he lay dead. Children and wife, and the slain, and the soldier's saber, and his dagger, and his dagger's blood, and the blood's curse—this world to ruin, this whereof all sorrow springs. Those who read the killing as God wreaking vengeance, or as the price of victory, and those who feared the worst, as if this was not it, fearing that war was still to be fought, or that war was still to be won, and those who knelt at the tolling of bells in the rain everywhere bells could be found from one end of the land to the other where rain could be found—all prayed to be forgiven or knelt to assign themselves to God as the unforgiven and impenitent. He died in a stranger's bed in a stranger's house, and this was nothing to death as the deaths by hundreds of thousands in marshes and woods under peach and apple and cherry trees till the dead grew one with the ground that were not devoured, no, but lay rotting in the earth as offal no less than a dog's or a pig's as he had seen when walking the field of Gettysburg and charred streets at the end of Richmond.

The sixth whom Mary Lincoln invited as a guest to the theatre was Secretary of War Edwin Stanton and his wife Ellen, but they declined.

The last conversation between husband and wife overheard by their carriage driver regarded life in retirement during which Mary recited again her desire to travel the world, to see first London, and then Paris, and then Rome, and she implored her distracted husband to say at long last where in the world he wanted to go. He replied one word. When he died Mary, the mother of his children—two of these dead, one by pneumonia, as you know, the other by typhus, as you know—*died in her heart*, she said to all who would listen, burying her heart in the coffin with her husband whose own heart he had buried with the woman he loved decades and decades before so that at last buried inside his own coffin with his widow's heart inside his own chest all was in its place, like sun and moon whether they could be seen or not, and flowers remained flowers whether blooming or withered, and sadness set everything of joy in its place and time too.

And so it was this then, that the derringer fired, as you know, and Abraham slumped in his rocker that ceased to rock, his beard leaning to right, his left leg to left to straighten, and by this on the instant he entered all that is memory, and all that is unconscious, whether meaning therein exists, with misprisions and delusions, the unconscious of deepest dreams unto death, where dreaming ends till his was the sleep without dreams, at last after decades and decades of dreams or of no sleep. Since the bullet cracked his skull without killing him on the spot, as he had foreseen it would, foreseeing it would because he had dreamt it would kill him on the spot night after night for years and years, and when he did not dream it because he did not sleep he saw the scene before him, and so instead of dying where he sat that Good Friday night he began the last long dream of dreams whereby he had not yet become the wandering soul among wandering souls that day and that night in the city of dread, but passed what existence remained of his existence marauding his mind from darkness till dawn. When before he lay dying he lay dying, but he did not die beside any of those mortally wounded at every midnight in gashed battlefields, those many faces in anguish he saw as he lay dying without dying, as he saw again and again without dying the indescribable eyes of those on their backs, arms and legs thrown wide under clouds descending as dark and thick as bats and birds.

Here ends the bloody business of this day.

yey tall, where the pointing lights, this cottonwood in this holler whereby I rest my spine so as to view once for all the harm to my limb and to the brokedown horizon of here now smoking as far as the eye can see into the set of the sun, my last set I spect for the vermin and critters alike come to feed of us done by cutlass and bullet and for me shrapnel so that there be my boot, where the pointer goes, with or without the foot in it since I feel nothing of it at the end of the ankle, if there is an ankle I also feel nothing of at the bottom of my leg that I see still attached to the hip of me, and so I am not yet the dead man across from my dying, him I shot not saying or hearing a word   not the smell of roses arised from the horizon, soldier boy, no, but the blood hot out of corpses piled high like twigs for to burn like witches in their evil doings, and so the red of the fires signing them to ash and bone and to the devil, that on the line at the edge of the world yonder whether it comes up sun for me or draws it down as the last sliver of God's glimpse of me or of all of us even, but that is the perfume of blood and bellies bursting in the far, human misery on fire so as to put to peace the mortal uprights no longer up after one and another braced against cutlass till one after another pledged his innards to it   for him at my foot as for my own self I have time to think on it so to say in my mind what I can't say now to any but me and the dead man here at my missing foot, and there be more than him and me in the next holler and ditch and pothole till the scape everywhere is awash in the buzz of flies and skeeters drawn to the stink of open wounds on dead men or to the prayers and cries and moans that stink of men dying so fearful they believe in God, in God's mercy there if not here, dreading the loss of this pitiful life they come to believe that is why God made another place to think on   and so there is this to think on if you are me in my holler surrounded by suspecting moles, and it is this, that we conscripted boys by circling schools so as to march them away to war, and we conscripted the old by circling theatres and parks and bars and brothels, marching them away from checker boards and beer steins and boiled eggs, and then we hunted bounty upon deserters who missed their mothers, these that we heard shot after drumhead trials of one or no minutes to remember them by, those suffering nostalgia, so they confessed, missing motherly cooking, so they confessed, or jealous of their wives and sweethearts that they might run off west with the

Gomorrah they fell into love with, so they confessed, and afterward they stood as best they could to be shot as best as the shooters could shoot them one after another by dozens before hundreds—nostalgia of that ilk   now he knows the underworld I thought after one shot before another, each shot whereby I said it to enter their sad souls into eternity even though none will say it of me as I have said it of the man I kilt without knowing his name or him mine, or what he was before he lay dying with my bullet into him who knows where, but there was smoke out of his shirt and the look of the loss of his being in his eyes till I will remember it till I die, but nobody to remember my look at the loss of me till they die   before I kilt and hunted to kill and conscripted boys and old men I mucked stalls and barns and such, and now there be nobody to tell my life to, not that man but one in the culvert one over, he that cut himself at the carrot of his neck so to end the pain of it, or the fear he wanted to end, dreading with his dizzies and hypos and trotters day in day out what with the noise and stink of himself and the earth shivers closing in for the bombs and long guns, and that is to remember the great groans of the fresh maimed man dying newly for how long who knows, and at how much suffering who knows, but no less I saw him sicken up before he struck with the Bowie knife long and thick and shinier than out of the Bible, so only after did I see the vermin in his nearby, dozens of them drawn to his privates so as to cleanse the woods of them, reclaim them to the soil or to heaven, or to nowhere   cadavers in their becoming baying like hounds *across the woods blown by cannon shot and great guns from high hills, in scapes as wide as seas, so it feels, noisome waste of that ilk year in year out of this war till we are meat for the hoofed and clawed that maraud through darkness among us war dead and war dying and war weary so as not to move even to save ourselves so we become sustenance for God's other creatures in culverts and ditches and hollers, them that eat and drink of us, not only the dead but the silent sleeping motionless dying, what with buzzards above and beasts below all beloved by God for enduring the stink of us in our wounding and dying, and drawn to it as to dinner, scavengers who put order to disorder   dog packs before dawn, themselves on the run from the smoke and the heat of fires, and from gunpowder, that smell that burns noseholes and eyes alike, theirs too, the four-footed, all that leads them to yap and growl and slather among the garden of our dying and dead so as to consume once for all whatever thing lay fragrant and helpless*

And there is this, that as he lay dying in a stranger's bed in a stranger's house, Abraham underwent the becoming of one of the slaughtered warriors delivered to the same great tomb of nature that he spoke of when he spoke of the tens of thousands of unnamed dead in the surround of woods and fields and creek banks for as far as the eye could see. Here and there bones and more bones strewed that site that day when he addressed the conscience of the living in the presence of dead facing dead across the vast expanse of one cold killing field where brethren slew brethren in the worst battle in the history of battles that anyone had fought or seen. The doomed commander spoke at the common grave of men who had lain scattered from one end of the landscape to the other for months after the battle, and that common grave was the naked ground itself, and so more who died there many months before, when the battle raged in grueling heat and damp to ravage the land and waters poisoned therefore by blood and innards, lay scattered unburied, rotted or torn asunder by varmints and critters, devoured night and day between wolf and dog packs, and hogs and housecats too. As he spoke, and others spoke, all the speakers and all who heard them who had ridden horseback against the mud of the rain of the days and nights that rutted the dirt roads, gathered together in the surround of human carrion, bodies not gathered or piled or carted, no, but innards and blood soaked into the earth of the countryside as far as the eye could see, even if the eye could not see any or much of it till you stood straight over a limb bone or dead vegetable black with blood.

They had walked, the gathered and their leader, pacing the site and nearby woods and nearby clearings, now and again seeing what remains there were to see clustered as bone piles uncollected, though whose bones connected to which soldiers no one knew or would know or could know. Pacing the fields, they held their hands behind their backs in respect of grass black with the blood of mayhem in one place where corpses had been laid on top of one another for burial or burning, or for another place of respect where innards and brain matter all those months later still glittered in the gun metal gray sun of November. As they toured the site in silence for so many deaths in so few days they saw therefore more than their eyes could show them. Signs and symbols divining woes to come if the curse did not end—these Abraham saw everywhere he looked and heard everywhere he listened. Slaughter begat slaughter, and yet slaughter had issued from the first hour of the first day the first diapered slave walked on the earth of the country. He saw the signs and symbols everywhere in woods and meadows and on river banks, and on all manner of killing fields of the reckoning that rent limbs from torsos or burst bellies by boar snout and wolf muzzle among the unburied dead and the undead wounded motionless on the earth of the country, some starving and thirsting, unarmed against predators, at some point unarmed against any and all who neared to prey upon them.

When he came to see and to speak he buried them by word, not by deed of burial, no, since the bones of the dead met the bones of other dead gathered together wherever bones could be found, whose bones did not matter in the least since even animal bones they gathered to bury, or not. In that ground of battle that was the bloodiest in the history of battle he saw signs and symbols again and again that his was a war of atonement, neither of vengeance nor of territory. Others spoke and he spoke to bury the dead where they lay or had been eaten months before, speaking words to rewrite creation, so many wrote who hated that he spoke what he spoke, making over the origin of the country in his image of it, so many wrote who hated that he spoke what he spoke, since it had not been true, as he spoke that it was, that all were equal here, unless he meant on the battlefield of dead, remaking creation for the godly alone, thereby serving up the ungodly to the ash heap of blood, innards and blood guilt, that ancient morality play. Those were not butterflies inside the mouths of dead Hebrews and dead Greeks that he recited, and read, and memorized, and imagined day in day out during the war of atonement, no, but monsters that harrowed hell inside the dark heart of humanity so that some should flourish because others slaved, even if it came to mean less that some flourished than that others slaved who were meant to slave, that some among the species were made ill for the sake of ill.

Now all those in vigil at the deathbed spoke to each other of the speech he spoke at Gettysburg, having before them midnight till the hours of the night stopped at sunrise, whatever sunrise meant to them then at midnight while watching the last warrior of the atonement atoning, those about him in his dying thinking aloud that the lolling tongue in the open mouth had cut loose the guff of threat and rapine to undo and overthrow two hundred fifty years of wretchedness by which millions of his brethren overcame millions of his brethren to comfort their needs, that these beat, hanged, burnt, and raped those other millions who were none other than those to torture and ruin for ill and profit. So said the commander again and again, who in saying such came to lose all that he had to lose and all that he loved till all and sundry hither and yon whether on the battlefield or across the country in the newspapers of the coming days listened and learnt.

Where he lay dying on a stranger's bed all others stood, knelt and paced unknowing of his condition minute to minute other than by this or that physician overhearing the beat of his heart or the shallow breathing in his lungs or the fever rising in him more and more as hours passed till the calm conviction of his face succumbed to the bullet mounted under an eye, the right, at the front of his brain, the right front of it, and so his right eye and jaw and sinus and forehead and nose swelled more and more, blackening his skin with blood and infection and bone ripped open at his cheek, the right cheek, so that hour after hour the globe of his eye swelled whiter and whiter as more of the globe rose out of the socket of it till all who saw him looked away and held kerchiefs to their faces from the stench of his dying. Then it was that he ceased to groan so that Dr. Leale never again fingered coagulate from the bullet hole behind the ear, and so many heard Leale wonder for the first time if he should have revived the dying man who was not breathing when he, first to reach him, had reached the box in the theatre to tend his wounds. *I brought him back to life,* Leale said, pointing to the deformations all who saw would remember till they too died, the meanwhile telling all who would listen that they had seen the victim's deformations at the end of the end.

Of the war of atonement that endless night, its evil core had ended two years before, an evil that the dying man could not abide, a godly end then that the ungodly enemy could not abide, and so on Good Friday night the ungodly avenged the undoing of the curse that made some godly and others ungodly, yet all countrymen, never more than in death across the vast tomb of the battlefield where the dying man had spoken to the gathered who gathered to listen, and just so Abraham's loyalists gathered at the site of his final battle, that of the deathbed battle, of dying on a stranger's bed, unconscious and dying in a stranger's room, as Henry Rathbone for a time lay dying in the surround of a puddle of his blood, or so he informed his sons, after trailing blood from his dead arm from the box in the theatre into the damp street so as to collapse once inside the door to the rooming house, or so he described to his sons who sat at his feet to listen, and yet neither man lay in danger of dying among twigs and leaves and stones over earth black with blood, or at river banks or in creek beds, or anywhere else that predators waited for sundown to prey.

And there was this, so Rathbone told his sons in the Germany of his exile, the he himself commanded Company C that held the bridge at Antietam Creek, afterward called Burnside Bridge at Antietam Creek despite the drawn battle among the single worst day of casualties in the long slog of the war, despite the grays outkilling the blues, and despite the so-called dog fall of the end of it. *If not a battle won*, said Abraham to their father, their father said to them, *not lost either*. It was, so the sons heard their father say, the first occasion when the commander spoke to him and to him only. Rathbone said of that day that he marched himself and his men by Sunken Road, so named for the slop of it in a rainfall, from Miller's Cornfield's to the West Winds, so named for the sturdy blow of it in a gale, and on then to the bridge that crossed the creek where their father stifled, smothered and repelled any attack of General Lee's army. *I survived visibly unharmed,* he confessed to be the purpose of his recitation to his sons who were too young to understand why he recited it.

One tomb for all, and that was nature, in the surround of which Abraham spoke of corpses still unclaimed and unnamed except by nature and nature's cruel summer of high heat and damp, and nature's hungry creatures among woods and fields, and its autumn of torrential rains and early snow—*nature* of that ilk. Such bodies were not yet assembled when he spoke, and others spoke, to be graved together as a mass, not to speak of those who died far from the field of battle where wounded men collapsed to bleed out or starve across meadows and fields for miles and miles farther than the eye could see, as if the war ill-used nature whereby instead of wheat or corn or cotton nature grew corpses across a wide swath of earth, corpses that begat corpses across the blood black earth, as you know. When he spoke in and to nature, nature had by then become signs and symbols to him of barbarism that had only its own nature, of cruelty and murderous intent day in day out, whether among godly or ungodly did not matter to the ruin of nature in the least. He spoke this in brief where thousands and thousands of corpses took root that could not overhear a word. *Until every drop of blood drawn with the lash shall be paid by another drawn with the sword, as it was three thousand years ago*—Abraham spoke this, an exhortation to God and to his gathered at the site of battle that foresaw the end to discord and insurrection and the murderous intent that incited cadaverous fields of weeds, rats and snakes.

He spoke leaning toward ancient wars of atonement so as to seal an ancient covenant that designed the death of ungodly deeds, even his ungodly deeds fighting a godly war, his own death the last measure. The man lay dying, murdered by yet another dying man, who even in his flight on horseback had begun already to die, knowing he was dying in spite of his flight since there was nowhere to flee, nowhere to be saved and nothing left to reckon or avenge. And so Abraham slept reconciled, most said they saw who saw among those who said they saw who saw nothing, but these were in hundreds before the year ended, but he slept like a long hairy infant whenever the groaning ceased and his breathing calmed to slow shallow exhalations, as if he did not or could not inhale, till those in the room about the deathbed witnessed him leaning into the last of life without resisting the end of things that he wanted to end. He would not have feared this end, so most said, or would have said that his violent end did not need his fear of it to happen, and it put many surrounding him to remember that in such thinking he measured his life in wait of a singular act in a singular moment of atonement and redemption or even of a righteous vengeance out of a nameless ill-directed act of destruction that he identified as primordial between himself, his country and God, but always beyond his understanding or power to rectify, instead something disclosed in an everlasting memory with inscrutable will and malice. He knew these sinews to sense day in day out their remorseless anger for the crime of being born or of being born only to die, not to die as a consequence of living one's time, like rodents and elephants, but to die as the intent and purpose of being alive.

Soldiers and soldiers' wives, and dead soldiers' widows, look there, as those gathered outside and inside the rooming house bore witness to that spot in the fallen world where the dying man angled left to right under a coarse blanket, his hairy overhanging feet not only too long for the deathbed, but for its blanket that otherwise elsewhere covered his nakedness—memories like these, brethren, if you saw what they who were there saw, what they who were there testified to having seen, a man who lay dying with a conscience written on his skin, who decried his brutish features and still more brutish deeds in sending thousands to their deaths and thousands to cause the deaths of thousands more, all countrymen, and then all brethren in death, whether buried or not, some dead on the instant, but thousands more dead from the heat and damp of July and so from wounds infested with flies and their delivered eggs breeding maggots that nested to feed on the blood so as to grow into large shiny buzzless creatures of another generation. And that is only one lesson in death since many were cut from this or that limb of theirs by battlefield surgeons who were not surgeons, no, but had learnt to saw here before there through apt bone and muscle so as to cauterize with torch and even gunpowder the stump of this or that arm or leg or foot or eye or ear or member, and that is only another lesson in death since most of those who suffered it died too, of shock to the heart or brain at the wound and its treatment.

Killers begetting killers and corpses begetting corpses like lilacs beget lilacs—*atonement* of that ilk unto the hard limit whereby corpses bloated with heat and bile bloated too with mosquitoes one generation after another day in day out hatched from the same exposed distended belly, always the next of the pismires and mosquitoes, and the same glistening slow fat buzzless flies, as you know to remember, inside their laminated silver backs and bellies, the small insidious predators of the dying and the dead that fielded this and that meadow, wood and crop yard for days and days, and night after night. And this is only one lesson of death among soldiers who at the end of the end would have believed anything to keep them alive, even God. Of gods and men, brethren, men doomed by the curse to atone for it so as to redeem for themselves a future, and the gods themselves doomed by the curse of ungodly men to lesson them by blood and blood guilt across thousands and thousands of lives squandered and loves lost and beauty relinquished almost from the onslaught of creation, that creation the same gods promised to men and to their brothers and sisters to tend now ruined from end to end. The dying man abed and unconscious only observed the most ancient gods, whether pagan or biblical, since he fought ancient battles of the mind, heart and flesh, so he proclaimed, and biblical battles among the righteous tribes obedient to God's word, and the thinking of his mind traced a path from the earthly curse of slavery to the infernal curse of a bloody fate for the accursed whose blood had to run and did run for years and years in meadows and woods and dirt streets, and poisoned canals and rivers and lakes for as far as the eye could see.

Rathbone informed his sons that he had fought in battle thrice, among these the infamous Fredericksburg battle, named thereafter the butchery at Spotsylvania County, there whereby thirteen thousand men upended across four days of December, blues pegging out three times more than grays since grays held revetments from Marye's Heights to rain down cannonade and Parrott guns blasted down all day every day, deafening so to shiver the ground—these percussion arms of great distance by their caps, hammers and triggers made men vomit when not blown off, up and apart or curled faces down in rifle pits as cold as Christmas. Of this he informed his sons, *I survived it visibly unharmed.* And he fought Yorktown too, though that was more skirmish than battle, he said, killing only hundreds and wounding only thousands, but then there he had had to flee to bare woods and bracken while ordnance blasted low hanging tree boughs till trunks hooked as if in a hurricane to tear men by their heads and shoulders, so Rathbone told his children as they sat at his boots. *I survived it visibly unharmed,* he confessed to be the purpose of the recitation to his sons who were too young to understand why he recited it.

On streets and in the deathbed room in the rooming house rain and the sounds of rain came as they had the morning before so that on this day a dull sunless sky appeared when all knelt on brick, stone, mud, floorboards, and carpets as if a quiet voice whispered into their ears that it was time to kneel. As torches died and bonfires died and street lamps extinguished, these thousands outside and inside knelt to pray, none hearing the dying man die, but as if gloaming signed to them that Abraham could not live beyond another daylight or was doomed and destined to die of the Good Friday murder before an Easter resurrection of which he could not partake since he was not the son of a god, or a god, or a false prophet doomed to die, or a god mistook for a false prophet doomed to die. This would be the tale of the *black sunrise* that thousands told to each other for years and years, of a hush come over gatherings till nothing other than rain sounded, and of a stillness come over gatherings whereby none looked as though they breathed, such hush and stillness that only a barking jumpy cur showed it to them, of so many estranged expressions on so many estranged faces that none among the gathered seemed as human as before one to another, those who witnessed a translation to the color of the sky and to the blow of winds across treetops when a soft measured rain began that did not abate for all that day named Holy Saturday by those who believed in it.

And this tale of black sunrise was told far and wide across the city so that at the same moment thousands felt in their bones that Abraham had passed because a voice inside their ears said that he had passed, but some there just felt in their hearts that by seeing the sky as dark as dark gets without thunder and lightning to follow some deed like his death had been done once and for all, and then among the eldest there was their bone-weariness telling them to go home since the drama in them had now finished. They would have gone mad, some said, as Rathbone said of Abraham's widow that Holy Saturday, and of how in his near mortal wound he felt madness inside him too, but God was not kind to them that morning or any other after among those who preferred to derange the world as they found it, though they lamented as if mad, all at first hushed and motionless, estranged each to each who had embraced and wept together, and prayed together as long as the dying man did not die, as you know to remember, till some openly sobbed or shivered a fist at the rain or called out to arm themselves, shaking off the frozen moments till all began across the city to keen in grief by turns roaring and fearsome or murmuring in sullen exhaustion one to another after the timeless night. Theirs was grief not to be endured and so they endured it, many at last gone to sleep before waking for the first time to his death and that he was dead forever whom they saw stroll the streets of an evening among equals and countrymen inside bars and brothels against which his wife warned him every day that he went out, and he went out every day that weather or his health or the war allowed.

Those who believed in souls felt his swell away from horror and slaughter and despair, all darkness in him blown away, instead a deathless essence of light they believed they saw emerge from the top of the rain, so hundreds who believed in souls lay claim in letters for years and years, and this was because the tragedy underwent another act undoing the tragedy since no one could expect to survive the tragedy of his murder unless day in day out they understood themselves doomed as he understood himself to have been doomed before being born without refuge or rescue in madness, wars, this or that messiah, or even his urge day in day out to suicide from this and that nearby tree limb. The dying man, or the dead man, or the deaf and blind and dumb man, or the man blind and dumb only had filled up his thinking for years and years with violent death all day every day till he remarked to any and all who would listen that he was not to die from illness, cancer or old age or by his dread of waking blind, deaf, dumb, paralyzed, and buried for his relentless reading of fear-mongering tales of madmen in love with beautiful dead beloveds who no less resurrect before their lover's eyes. He woke in dreams to large carrion birds flying away with the globes of his eyes in their beaks or talons, or woke to his innards uncoiling as the same large carrion birds flew away with one end of them, or woke to his tongue torn from his mouth—same birds, same flight, differing innards. These things happened to him in dreams as they happened in poems, stories, epics, and bibles whereof he read day in day out, but then there is this that hushed any who heard him speak it, as he did to any who would listen—he dreamt all that happened across battlefields in his war of atonement, and so it was no dream when he spoke of blood, reckoning and the need of redemption.

Of his unconscious, where the dying man existed without salvation except in death across the time of his dying's timelessness there was no more order or mercy or law to it than to the falling rain or to his embrace of dead women he had loved and lost, ghosts his sleep lured into his mind, ghosts who came to life only to die before him again and again as his mother had always done again and again, and as Ann had always done again and again, and as his sons had done. Dreaming such as these with dark outside hour after hour, he did not quiet till rains came and damp black sunrise came with it so that the sound of the rain on the earth and against the windowpanes of the room in the rooming house signaled an end to his groaning and the onslaught of silence in him that would not end ever.

He quieted till he could not grow quieter between life at its end and death at its onslaught, so said the prayerful and the sin eaters praying at the horizon of the deathbed and calling from windows to the sky and to the crowds gathered below, all those believing in souls at a horizon between heaven and earth, even though to Abraham that same horizon divided earth only from hell since he was never not going to hell wound by wound and groan for groan like other dead warriors for three and four and six thousands of years, men slain and men who slew, breath for breath too like other dead warriors for the millennia of wars that he had memorized and recited, those of slaying and the slain now and later anywhere and everywhere always so that dust became the only fruit of living. Across those killing fields he spoke briefly among butchered bodies and the stench of thousands of years of annihilation such that in the end even horse slaughtered horse down to the ground—he had seen the carcasses beside a stream. Surveying with his long arms and long hands opened wide around him, Abraham saw that the charred and blood red landscape suffered scars and pits like the hills of Jerusalem and the vale at Thermopylae.

After telling his story again and again till his sons would remember it even though too young to know why he told it, Rathbone fell silent before them, speaking instead only to their mother till he spoke only to himself or to no one, passing first his nights in the farthest room of the consular house, and then he passed his days there too, passing days and nights on and on as far from his beloveds without deserting them or being deserted by them. His wife and children came to suffer his absence since through the door of the farthest room in the consular house they heard him speak to someone who was not there, and then he replied to someone who was not there so that a day or night came when he informed his wife and sister that he was undergoing visitations from the dead when not hearing voices from the dead who did not visit him. Clara reassured him that no one stood in the room or spoke to him, and since she possessed true conviction in the eternal resurrection of the dead he must believe her when she promised that there before their eyes together in the farthest room of the consular house in Germany when Rathbone saw a specter or heard a voice, none was present.

There had been no motion in him other than the

body rocking in the hands and arms of the seven, three physicians and four soldiers, as you know to remember, rocking as if imparted to a gently swaying slave ship, and the sea that sways the ship, and the inscrutable gods that sway the sea day and night forever. The sky is greater than earth, and the inner life greater than all the world about it, and in him who lay dying once and for all after decades of dreaming of dying, and philosophizing death, the inner life let loose in him to what end who knows, but those who watched and waited saw none of his mind's terrors and tortures come to life in his face, nothing that witnessed the madness and bloody images of his inmost mind day in day out that he suffered in silence or in thunder, but underwent so as to stir and drive forebodings that exiled him to his violent end and to his country's salvation.

In vain the mastodon clings to life, and so to Abraham's dying body plasters were here and there applied, and rubber bottles of hot water were applied, and soon roses and roots surrounded the bed, and against the stench elderberry, mullen and pokeweed effused the man's flesh that slowly had taken the shape of another man whole and entire, a stranger in a strange bed now, naked in jags under a coarse blanket bedpost to bedpost, articulated as a man no one knew to recognize. *If you would see me again,* Abraham often remarked to any who would listen wherever listeners might gather, *look next under your bootsoles.* The vigil silenced when he groaned less, and less often, since the pain therefore dimmed, and the measure of it too, till the swelling of his brain against the bone of his skull mattered no more to it that his nerves neither pained him nor did not, and so Dr. Leale, most said or wrote, now and again touched the deforming ashen face, a horse's face near the end of the end, and Dr. Leale left off scratching the hole in his head of its crust.

Before the black sunrise the sunrise widow wept in a drawing room the night long, as you know, waiting with Clara Harris, fiancé and sister of the unconscious Rathbone, women waiting to hear of their beloveds' deaths, as the son of the dying leader waited because the children of the dying wait, as the dying man waited to die since the doomed who know themselves doomed are always waiting to die, each in their place in their times, playing their parts as they know their parts to play, sacred idiots all. All who die and all who wait for all who die to do so do so as if in a dream like the dreams the dying dream wherein the sky is no longer the sky they knew before they lay dying, no, nor is it the same sky for loved ones before their loved ones lay dying anymore than seas are seas as before the enchained enslaved sail them, as the dying leader sailed the sea in the hands and arms of the seven from theatre to deathbed. Everything forgot of life in dying opened then a void more void than death itself to the living till sky was not sky, sea not sea, clouds not clouds of the day or night before. Had there been a moon that dark drear night it would have been a differing moon from the moon the night before, and stars too, differing from the last night that there were stars to be seen in a sky that was still a familiar sky when Abraham did not lay dying or dead.

As he lay in a stranger's bed in a stranger's rooming house, his whole and entire was that of a man abandoning life who had yearned to abandon it, so most said, and had practiced abandoning it during night after night of sleeplessness and the sleeplessness nightmares inspire, as all who die appear to abandon life to all those not dying there and then, those who are there and then bearing witness to the dying as they leave life behind. It is written on their faces that the dying leave behind all such things that only belong to the living, whether peaches and apples or stars and moons does not matter in the least, and did not that night matter in the least, but it was by his graduated vacancy across the long silent hours that the gathered took into themselves their inmost understanding of the dying man's dying while they watched him do it. When Leale felt the beating heart his hand foretold it ceasing so that each time he touched the victim's chest mourners everywhere in the room fixed on the medical man's expression, quieting till Leale touched his own lips with a forefinger to mark that the dying man slept, if that was the word, and only looked dead, at last without the thought of dying weighing his mind, unless unconscious he thought of dying as if he had already done it or was doing it in a dream from which he would not wake. There he lay while dying was happening without the thought of it in him to make it happen, as he had always affirmed that his violent end did not need his embrace of it to happen.

Abraham thought always of dying on the spot though since he had witnessed his mother lingering to die for days and days from the snakeroot berries that poisoned her and her in-laws, and he witnessed the woman who was his only true religion linger and linger to die for days, as he witnessed first this son, then that son both lingering for days and days before dying, and so he could not believe it of himself that he would linger and linger in his dreams and nightmares of death, and the mosaic of his readings that incited his dreams and nightmares persuaded the inspiration that his would be a sudden violent end. Never to be the first to die, a thought he thought aloud in this and that letter or note or saying, but always in his mind he would be the last man of the war of atonement, another thought he thought, wrote and said to anyone who would listen, unless God was making him mad before destroying him—this thought too he entertained for all and sundry to hear, as you know. He expected a deafening end to him, like cloudburst or cannon fire, and as immutable in him as bone dust, and yet the seven carried him in their arms and hands from here to there that would be his end place, a stranger's bed, as you know, the deathbed pillow, as you know, against which his head bled but little, as his head had bled but little against the cuff of Laura Keene's dress, as you know, and while it came by violence his death was not sudden, even though from the onslaught it was sure. If he dreamt the slave ship dream that he knew for decades in his sleep as he lay dying, he dreamt it with the dark dampness overlooking him, asleep under an unscrupulous sky that teased his freedom, as every slave dreamt or thought when seeing the sky, or the sea, so many said to Abraham among those who had been enslaved that he would meet on his walk at sunset past bars and brothels.

The vigil's end neared when the dying victim lived in word only and was himself only in name so that he lay almost nonbeing, nothing but the cadaver of himself that was and would become still more the most recognizable human shape in all the country over the country's brief story—tall, ugly, dour, and dyspeptic, wearing his darkness above his collar while speaking Poe's *Raven* from memory or reciting here and there now and again from Gray's *Elegy*, or reading aloud to all and sundry the opening lines of *Richard III*, or more morose than ever expounding of an evening at the fireplace in winter that his marital life reminded him of Macbeth's marital life, not forgetting either the mystery of the child found dead behind a door of the castle, no, nor the suicide of his wife by hanging, this reminding him of the suicide by hanging of Iocasta, the wife of Oedipus, and if he spoke of the Christ, though not often, it was the Christ in the vale of Harma Geddon, or at the hill of Megiddo, the Christ astride his stallion with the gilt sword born of his open mouth annihilating Satan's legions before annihilating Satan so that all evil vanished in an instant. Still for him the after of life only always meant a netherworld, that fiasco, and nonexistence, that fiasco, and the consciousness of nonexistence in a netherworld, that fiasco—*underworld* of that ilk, *nonexistence* of that ilk, *consciousness* of that ilk.

Long in their vigil mourners prayed because the battlefield in him had spread till the odor of cannon fire and gun powder and wet blood smelt on the deathbed at the end of those immortal hours of dying in a stranger's house, in a stranger's room, on a stranger's bed, on a stranger's pillow. *The sorrow of death compass me,* he knew of the psalm, *and the floods of ungodly men,* he knew of the psalm, *the sorrow of hell compass me,* he knew of the psalm, *the snare of death* he knew. The sun that rose as black as the inside of his coffin incited the onslaught of death to all and sundry who sensed in belly and heart that his brain thought no more whether of reason or of dreams till here and there again and again across the city mourners heard enthralling howls of that hard night's travail from windows, spinning wagons and galloping horsemen. In death came the abolition of dying, and of the dread of dying, and of the tragedy of living on after dead beloveds, and so of the end of the death foretold, instead once and for all the death finally told, his story of death to be told after a lifetime of slavery to the thought of death, of shedding the blood of others and of the blood guilt that would ensue on and on till this moment of this hour of this timeless day, that one after the one the Christians call *Good*.

As morning and morning rain rose and fell the room dampened to the touch in the dead moments after dawn, and a clock down the hall chimed whose chime had been stilled so as not to distemper the unconscious victim for the hours and hours of his dying. Now that he lay as dead as dead gets the chime marked the hour to remember when he began his death (if death can be said to commence), those moments before or after the hour struck since some said before while some said after, according to their memories or to their pocket watches wound or unwound, or wound down to unwound. His dead body, if *his* is the word, lay more rigid than it had in his hours and hours of coma, and now that gray dawn lit the room his dead face darkened not from the black night outside or from the shadows of oil lamps and candles, but from the damage deep into his skull and brain until the swelled skin presented blacker and harder than polished shoe leather, and it smelt stronger, smelt of the stench of death that the living find unbearable.

From the toe and arms of the deathbed's dead his mourners listened without hearing and looked without seeing, bearing witness and beholding so as to remember and recite decades on what it was that happened to whom, where and how, though few remembered the same memories even later that day *how it was* so that years and years later it was as much a story as it was a true story. So Rathbone had once told his sons who sat at his feet in their house in Germany, telling it to them that much written and said inside and outside courts and newspapers and books was no more true than the south's story of it, or that the Catholic church had done it to him, or that disloyalists among his cabinet had done it to him, or that he, Rathbone, their father, had allowed it to happen by sitting where he sat instead of rising to save him or only to learn if he could have saved him if he had tried to save him.

At the end of the end the prayerful had foregone their hopes for anything other than Abraham's soul resting at God's foot among the millions of dead glorified souls that rested there before his, and the sin eaters sang hymns of resurrection, no longer weeping as they had through the hours and hours of his dying. By the hour of the great man's death, so Rathbone recited to his sons till they could remember it the way he recited it to them, their father had been removed as if dead or nearing death, but as it came to pass he lay in bed at home at the other man's end so that he missed whole and entire the widow bellowing through an open window to those hundreds gathered in the dirt street waiting to hear of his life or death inside the new rain, the widow a small dark furious creature shrieking still till dragged by her arms from the window to collapse into silence once her husband's dying had finished. That then was when she had finished, when to bellow or to curse did not become the first widow to the country, and this she took to as if she had thought it through for years after hearing it from her husband for years, by this planning to outlive her husband for decades in depression, despair and penury so that she might outlive herself. And she did.

Through windows thrown open against the stench of dying a thousand gathered in the dirt streets heard cries rise from inside the rooming house just after dawn, and so the last sound of nature the dying man would have heard in his coma, if he heard in his coma, was rain on the roof and rain falling to earth and rain pelting the window pane of the death room. So began another day of storm at first as drizzle, but then not, and so of washout and backwater and overflowed rivers and canal banks, the so forth and so on of hysterical rain to kill all that blossoms, that drowns the errant cat and piglet and rooster while women seek shelter and soldiers in knee high boots dismount to rein their horses lest they flee and sink into mud and pig bowel sludge where rutting dogs flail to their shoulders before they die howling. Cattle too mired in the muck of the dirt streets till dead so that for hours carcasses among dogs and cats and pigs and cattle and horses swept into the river and downstream the river to the ocean. Naked mutilated whores, these too swept down canals in the surround of the hundred brothels and bars across the capital, and soldiers too killed by secessionists, and secessionists too killed by soldiers, all swept along canals that reached the river that reached the ocean and so the bellies of sharks and such life.

That flag, as wide and high as a wall, shrouding the corpse of him smelt of smoke, and so of war, and so of his war hard-pressed that killed or routed the ungodly by the hundreds of thousands, and killed or routed the godly by the hundreds of thousands, and among the killed all ended bloody forms and shapes of what were men bent and bowed into the ground, buried or not. All were children once, all green once, on both sides green, with the fear in them of all that are green so that the leader of the victors said to the green soldiers soon to die in victory, *You are all too green to fight, north and south of you.* Now who they were he really did not know unless they were dead from battle and he read their names, but then he knew only their names, and yet they knew death before he did, whether green or not in life, and so they knew what he did not, less than green about death than he till he too died to know all that there is to know of it. One gray and dim daybreak after another— these he did not wake to after death, yet everyone who did not die with him woke to these day in day out for days and days, and yet there was this, that when finally there came a sun at dawn and flowers opened and cattle chewed meadows, the day brought people to tears since he was not among them to take pleasure by it. Then the conspicuous and capricious round sun was too splendid to look at, dizzying his mourners, and all were mourners but the slavers and their kin, and all these had taken to ground after the death, some as far south as south goes, others as far west as west goes, as you know.

In their grief his mourners for a time found life too intense to live it, its sounds and shapes and smells overwrought and overripe, as when the blind are cured of their blindness and the deaf their deafness. These were sexless grievers too so that bars and brothels boarded up in patriotic memoriam, and whores hid their breasts in modesty who otherwise held one or both bare in their hands to tempt this before that client, half of whom suffered disease, half of whom feared it, as the murdered man suffered it or feared it, fearing that his youthful whoring killed his true beloved and addled his wife into melancholy and opium, and gave to him his hypos and the foresight of a violent end, even though there was this too, that the foresight saw he could not die till he had become free to die, and so this is why he walked the streets at sunset past bars and brothels since he was a slave to the end of slavery and to the war that atoned for the curse of it, dooming ungodly and godly alike to be alike killed and killing countrymen and their kin. Those who died under summer trees of fruit, who looked up as they bled to their ends, saw above them apples and peaches and cherries they could neither pick nor eat, but were the fruits of their childhood that they were losing to buckshot busted bellies and to blown limbs or sword-sliced gizzards, at least among those who lay knowing what killed them even before it did. All were under peach and apple and cherry trees at the end of the end, motherless child one and all, bleeding out into the ground and drawing by that varmint and insect, and sorts of nature better left unsaid. But for this, that muskrats invaded the bungholes of the undone by death or dismemberment under this or that peach tree wherever the dying befouled to do so. That is one lesson of war to remember, brethren.

So there was no life in him now except what moved the bed where his cadaver lay—the weight of those who prayed with their elbows on it, fingers clasped closed, and the final clutches of his widow across his chest that rattled the bed springs and the body dead on them. She asked for someone to shoot her too, though none did, but many would have obliged had it been a legal thing to do. The flag as wide and high as a wall arrived from the Capitol into which the body was shrouded for the ride to the manse in the damp dawn that no less felled leaves and branches into the mud and the dung of all manner of creatures. In wet streets bedraggled mourners would follow where the dead man rode inside his flag, assuming dead men ride, and most said they followed in silence, but if they had spoken or sung or prayed the rain would have silenced the sounds, and so the worth of their singing and praying and speaking would have been of a subdued exhausted literature of mourning, unrecorded and unremembered—sounds, all but the rain and the wheels of the rolling cadaver, lost altogether forever.

Mourners of dead sons and husbands and brothers of the war of atonement followed the cadaver and the cadaver's widow to see also among them wagons of dead and wounded on battlefields at all compass points bossed down in mud tracks, rutted wet or dry did not matter in the least, wrestling the landscape against flies and mosquitoes and vermin that came aboard to devour the meat at the wounds, coveting the open holes of the world of the dead and dying. Such grievers grieving still the death of loved ones had wearied of grief till now they could not be wearier of grieving and memorizing and remembering the memories, so in this death wearied through the night by the shoot and by the frenzy of shock and by the hysteria of fear amid gas lamps, torches and bonfires doused by the dawn rain, at last put out for the drama to be done, if it was done. All there saw ghosts gathered to grieve his death, and their disappearance too, ghosts of soldiers bowed down by the millions, and ghosts of slaves bowed down by the millions, all walking bowed behind the cadaver and the cadaver's widow so as to put out the lights that the drama be done.

Even by his death all was in its place, as he pronounced time and again to his unmoored wife, that from redemptive war to dead children to devouring opium and the madness thereof day in day out all would be in its place. These afflictions he had a lifetime of, suffering the consciousness of on and on so that it was in its place he should not know his own dying as he had known others dying in their time and place, even by his orders dying in their time and in their place. Though he lay for hours blind, mute and deaf, if deaf, he rested in his place too since he had seen the elephant and heard the owl silencing crickets and frogs and mice in the middle of night, and his hands had filled the circumference of Ann's flesh whether he lay beneath her or above her or mounted her from behind before expiating and pledging love and lamenting her death *sacredly,* as he had loved her that way, so he said to all who would listen, and he had whored among whores and carnival acts, gathering there the pox, if he had it or only feared he had it, fearing that his pox had killed Ann and later unmoored the mother of his children. Yet now all was in its place, as he had pronounced time and again to all and sundry who would hear, even not knowing the place and time of his killing, yet knowing he would be killed after waiting and waiting for it year in year out, desiring to know of *the last bitter hour, the stern agony, and shroud, and pall, and breathless darkness,* so the psalm promised, but did not fulfill. He died unknowing that he was dying, and so died denied the final huge nothing before him unless he dreamt tombs, jackals and old men shouting into the sea's wind.

Some said silver coins closed his eyes forever, others that these were gold, but which gold coins from where by whom no one knew, and if silver, which silver—dollars, halves, quarters, but then there were those who spoke only of pennies closing his eyes, pennies sealing his eyes from seeing again while he lay shrouded neck to bare feet in a national flag as wide and high as a wall, as you know. Then there is this, that pallbearers bearing the pine box to return his cadaver to the manse removed their boots in the doorway so as to evade the widow removed again to the drawing room down the hall away and below from the death room with its deathbed and death pillow and her dead husband. As a consequence she did not know till the body began its death roll that her husband had been taken, or that Clara Harris had been taken to her wounded lover and brother who did not die, and then in the handle of her eldest son and eldest friend she hurried to a carriage to follow, as she would hurry weeks and weeks later to follow his body, following Old Bob, her dead husband's favorite horse, weave and fidget as the horses of dead soldiers know to do, seeing thereby her husband's riding boots facing backwards in the saddle's stirrups, the symbol and sign of a fallen leader—all this so that in an instant she knew she no longer laid claim to him, no, but once and for all he was besieged by loyalists, idlers, stragglers, and braggarts whom she despised, as they despised her. Those she blamed for his hypos, and the onslaught again and again of anxiety and guilt that bred his nightmares and daymares whereby this and that drama of war or nostalgia suffered him to enter, among them loss and death, and to the last torment over a life not led, for the marriage of Macbeth led instead.

Of the coins closing his eyelids, it can be said that dozens who lay claim to gather at his bed lay claim to placing them, whether silver, gold or copper did not matter in the least, so that dozens lay claim to playing another part in the disaster than the part they played, as hundreds lay claim to sharing the death room at the instant of his death, as dozens lay claim to carrying his mortally wounded form from theatre to rooming house in the mud and dung of the wet dirt street, as thousands lay claim to hearing the shot from the audience, each laying claim to playing a part in the disaster that they did not play that long hard night full of dread. *Who knows but that my words may make them yield,* he said old blind Homer said, but he did not believe that conviction anymore than did old blind Homer. *Of tumors and mice I sing, of God who shatters by thunder,* Abraham would read aloud across breakfast to whosever baffled faces met his. *David against the Philistines in Gaza,* he alluded with a smile—*the king who danced naked in the desert among sacks of foreskins in thousands,* but he explicated this footnote only when someone asked. *I will divide Shechem and mete out the valley of Succoth,* Abraham read that David had written. *Gilead is mine,* he read over eggs and toast since David had written it. *Manaseh is mine*, he said after battling its namesake, that battle in the war of atonement, as Shiloh too meant something more of ancient history than nothing to him. *I will not be moved*, he concluded, rising from the table. And he was not.

till now by my hands I lived, by livery wherein I sponged donkeys and horses, raked stall of shite and such, and mice and such, straw made stinking wet by pizzles fuller than a child of animals pissing loud, long and smoking with heat of the sort little sister beheld, afraid of the monstrous thing but drawn to it too so that in the stable next she drew the farrier to her, him darker than blood at sundown who had been bred at half tones therefore, proof of the slave blood running through him in his past, him free as thunder though, how so who knew but he were as free as a sky, him my sister's Gomorrah she loved since the mud of childhood where they looked like each other at day's end, him that spared her drowning under the crick water floods so he won her heart before her flesh that he won too—love of that ilk that by my hands I fought against and for since who knows what but that now by my hands I be dying here in my holler boot to boot with the man I kilt by my hand and little sister gone as west as west gets where maybe nobody cares who they are or what they look like or howsome they speak or that their babies make no sense at all—love of that ilk   that called battle sweat whether of the heart or spleen or bung hole does not matter in the least but it pumps fast and hard and loud inside a soldier so outside what runs near as black as the sun at midnight mixes with the nature under it—leaves, twigs, bug crush, the earth beneath us, him and me, the dead and the dying, and there is this, I hear a crick nearby but so what, manful in my doom, made sanguine by it, turnt inside out so I can see some boot with a smoking bloody foot inside it, my foot in my boot by my head bent from this tree trunk here without which I fear I were to fall east or west never to see nothing more again, what there is to be seen, my foot say, the missing one, and the boot covering it, a dying man's boot therefore, a right boot with a right foot in it, numb as rocks though where the scalding metal tore across my ankle I guess and scorched the stump all in the same I guess where inside the mangled boot the mangled foot I guess looks a paw in a bear trap or some other roaming marauding creature in the wrong step forward, or backward, and that would bespeak all of us not able to go back for a missing hoof or paw or foot so as to flee, no, but to flop down like back shot by rifle, thereafter to lay shored up by a cottonwood trunk or an elm or an oak till the umbrella of heaven sheltered us one and all against *our dread and abhorrence, we who do not think on heaven till we think our last nor pray neither in our quiet breathless hearing and seeing that is all in all waiting to die   them of us who bible think into the hardihood and manliness of dying flat and alone in the surround of others dying manly too, by such breathing and groaning and coughing as all those done fleeing or fighting, now only God's creatures like all the others that walk or trot or slithe or swim, us tracked of God by signs of our sick up and shits and all the stomach ills that laid waste to us roadside without bombs bursting or bullets whistling or shrapnel burning like a torch, or those still staggering on and on sicker than chinamen from dead goose and hog and dogs kilt in ditches full of dead bodies they fed on before they were feed, scavengers eaten that ate the corpses so as to make more corpses of them that ate them, on and on day in day out of that   from that first pitch of distant battle that was the elephant in its graveyard we grew scrofules on our skin from such diet as the dead living off the dead so that we scratched itch and groomed away flies stuck to our sweat and jiggers of blood crossing our faces, but of this if we lit a match to burn off a swamp leech or maggot a shot rang out from them in the dark to us in the lit so we learnt to be food to the bugs to forage on our skin except at the bollocks and bung hole where the itch agonized or bites festered into blisters and such, like as we was toiling away at women we toiled into, them who saddened us by their mouths and up their backsides but even when we didn't toil in them we saddened too because we didn't, saddening before, during and after therefore till we suffered instead the picture book drawings of bucks ravaging women like the sisters and daughters of us while we lay in darkness smelling up our britches with our hands on our whistles, us by the thousands in our blankets who had done enough harm to females we didn't know or want to know or loved or desired to love, all of us dreaming awake of home by it, waiting for sunrise by it, yet a rise without a sun to show for it in the forest or for the smoke of fires lit a day before so as to unforest our concealments or their concealments, leaving us and them stripped bare of hope till ours was the sky of hell we looked up into, that of murder done and murder to be done, done just by following the sickness sick men left along the trail they did not know they were leaving, it lit by the devil sky so it came to be that I never before shot a treed squirrel let alone a man with eyes like my own, and so my hardihhood they named it who conscripted me before I conscripted others, my hardihood that were my will to kill men dead, to sit unblinking for hours so as to do it, to say nothing so as to do it, and then to do it   impedence, a tree say, or say little sister, the that of this or that showing my life to me when I lived without a name note stuck to the chest of my shirt with the who and where of me so as to say what of my carcass if I am not ate first by varmints of the earth or fowl of the air, and yet I have transgressed, and so I am a transgressor, and so he transgressed it is written onto the note, by this informing God and whosoever that the bad monkey inside me ended*

in the lion's mouth, that I die less for the loss of some part
of some foot inside some boot, though it is the right I am
persuaded, than for the sickness called the onslaught of the
flux that glooms me, the homesick bracing the spirit to kill,
not only robbing cradles of them I kilt or conscripted but of
the graves I robbed among the half dead too, the boots blown
off, though it is the right I am persuaded, them I retrieved
from a gut shot groaning man on a hillside—homesick of
that ilk I am dying of, for my missing foot past bleeding now,
and that is the good news, and the man I kilt I did not back
shoot, and that is the good news, but I can fight nor flee no
more, and that is the good news too

What Sumter had been at the onslaught of the onslaught became the *infernum* the atonement war's creator dreamt year in year out across decades of dreaming, or when not dreaming while he did not sleep Sumter became the *infernum* of his wakeful sadness that remained day in day out as dark as dark gets. There, where the first shots fired and the first dead died, Sumter made Abraham weep for both sides killing both sides on and on as if for forever since killing would beget killing as uprights beget uprights who would execute the killing till enough souls rose up into their own forlorn nation overdone with killing, corpses and the grief that ensues. Then, brethren, the guilt in blood guilt would issue to end the war atoning for the iniquity that cankered the country's heart even before it was a country, as you know, when it was only wilderness colony after colony, as you know, whose founders founded slavery the same first year of the first colony—*new world* of that ilk. Where Sumter fired the first shots and so knew the first deaths of the great divide there came after the beginning of the end of the war that would lead to the end of the end of the war the overgrown burden of prisoners there, on this map here, that translated what had been an armory of the country whole and entire into a captive camp that translated by the end of the end of the war into a death camp, itself iniquitous and so in need of the atonement that the country whole and entire had needed for two hundred fifty years.

Begin the tragedy.

Now therefore we speak of Andersonville, so-called, and its deplorables one after another among grays and blues alike across the dust of the camp infamous for starvation, disease and death, and yet where no battle happened after the first skirmish to open the war's theatre of the south, as if those first shots fired and first deaths done foresaw atonement by the deaths of more than ten thousand captives, wherein the only potables were rain and snow and urine since Sweetwater Creek akin to the camp flowed sweet while the spillway inside the stockade ran as poisonous as snakes for the dung, blood and corpses swimming through it. While battle was as worse as worse gets the captive camp worsened the worse till the death camp made of Sumter that was no more Sumter therefore the worst that worst gets. Those hung by thumbs or heels or one big toe in the sun or rain or cold snow saw it easier than most in that their bones only dislocated so as to elongate forever that they would not walk like others or grip this and that like others whereas dead bodies from starvation and thirst and the diseases thereby flamed in bonfires from one end of the camp to the other, and here some could keep warm (God forgive those) till flesh and bone at two thousand degrees for two hours among the corpses piled higher than men's heads burnt to bone dust once and for all. Captives resumed their shivering again therefore, all in their shebangs of tin and tarp, or of none and nothing nowhere to protect them from the climes of the seasons. War such as this that is not war anymore is never far whether here or there before us in time or in space, by which we witness the overgone again and again, the forever ruined of mind and body from one end of the world to the other, even though the world does not end except by time anymore than the sun and moon rise and set.

Among those green youngsters for whom the onslaught of atonement was worse than worse during battles here and there months in and out year after year hot and wet as salt sea or as cold as Christmas, when they prisoned up they knew the worst of the worst, as you know, not only in others either, but in themselves too, so that blues beat on blues for next to nothing in victuals and brine with ax handles and wheel spokes or gutted some and sliced some with Bowie knives after watching these dig their own graves, and then too by hundreds these raiders, so-called, force fed fellow captives food that killed them deliberately or suffered them to drink water that killed them deliberately, this to steal from the dead whatever they had that the killers did not have. The grays stockaded those that the blues did not stockade or maim or kill by arms and legs in cold and rain and snow till these died of thermia, pneumonia or thirst that choked their throats with swollen tongues black below eyes swollen black for all to see who were forced to see at gunpoint, or who could not help but see.

One hundred twenty thousand Midianites Gideon killed, the Old Testament reads, so Abraham read.

Look, here, where the finger points, we find bones, brethren, collected into a hole as deep, wide and craggy as the man in the moon, and so we gather to our sight clavicles and hips, here and there a ribcage or a knee, and there, yonder by the length of a leg several bones that belonged to a foot when it had skin across it. Now some who died died from not eating even when they could eat since their stomachs and bowels would not take food into them for the parasites living inside, and those who died died from sleeping on and on or from never sleeping, going mad thereby, and going mad to challenge the guards high up in pigeon roosts to shoot them as dead as dead gets when they crossed the dead line, so-called, that fence beyond the fence of the stockade, where the stock gather whether cattle or horses or men did not matter in the least. In that year, the last of the atonement, thirteen thousand captives died in that space, and after their redemption thousands more died after not dying in Sumter Camp from shredded hearts, lungs, bowels, minds, and all after. These made for home and died before they arrived or died the day they arrived, or the day after by the thousands. The war nowhere failed to inspire barbarism till none who spoke well of fighting did other than lie from their teeth to their boot soles, as they did to their sandals thousands of years earlier, and they all who laid claim to massacre and torture by order of others did it without guilt till they were made guilty, among whom thousands killed themselves or their families, or took to banditry.

It was the same at Andersonville, so-called, as in Bengal for hundreds of years where Sati burnt alive eight thousand widows because they were widows, as in all Islam eighty million Muslims have martyred for being Muslim, as in Christianity seventy million Christians martyred for being Christian, as in twenty million Hindus, and ten million Buddhists, and nine million Jews, and two million Sikh, and one million Baha'i. One million followed by seven hundred thousand died for the city of David and the Christ and Mohammed out of Ishmael in the Holy Wars, so-called, across two hundred years of blood-letting so that half that number measures those dead of the atonement across four years only—*atonement* of that ilk, so Abraham read. David slew sixty two thousand Arameans at Damascus and Helam, reads the Old Testament, and then eighteen thousand Edomites and another hundred thousand Arameans at Aphek David slew, the Old Testament reads, and the Old Testament reads too twelve thousand Ai died by killing, and all those at Makeddah, Labnah, Lachish, Eglon, Hebron, and Debir who died by killing— one hundred thousand, reads the Old Testament, so

Abraham read. One and a half million Greeks and Trojans at Troy died across a decade of warring, unless there was no war, no horse and Helen never existed. Two hundred fifty thousand Persians died fighting Greeks at Marathon, Thermopylae, Artemisium, Plataea, Salamis, and during their retreat across Asia Minor, and two hundred thousand among Persians, Indians and Greeks Alexander slew, so Abraham read.

Begin the tragedy.

Picture now that clear stream laughing over rocks and its rock bed on that side of a fence running as far as the eye can see, a raw tree fence it is, rough hewn and barked still, this called the dead line whereat a bare human foot that reaches under becomes a shot foot or the man that waggles it toward the clean creek becomes a man shot dead waggling a foot by any of dozens of guards hoisted thirty feet up ninety feet separate, these in their pigeon roosts, so-called, guards who keep law by rifle high and away so that starvation may order things, and thirst may order things, and disease may order things, all these derived of nature that orders things here in the death camp, and not those derived of human nature that order things as beatings do, and tortures do, and maimings do, the order of things that murder measures even from roosts high and away day in day out—*human nature* of that ilk, of that curse, of that fiasco.

Now in his dreams, so many said, Abraham lay in the mud, muck and human dung beside his fellow captives sinned against by all who saw that chose not to see the sin as they had chosen not to see the sin of enslavement, those who had gone from men to *golem* to become savage of mind and stone of heart, and who would themselves go to prison at hard labor after their commander twisted by the neck in a winter wind. Then too some said that Atlanta burnt for the death camp, though some said not, and history *qua* history said not, and yet it persisted and persists that Atlanta burnt by order from the manse down to Maryland and to Virginia after and then to Georgia and so to Atlanta that Atlanta be burnt for the thousands dead in the prison at Sumter and for the thousands who were yet to die there after Atlanta burnt, those in the thousands who were to die there after the surrender even, one month after the surrender and the death of Abraham, and the death of Booth, more than one month after Richmond burnt itself nearly to the ground. And when the death camp came free those who freed it in the month of May found among the captives little else than bones, vermin and sores wide open the size of a silver dollar. Where there was hair were lice, when not worms among the naked and dying whose corpses then were robbed of the rags they wore by the living who beat, maimed and killed others among the living to wear them, slicing and stabbing each other among the living still, if that is still living since many who stabbed and sliced said and wrote after that life was most like death in the death camp than on battlegrounds full of dead rotting from one end of the war to another.

Ten thousand Canaanites slain, ten thousand Moabites slain on the banks of the river Jordan, four thousand Israelites slain at Ebeneezer, three thousand Israelites slain by God for worshipping the idol of the golden calf (Moses was his means), so the Old Testament reads, so Abraham read.

Blood stained the country year in year out even before it was a country, its woods and fields and bracken littered with limbs or only the bone inside the flesh of them, the remains of remains nature devoured by its climes or by creatures in nature who devoured them by their teeth, and then this, here and then now, the close in face to face carnage by disease, dysentery and the dying that ensues. So some said and wrote that Sheridan asked Sherman and Sherman asked Grant and Grant asked Abraham who replied, so those said who came to believe it, *Burn it* of Atlanta to atone for the death camp at Sumter named Andersonville for the nearby town, not named Sweetwater therefore for the nearby creek that remained for years not so sweet as once it was, or was believed to be, what with not only now deer piss and varmint carcasses flowing down, but human ones too of the dead from disease, starvation and thirst.

Since these were armies once, both johnnies and blues, they did not think of doing such each to each on the field of battle, no, but that the killing alone atoned for the enslavement galling God, and so galling Abraham, till one became a vengeful God and the other God's minister and scourge not against the slave south alone, and then not only for the blood by which the slave south atoned, no, but for the document of all sides agreed to that promised slaves their enslavement forever (that would be the Constitution—that curse, that fiasco). This war atoned for the two million slaves in the first century only who died in the passage out of Africa to the new world, so-called, and this war atoned for eighteen million slaves who never slaved because they died on dry land before they put to work, and this war atoned for thirty million slaves who died slaving on the slave south's sacred soil, so-called, of the so-called new world, and this war atoned therefore for the fifty millions of Africans who died slaving on the sacred soil, so-called, of the slave south's so-called new world—that curse, that fiasco.

There, see on the map where they are bred and reared only to be kidnapped across thousands of miles seeing freedom in stars above and seeing death in the sea below, and then see on dry land this place that on the map marks the country even before it is a country till weary, sick, surrounded by white men who speak no language they know other than violence by whip, stick and gun these hopeless millions fall over dead on the march to nothing nowhere. This the south states claimed as their right and heritage and history worth warring for so as to die in their time in their place at a half million and more till those at the end of the end could not remember that they had mothers or had been born children. And say this therefore, that all these had the need inside to leave their beloveds so as to become killers in war and killed in war when not torturers and tortured, doing all that none could see their beloveds doing and killing till they were killed, and seeing men die till they themselves lay dead or dying among the dead, and doing all this till it grew too late to forgive or to be forgiven under peach, cherry and apple trees.

Some who call for peace mean peace, some who call for peace mean surrender and some who call for peace mean the peace the dead alone know. And so Abraham was put to peace, and all across the Union those living rather than dead meant by peace to avenge the vengeance of the dying south, but all those of the wandering Union dead, all those souls risen from the wet grounds in the rainful days and nights during and after Abraham was put to peace, those who of a sudden knew all there was to know knew the wisdom of the war commander who remarked to any who would listen where any could be found that Niagara Falls had been falling since the onslaught of time and would go on and on over and over falling till the end of time, even though not as uprights know time or even as dogs know it, but as the universe knows it, and that was as near to believing in a god as believing gets.

Thuggees slew one million in India and in England across four hundred years, all by strangulation, so Abraham read.

In battle landscapes separate enemy from enemy, and ordnance flying across lines among canisters, cannonballs and bombs separate each from each, and bullets round or elliptic separate one from another among blues and grays till only by saber, cutlass and knife does soldier meet soldier at the eyes and all that lies inside or behind them of fear, ferocious will and brute strength. In the captive camp that became the death camp moment after moment leads to knowing, among captive and captor alike, that nothing has been left of the distance between enemy and enemy, that day in day out blues look at grays and grays look at blues so that each knows the same differentness and the differing sameness of one to the other. Now this is why, brethren, repeat to learn so as to remember as if it were a foreign tongue, now this is why when the captive camp swelled with captives before shrinking to a death camp no eyes met others, not even gray of gray, no, but instead of eye meeting eye there grew a fence beyond the fence till grays and blues stood like the blind one against the other. A fence as barked as a tree grew to become the dead line keeping blues from the only clear creek that captors guarded beyond the stockade fence wherein the polluted creek crept as if it were not deadly to drink or even to wash from.

Now there is this to learn so as to remember, that no food came beyond the stockade fence, and no fresh water to drink of, neither clothes nor medicines came, or cots or blankets or wood for fires or wood for lean-tos, and it went on and on as such for a year and more, that nothing came, and that is four seasons of the overburden till thousands on thousands starved and thirsted and diseased before dying till dead, yes, and while they did this those without rags wandered naked in rain and snow alike since no shelter came for any storm anywhere till each of them that wandered sickened too and died by thousands, all of these while Atlanta burnt, Richmond burnt, Lee surrendered, Abraham lay put to peace, his assassin too. Month after month and season after season naked men little but bones, toothless mouths, hookworm innards, and skin sores as wide as a silver dollar wandered like the souls they would become even as some, and more and more when time grew measureless, when time measured only if this or that one lived this or that day or did not, that some therefore drew a foot under the dead line thereby to be shot on sight by a rooster in his roost as an act of mercy, some said on both sides when time returned and it was time therefore to bear witness to these horrors inside Andersonville.

Of that last month beyond the end of the atonement, the thought across the camp among the grays awaiting a thousand armed blues bent on redress was to hide the dead inside mass graves as deep as hell and as far as the eye could see and to heal the living by what means no one knew, and so to hide and heal the death camp commander would order day in day out awaiting capture, and the guards about him obeyed since when they heard they obeyed, as soldiers have done for tens of thousands of years even as the death camp commander reminded one after another week in week out that they too faced death once captured. Know this so as to remember, that those captives who lived to speak were the last to arrive so that what they spoke they heard from the dying who arrived before them and who spoke of themselves and of the dead therefore before them, of how and why they lay dying and of how and why the dead had died. Now hear this of that, how defenders of the death camp spoke of lies and madness that the dying spoke to the living, speaking before God and sundry that the tales were unreliable since they were spoken by the dying who were later dead and of the dead who had spoken to those then living who became dying before they were dead.

Begin the tragedy.

Of when and where Abraham lay dying those dead souls that knew rose from flooded graves to roam streets, churches, bars, and bordellos not a mile from the manse, so hundreds said again and again year after year till they themselves became dead souls, and so before he lay as dead as dead gets from in their place in their eternity these that rose to walk the world knew his peace had come upon him or that he was now to enter once and for all the *infernum* of an underworld that he foresaw too often too well to be met there by warriors and kings thousands of years without flesh and yet thousands of years mindful of all that they had lost in death and of the crimes and sins they had committed in life. Dead souls rose from the graves at Andersonville even, and from the graves at Richmond, at Gettysburg, Antietam, Bull Run, that battle and those battles on and on, brethren, till all these dead souls drew to the city that night from a thousand miles distant to bear the soul of the commander of the atonement that atoned by more than a half million dead and a half million wounded, and atoned by millions more and more millions by loss, grief and hardship far from enemy lines, but not far that they failed to hear the bombasts of cannon blast or bomb that could still the hearts of old, young and dog alike. These millions of war dead and their ilk rose up to succor and to quicken the dead Abraham put to peace at last so that they wandered south to north as had the slaves the dead man set free, and hundreds before thousands saw them walking as featureless figures of clay or as shadows where no one walked, saw them by thousands in the fog and drizzle of night and in the dewed gloaming before dawn, walking as if mindless though no less driven south to north thereby to lift Abraham's soul once and for all that he foresaw in the *infernum* over and over for decades, never more than during the atonement that he ordered and commanded till he lay dying before he lay dead.

They knelt in torment, those at the bedside because the drizzle began that sounded to their inmost hearing to begin the hour of his death, and they knew it inside their bones, and they saw that each of them bedside knew it when each looked into each other's eyes that because the day dawned without a sun to show for it and drizzle as soothing as a lullaby began along with it that Abraham must be passing from life to afterlife, and they saw it happen there kneeling in torment bedside, and they saw that each of them saw it happen when each looked into each other's eyes. Each in their time in their place saw themselves dying as he lay dying and because he lay dying that was how they learnt to mourn themselves their own deaths, by mourning the deaths of others as Abraham had learnt to mourn his passing before he passed by mourning his mother and his only true beloved, and mourning his children one after another, mourning for the child and the adult and the father inside him, and then mourning himself who became the minister and scourge of a god he doubted except as the inmost voice of his mind, that called conscience, till even though he named himself a murderer of hundreds of thousands of men he suffered a conscience, that called guilt for the blood shed by more than a million, as you know, so that guilt shaped the measure of him, the inmost voice whispering into the deepest well of his ear that he must atone to be redeemed.

The bane of his thinking, those born to kill and no

less and those born to be killed and no more, these he feared from the onslaught of the atonement, fearing that the enmities of north to south and south to north among all who could neither understand words they spoke nor what words meant anymore than they could on common ground understand whose god was God even as they found only the orchards of corpse and bone ground to share. Once warring ensued corpses issued that could not be recalled to life other than as souls aimlessly wandering the nowhere and nothing of the *infernum*, so Abraham saw it at least, saw no God's paradise or Satan's hell, but a penumbra that the dead stood in or walked in seeking others there that stood or walked, all who wondered why they did so and wondered for how long they would do so till one by one they came finally to know the purpose of their eternal wandering, and that was renunciation. And so the living witnessed across the nine hours of Abraham's dying his gathering renunciation as he had failed in life to witness it when the south failed to resign after Gettysburg and failed to resign after Atlanta, and failed still to resign on the spot at Richmond that became no longer Richmond, as Atlanta became no longer Atlanta, instead grays fleeing south and more south or west and more west, as you know, either into swamps ruled by snakes that struck at the water's commotion or into deserts as dry as the moon. Abraham could not reason this as he lay dying since dying is unreasonable, but he could see it on and on over and over till even his unreason failed him.

Tamerlane the Mongol killed fifteen million Nestorians at Byzantium (1358), so Abraham read.

They knelt in torment at the deathbed, at last the deathbed if the drizzle meant anything, and the sunless dawn meant anything, with windows thrown open wide against the odor of death and so too that his soul swept away the world of his leaving, an open window as wide as the maw of death that invited his soul from the room till at last the bed named the deathbed had become the deathbed, so pictures and sketches and paintings would say for years and years to come and go, and the pillow whereon his head bled but little, it too pictured, sketched and painted over and over, as was the room, as were the gathered who knelt in torment so that the soul alone his mourners came to remember for themselves as it swept away the ills of the world from its path, sweeping the world and all in it till those who knelt in torment remembered whole and entire for years and years nothing other than watching his soul depart his body.

Conquistadors killed fifteen million Amerindians (1560), so Abraham read.

Many measured differently which minute he lived before he died, or that he did or did not groan at the end of the end, or sighed or did not at the end of the end, or slumped at it, or if he opened his hand to offer his naked palm to all who looked into it, offering his life to God thereby, some said who believed this of what they saw, and some said he opened his hand to show his palm that a coin be placed in the pool of it for his boat to the underworld that he believed in if he believed anything of life after death, and still there were those among the kneeling who saw no open palm, none offered to anyone for anything, and then those too who saw the palm open said for years and years that Abraham opened his big hand to undo the life in it as he had done with birds that he found hurt so as to heal and to free, that once healed they were as free as air unless they would have been truly free only if it was not for air. After the end of the end, unless here was the end of it, Dr. Leale sought to clarify the head wound for history with water and a rag, parting the cadaver's hairs crimped by blood and leaking brain. The room cleared for the doing of it now that the man was only the corpse of himself, closer to nature now than he had been alive, as far from humanity as far gets now that he lay dead, so that Dr. Leale could bathe the wound and wipe the last congealed blood the size of a newborn's thumb from the skull for the last time. And he did.

To the Andersonville of body and of mind at the hour the captives sussed out that Atlanta burnt for them and sussed out that Richmond burnt for them, that Davis and Lee had taken to the long washout wetleg run to the end of the end, and then at the hour the captives sussed out that the south had surrendered and so atoned once and for all, and then at the hour the captives sussed out that Abraham lay dead and put to peace thereby, and his killer lay dead and put to peace thereby, and yet at the end of the end of atonement these thousands remained no less captive, as if they were not war captives, no, but captives of another ilk, like slaves for whom they fought were captives of another ilk, though these millions were of a sudden as *free as air*, so Abraham said to them of them when he greeted some going north as he went south the two mile walk up the high hill to Richmond that no longer remained Richmond, as the Confederacy remained the Confederacy only on a map, as the sacred soil remained sacred to none but true believers in a god who was not God.

So no gate opened for the captives at the end of the end that was therefore not the end of the end, and yet the war was over, and no roost emptied of long rifles and their balls and bullets, and yet the war was over, and no fresh water arrived that flowed just beyond the stockade fence, that fence beyond the fence where fresh water flowed, and yet the war was over, and guards did not share food, clothes or medicine with these thousands still captive as if captive forever, and yet the war was over, and so at the end of the end of Andersonville the war was over and it was not over, and so it was not the end of the end of anything till it was the end of the end of everything that atoned for the iniquitous birth of the country even before it was a country. This is why hell must have been empty, brethren—all the demons were here.

Wars wherein Greek killed only Greek across three hundred fifty years three hundred thousand died, most slain after they slew (500-146 BC), so Abraham read.

Begin the tragedy.

Abraham done and gone, and Booth done and gone, and war done, war gone, and slavery, it too gone, it too done, and the Confederacy as done and gone as done and gone get, and so the atonement done once for all. At the end of the end therefore ran the longest darkest widest river of the country since before it was a country, and on this river the largest steamboat ever rolled on it peopled four times the most people it could move from here to there and expect to move them from there to here without the death of many, if not most, so that by these measures of river and boat and passage *Sultana* gathered to it paroled prisoners of the war out of Andersonville and Cahaba now that the war had been done and gone for weeks, what with Lee gone and Davis gone, Jackson too gone, and on and on the gone grays some as far south as south goes, some west to the setting sun, all gone so that from Big Black River beside Vicksburg carrying hogsheads of sugar and molasses that largest boat that ever rolled the Mississippi stopped first at a Memphis barge as big as the ship it served to assume the burden of coal so as to safe drive these near on three thousand uprights and the souls inside them.

And these more than two thousand prisoners now could see and smell the getting to of home, of home's beloveds, even watching the water rise and fall like the ghosts of war were turning the wheel and steering the rudder toward the going home and those beloveds, those who mothered there the men in their going and those made into mothers by these men, those robed therefore and those therefore not.

Only beyond Memphis by an hour or two, hard to measure in the dark night that is three of the morning or thereabout, steaming to Cairo to the north and west, rushing out of the slave south that existed now only as a map, that boat's boiler blew till that boat by wheel and house and cabins burnt like Richmond had burnt, and Atlanta had burnt, and one after another Confederate fort and city burnt, so that those remnants of starvation, beatings and torture began of a sudden to roast alive, of a sudden to inhale black acrid smoke that keeled them over by hundreds or lurched them into the river near to freezing to drown or even to quench their burning by drowning. And so there is this, that those from Andersonville and Cahaba who were only now set free in spite of a peace weeks old, and who still starved and thirsted and sickened in spite of the peace weeks old, these who had survived battle wounds and had survived death camps began of a sudden not to survive any more by hundreds before thousands. Those in the big river in the long dark saw the nearby only by the light of the flashing boat and the bursts into flames of the hull, wheelhouse and bow after the eruption of the boiler deck till the cedar and pine from one end to the other end fired, but this is not to remember the red coals themselves raining down like shrapnel hot from a cannon or big gun mounted overhead as from a hilltop. Who saw therefore bodies blown to the air, bodies aflame, and heard thereby the cries of burnt bodies doused in river water singe as they submerged, some to disarticulate like boiled chicken parts or screeching like crabs dropped into scald pots, and this till cries came fewer and fewer out of a darkness cramped with burnt dead floating and drowned dead floating and those choked to death by those hoping not to drown by strangling the living like ballast or driftwood, and so those who died killing those who died with them cramping the widest longest river in the country since before it was a country.

Those who swam dressed died more than those naked, and so swimmers disrobed even to the water only more than freezing and rushing against them like a flood for the rains of days and days that overflowed the banks of Tennessee and of Arkansas, and so at the gloaming those naked drew snow skeeters in the banks and bulrushes down river towards Mattoon and Muscatine and on to Cairo whereby the cold and scalded and arm and leg weary lay beset by insects as hungry as those they fed from, those who lay wounded by flames or debris and so who lay till they died as if it were the onslaught of a last battle among the blowflies and swamp angels that came to people the burnt flesh with eggs to lay so as to hatch for worms and maggots to prowl and devour—last battle of that ilk.

Till the river roll drew corpses more and more distant one from another and the cries grew to whispers and prayers and silence the dead made a thick damp floor the living crawled on and across in search of driftwood or dams such as beavers make, boat debris too that the weary, cold and wounded bellied up to to paddle by or even by some only to drift nowhere but to sleep against, and then too some of the living rode the dead till their own hands and legs were numb as death and so till the dead rode the dead, all knowing neither land nor sky till a dawn without a sun to show for it rose out of nowhere and nothing like a horizon these cold dead could not see. Hundreds of naked men scarred by torture or starved to their rib counts came dripping out of the river then at banks left and right, hundreds of naked men emerging from the river like new life from the mud bed itself, and there were seen naked men by dozens clinging to treetops like monkeys and squirrels since levees bursted ten miles across so as to lower strong limbs and lower spinier limbs and bobbing limbs that reminded the men clambering onto them by hundreds that they had climbed trees before, climbed so as not to be torn by dogs in battlefields, no, but to set captured away in the no more of bombs and bullets, and so graced by God to die another day, these being the treetops of Eden therefore to them after the boiler blew, whether or no they found high hanging fruit saved for lesser creatures who could scamper or swing or fly day in day out.

Those that lived who had smelt the burnt flesh of the dead, them at peace in spite of the smoke and char and sizzle at the river's surface said later to whomever they said it so as to remember that it was not the aroma of beef or pork, no, nor even the roast of a duck or Sunday goose, no, but the stink they had never smelt that war taught them till they learnt it like the roof of their hands from anywhere in the surround, that of rotted or scorched upright meat bending the knees of every man who inhaled it, the unmentionable irrefragable odor of human skin, gristle, muscle, and such innards as remained untouched by varmints in nature, that smell of dead humanity that made men sick and drew other species to it so as to eat and be nourished, and by this cleanse the land of its carrion. At the end there were hundreds who lived among more than two thousands who did not, and those who lived dreamt unto death of the dead they saw and smelt and held to or pushed away since all that could float floated, none better than corpses bloated by this and that gas within or touched bottom in drowning so as to surface like a great fish from before creation that caught in the current some of those who were arm and leg weary and held fast to feet and legs rushing the river as if from one end to its other, this till cottonwoods passed rootless from the rains, their limbs thinner than a man's arm.

Some naked men hung like pictures high in trees, as you know, till their grips gave way to cold or scald or weakness and they plunged to death after all, after believing they had been saved from death, or those who fell snake bit by cottonmouths and mocassins so as to sicken while they turned ass over shoulders down the river, them that would not know if they died of drowning or burning or venom, dead no less, or those who rode naked and bareback on horses and mules downstream, these creatures tossed dumb and wide-eyed by currents too, who kicked at the water and the bodies in it, paddling by the hoof till one after another upended, inhaled by its big noseholes fatal doses of backwash and debris, gathering their riders to them, taking them under with them or without them, but in the end all gone under, men and horses and mules as dead as dead gets or as near to it as near gets—that would be the living, brethren.

Paroled then from purgatory, so they named it, those from Andersonville and Cahaba and other miserias did not know a first hot meal of beans and cornbread and bacon grease from a last hot meal, no, as that first night of freedom they did not know from the last night of it forever, unless we name death freedom, that fiasco, since they ate by thousands and drank fresh water by thousands and so slept by thousands to wake to the sound of bombs, so they named it, and woke thereby to flames and scald and drownings among those who failed to burn to death first or be concussed to death first by flying debris as hot as the sun, so they named it. Of those who neither died then and there nor sooner rather than later hundreds were saved in the screaming darkness lit by the burning boat for ships that followed the fire named *Siver Spray* and *Bostonia* that drew the living from the dead, all rushing the river at ten and more miles of speed, and so more than the strongest swimmer could navigate even at high warm noon wherein none maimed or scalded or freezing would not drown, and so these drowned hundreds at a time clutching each other, choking each other, strangling one by one before going under to who knows what at the bottom.

The steamer *Pocahantas* saved lives too, and the shorelines of Tennessee and of Arkansas saved lives what with bramble and bulrushes lining the banks, snakes and wharf rats heading for cover from noise and fire and the turmoil of uprights distressed. Then too farmers on both banks of both states threw ropes into the turmoil of voices, calling into it to halloo or pray or sing, and tossed into the dark water limbs and bark boats such as children row, and men with axes persuaded narrow tree trunks to fall that were floated into the water whereby three and more naked cold terrified men rode the whole of the night till dawn showed each of them who it was they had been saved with if not by, and they recited that none killed any others on these logs or trunks or were killed by others to save themselves. Some in need of saving called to the shoreline that they were prisoners going home and so later recited their surprise that defeated grays had spared them nonetheless, wondering in them why any had fought the war at all therefore. Those burnt deep into their flesh were coated with flour since there were neither nurses nor medicines anywhere, and some used lard rather, and others tarpaulin drenched with cold water, any and all things applied to skin that fell away like boiled chicken skin and stank already of infection, but they gave them corn liquor too to put them to sleep or to numb the pain that could not be lessened no matter what till up and down banks and boats naked men cried out for the deaths they had escaped till it came as the only medicine worth anything at all.

The *Essex* saved men from the river, drawing breathless naked victims from it, all trembling and so till they were seen close by none knew if they shivered from cold or burn or scald or terror or that they still lived—quaking of that ilk, and these not burned or maimed were stuffed in the belly with bracken of the river, and small fish even they inhaled when they breathed. And gunboats saved lives so that men by dozens clinged to yawls and rudders and to the oars of outriggers come to rescue them, or from poles and fish lines cast to them from fishing boats by men who lived on the river day in day out decade after decade, yet never before hauled humans over the side, some of these rowing and paddling from as far as Meridian and Vicksburg itself where the burden of the *Sultana* had begun.

Wharf boats patrolling for thieves of the armistice saved lives, those that caught or killed bushwhackers and bank robbers and rapists up and down the river, and pocket boats cleaning debris day in day out saved lives, and the relief boat *Jenny Lind* saved lives, plucking men stranded in the vinculum of tree trunks spavined by war and flood and the rot of both so that up and down the waterway the living and the dying were drawn away from the dead after which no sound came from the river since all who floated or rushed or bobbed or rooted at a dam such as beavers formed were none but the meat of nature's leaving. Now this meant that dawn opened onto the roll of the river flooded over to left and to right with corpses, a sight the sky had never yet seen, and yet the war was over, and so those neither dead nor dying but yet adrift on logs and such along the river for four hours now saw corpses to left and to right, some more of Arkansas than of Tennessee and so the other as well, but none with sound beyond river sounds of flowing and rushing and overcoming rocks till it reminded those yet alive careening down stream of Babylon or of Eden in the Bible so that the voice of God quieted them in their survival, succored them in their not being dead like this or that man nearby turning belly over buttocks and back in the churn daylight lit for the first time. *Belle Memphis*, that steamer, it too saved lives.

The *General Boynton* took the living to a wharf boat that took the living then to Cairo, where the doomed and submerged *Sultana* was destined, or not, as fate said to the birds captured by a breeze who wanted their freedom, and on and on by another boat and on and on by train to Indiana and to Ohio where more than most of the living lived, and those who were still not dead boarded finally the *Belle of St. Louis* that saved a gather of imprisoned Jews and imprisoned Negroes, these bunched like grapes first in the death camps and then on the death boat, kept from the white prisoners who were at least fully human while these blacks and those Jews were not, and more like each other than not, if you knew your Bible, till all of them, the last of them who did not drown or burn, debouched at Licking County, Ohio or at Bucks County elsewhere farther east in the direction of Philadelphia and New Jersey whereat the Negroes and the Jews breathed more easily in the salvation, and yet these two witnessed the wheel keep turning that drove the boat on fire after the blast, witnessed the ship's pet gator stabbed three times at the belly so as not to eat the dying or the dead, to say nothing of using the crate he slept in to float down river by.

Those who lit afterward to Boone County and Mt. Pleasant were delivered from death by the *St. Patrick* and may have been the first big boat to behold near on two thousand dead in the gloaming before dawn rolled over and backward and over again, racing toward nothing but the immeasurable distance the river knew before the country was a country and before the war fought on it was the war fought on it. The steamer *War Eagle* saved hundreds first from the *Henry Aims* that saved dozens and from boats carrying light, the *Lady Gay* and *Pauline Carroll,* from as far back as the Black River and Meridian, and the meaning of such measure is this, that there were more boats light and empty that could have stopped the biggest boat from blowing, and yet these that saved those who did not blow with it, those who day after day afterward delivered themselves to towns and cities across the scape of the war, to the hospitals and soldiers' lodges beyond the scape of the river and its disaster of that April twelve days that Abraham had now been dead and himself delivered to peace.

Those from Athens in Alabama and from Little River out of Georgia and from Chickamauga, those from that battle, and from Blackshear and Americus to La Vergue and Mt. Pleasant of Tennessee, and out of Selma and the Dallas of the Arkansas side, and Sulphur Trestle and Shoal Creek (Alabama), and so too Stone River (Tennessee) and Rocky Force Ridge (Georgia) and Guntown (Mississippi)—all and more blue bellies captured in thousands across slave states and confined to Cahaba prison and to Andersonville prison paroled so as to burn up and blow open like slavery itself, these depended in the end on the kindness of those that were the enemy weeks before, those who came in boats in darkness to save their enemies, or by ropes pulled their enemies to safety, and there were many who swam in the cold river darkness to voices nowhere to save their enemies.

More or less and give or take, one thousand two hundred freed prisoners perished by the *Sultana* disaster, so Abraham did not know, dead twelve days before, so Booth did not know, dead one day before.

by the tombolo from that river there to this ditch here, where the pointing starts so as to finish, I left behind bombast and smoke and shivering earth, the trouser backs of other fleeing militias to my fore, us flying out of harm's way like as shot from a cannon till we come upon the last herd of dead so dead they was beetle eaten, the last bugs before there be nothing but bone to gnaw at such that a stray cur might gnash to sharpen its teeth so as to tear other flesh of other dead elsewhere, but as for this gather of the longer gone no bugs more and no butterflies neither, but no dogs barked and no birds called   and now eyes fail the world above my holler till there is only grass at my sides that rolls now and then in a breeze, and that is a nice thing, and mud ruts in the nearby saying the wagons and ass carts have fled long before, and that is a nice thing, and clouds over me sometimes high, sometimes not, sometimes awash in turkey buzzards, and that is not a nice thing in my holler wherein I were blown by long gun shrapnel from who knows where how far off by a soldier never knowing he hit anything or anybody—a day before a night times two now I am persuaded since bearing witness to the congregation of moles at the edge of me, those same environs at the horizon full times three of dawn and of not dawn, and so do I still live or do I die asks the ox of the knife on the stone altar, this where in the far off explosions report that are the retreaters blowing up feed behind them, such being hog and ox and ass, feed of that ilk strewn as sick beef and so forth, burros too, across the wide fields put on by the victors coming in the hundreds in thousands, those among creatures that did not fall forelock to fetlock or haunch from cannister bombs exploding fields of wheat, corn and succotash, though that is when by what it was I saw my foot fly to the air in the boot of it and knew of a sudden I had took my last step the step before, that step that raised me from the ground after sitting beside the corpse of him I kilt, prayerful over him, doing my regrets to him for it, needing thereby to flee again farther off from the cannon fire and the shivering ground that were wagons wheeling and horses thundering by thousands like pharoah's army chasing Jews in Egypt, all coming at me for me, and so I stood over the cadaver of him thinking now he knows the underworld till I lay footless and backflat, sussing out what abomination has burnt the stump where a boot was, and so the likes of me that raked the scat of ponies and horses and now and then the muck of sows and goats, and only once at a far walk did I ever see one of the enslaved, I lay bootless and unmanned in the surround of gophers and moles and buzzards, all this

time breathing in the puke smell that was me whereafter
I crawled to the trunk of the cottonweed here, where the
pointing ends, but the noise and the feel of the foot in its stole
boot were nothing like pain as yet, no, just an empty space
at the bottom of me that smoked and looked raw as gizzard
of a Sunday, it that lopsided me for all my days left, why I
sat me down grateful to God for a tree and grateful to God
that by its own volition the shrapnel burnt my wound so to
seal it that I could slither on the stones inside my breeches
to the trunk of the overhung tree whereby I could see as far
as the holler let, the sky therefore where the fowl wait for
the darkling of the world for the second of my nights dying
takes, my own self concealed whether from the end of me
or from God's trial of me I don't feel to know, disenthralled
of the bleeding at my ankle since it is dry as bone and none
of the bleeding I learnt of day in day out were that little
less it was in water where we sighted hour after hour those
corpses back assward knee over skull bobbing and rocking
downstream one or another river that we could not drink
of therefore, but bloodless bodies too, disenthralled of their
blood too, nothing like that man shot at close range, his
eye whites gleaming in tears where he lay supine, how it is
named, among crisp yellow leaves so that critters might lay
their gametes into the wound I opened nearby where I will
make fodder too I am persuaded, where I like as feel to soon
be gone seeing him I shot dead gone already, and the quiet
of the men who growled and moaned and cried out for a sun
and a moon at least till I measured myself the last man in

*the last ditch off the last war pony whose shank exploded
like my foot were to do later, though not much, a reckoning
of that ilk such that here in my holler as far as the moon
from home I am saddened by a new soft drizzle sensed on
my skin like the touches of loved ones at a sickbed   stall
mucker, scat cracker, the gloaming, the holler, soldier one
day dying the next, and the next, last day of days, end of the
end, him when he did not bear a musket nailed hob to boot
heels or battened wood for coffins the insides of which I don't
now expect to see on this ground where it is not even a battle
to memorize so as to gather the dead even to fire the corpses
in a ravine as long as a corn row cause there weren't wood
enough nor nails nor pegs enough to border up cadavers
day and night, no, and the corpses measured too many and
hardly in one place in one shape, but too we who put them
in piles and wagons and on pyres taller than two men stood
foot on shoulder we weakened and sickened till we was
called to kill strangers at a distance, those that wasn't kilt
by them at the same distance, and so for me the elephant
came at Port Hudson and that was shooting black soldiers
at a distance so that till we overrun the dead who knew
skin from skin, only blue from gray, and then only alive
from dead where the dead looked like babes in cradles and
the living as old as Moses, and then we was the afterwards
brigade that gathered weapons and kits and grub from
the dead who still smelled of living, and those things of the
dying that we took since they was dying whether some said
take this or take that—how I got my boots—, marching*

*through rows of the dead for as far as the eye could see,
so far that another day's dead met this day's dead that we
came to know cause the older corpses was as black as slave
skin, and so we conversated on God's sign to us till we knew
it were time to assay the earth paved black with dead men
and the creatures moving through them with their muzzles
bent low at the drop of the sun, and by this only now and
then was there a cry from a dying man took for dead by a
coyote or wolf or raven as big as the moon*

Jimmy your suspenders, redeem the fat pouch of belly so as to relax the biggest stud of those pantaloons that Sunday wants, and extend then the kneepans of you, brethren, so as to loose your go to meeting boots, or at least thy spurs loose, and let us home the children, and the children's children, and their mothers, and their mothers' mothers that we may speak of the last dark night of that dread city of his life, he that saw only so to see the world's need of redemption and of atonement therefore, and saw thereby blood and blood guilt that issued for as far as the eye could see from horizon to horizon, and saw there the long dark well of iniquity that gave birth to the country before it was a country, saw far and deep of space and of time therefore.

And he said to his wife in the dark of the carriage those last hours of life in him—Jerusalem he would travel to before Paris or London or Rome, Jerusalem the city of David that he had come to imagine while he walked at sunset past bars and brothels day in day out for year after year of his war against the lower states of the broken land, Jerusalem that then was little but desert with a sea in front of it, without a hotel anywhere in it to sleep inside, without more than one eating place anywhere as far as the eye could see. Walking with the stick his distressed wife presented so as to fight off assassins and well-wishers alike who came too near to view his face, or to touch his coat, or to address him as Father Abraham, or Prince Moses, or King David of the New Jerusalem, that Jerusalem birthed in iniquity that called for enslavement, enslavement that called for atonement by blood and blood guilt, as you know, and so the atonement too of father, prince and king who commanded that war, for commanding that war, of what then elicited the death of the iniquity that birthed the country, that emancipated the country from its craven birth even to the Rio Grande of Texas, and to the deserts of Kalifornie as raw as the moon, and to the Keys of Florida that were as south as south gets till even the unforgivable got forgot so as to calm lands north and south and east at all compass points, if not west, that compass point, where instead of millions of kidnapped black men and black women to enslave there abided indigenous Indian men and Indian women to kill or to be killed by, that fiasco, and so unto the blood guilt that would ensue.

Bells tolled in the calm bedrizzled dawn of that Saturday named Holy after that Friday named Good that was the last Good Friday of his existence, and the last good day of any day, Friday, Saturday or other for months and months that anyone knew to speak of, a dawn of such darkness so as to eclipse the sun on the far side of a fleet storm descending from God, so many said they believed of the morning after the mortal wound from the fatal pistol that fired the last bullet of the last war of independence, that report of smoke, smell and sound that began dolorous rites of despair among all who chanted or prayed or wept. Solemnities as silent as secrets stirred from one end of the city to the last of it so that windows, balconies, rooftops (their chimneys), and flagpoles, and balustrades, and long ladders—all manner of exhibition from churches or homes, or from bars or brothels, these hung draperies that trembled in the wind like wide wings of ravens come to cast the pall of dark angels. Death drapes glowed against plumes and fumes of flaming oils and snapping wood, shadows stood upright and smoke shaped into lost souls risen to bear the dead man fast to his grave out of the low narrow small bed wherein knelt and wept as many as twenty, so many said, at the foot and at the head of the man and of his bed so that all who saw and stared stared and saw as at a shrine. Grievers by their inmost silent oaths mourned those quick and those dead among the numberless scattered or numberless floating across canals and spillways of the city, Abrham but one among thousands of dying and dead in the city that day.

On that long hard night, while those who recited one after another elegy or sang one after another hymn to death and its undoing by heaven, streets and byways flooded this and that way here and there till there was none but remorseless weeping and the crack of wood to break the spell of flow and ebb across the city, wood that split like bones in medieval bonfires, bones that snapped where witches burnt to lift the curse of an accursed hamlet, an ancient city speaking a forgotten language haunted by pitiless gods who first made men mad that they would thereafter destroy for crimes despicable to recite. Thousands of years later, brethren, mourners came this night together to think the unthinkable hour after hour from midnight till dawn's sunless rise in a drowsy rain as monotonous as tears. The destiny that was living, and enduring living, and doing whatever with life, and why this or why that, and why or why not, seemed of a sudden less obscure to all who stood, or knelt, or roamed like lost souls among lost souls because, and *because* is always a dangerous thought, for all the mystery of its meaning death was as clear as clear gets, even in the gloaming and the rains of the day.

Death mistakes human nature, so Rathbone had informed his sons years later in the Germany of his exile, explaining to them who were too young to understand and too young to know why he explained it to them, that no one thinks of death till they behold it in others nor does anyone fear death except by first knowing loss, and fearing it, so that only after we have known and feared loss do we mourn the loss of ourselves who are doomed to die, or so Rathbone had said to his sons years and years after the unconscious man who lay dying jagged on a stranger's bed had mourned the loss of himself day in day out for decades before he lay dying. Abraham's dreams over dreams reassembled the life of the night vigil as he lay dying in the surround of wails (that would be his wife) and prayers and barking dogs, not to say of voices familiar to the war that he heard day in day out year after year regarding battles and deaths, and of battles and of deaths yet to come, and of the aftermath of battles and of deaths past, present and yet to come so as to dream battles and deaths whole and entire.

Of the pointing lance he saw this, the drive through forehead to jaws from above till the eyes darkened like starless night and the face shadowed the ground to which it fell, and then he saw this, the bellies of thousands grazed on by thousands of animals in one confession of deaths across battle fields, with scattered here before there bonfires of other dead spared dogs' teeth till a black ink choked the sky with gloomy clouds of stench that were cooking flesh, innards and bones raised high by gathered winds driving to heaven, if there was heaven in that dream, and thereafter the dying man saw this, the on and on mad gods of violence that from unhappy stars of human fate form tools of war that leap on their enemies, enemy after enemy, like lions tear oxen and steer to wring and bite their necks. In these dreams one after another as he lay dying, he lay dying over and over across centuries of soldiers who lay dying as if now, this moment dying, torn asunder, speared through the mind or rent at the innards by the claws and teeth of God's greater and lesser creatures.

Our discontent, that winter, *glorious spring*, that April that expiated blood by blood day and night over and over unto the great nothing that was the death of dreams, that which was the conscience at rest, at last after numberless deaths at all compass points the last of Abraham's mind born into guilt, his guilt that could and did destroy cities, and his anger that could and did destroy guilt, that at the onslaught of the slaughter he possessed, so he said to all who would listen, a madness to outdo madness, that nothing living should live born of iniquity like the iniquity that birthed the country and the nation, so-called. All creation that needs to bleed bleeds, so those who said they heard he said, and by this mystery he and he alone, or so they said he said, drew an absolute nearness to God, but that the God not of vengeance no matter how vengeful, but of reckoning and righting the world, tilting the world so as to stand upright. Yet he remembered this of the ancients that he remembered best, those that taught him most, and it was this that he recited to all and sundry: *The murderer you seek, my king, is here, a stranger among strangers, who has no eyes to see what kings see.* Even at the end of the end that was the destruction of the evil men had done in the name of freedom and God's will, he took the lessons of Oedipus to heart, that the curse of the accursed could lift only by blood, and he that had taken blood everywhere as far as the eye saw could lift the curse of his own accursed person by shedding his blood too.

So many lay claim to his bedside as he lay dying that there would have been hundreds kneeling and pacing and praying hour after hour so as to measure first the silence of the sky and then the drizzle before dawn, and yet none knew to be sure when he lived one or another moment or did not. His heart beat or it stuttered only to beat again, or his breath stopped only to start, and there were those who when they heard rain against the window believed that the dying man heard the same rain against the same window. Of that last dawn of his life, of the last rain of his life, the ground ran already drenched by days of April storms so that the soft constant shower set the streets running red with the blood of the fresh dead who had risen in the floods of days and days of cloud burst till the city of floating corpses and lifted souls seemed itself a field of battle. So when pigs and dogs and chickens drowned, those creatures that did not drown chewed the remains till blood ran red in the streets of the city, and now when blood met blood on streets, avenues and byways no one could say which was man and which was not whereby to remind his mourners that the dying man, or the dead man, said to all who would listen that he had read somewhere sometime by someone, *Whoever hears me let them search out this day this, the moon I see and the moon I cannot see.*

They who like to drink of it (the war), who like the stench of it (the war), the earth of it, the blood of it that sinks to soak the roots of trees and waving flag grasses from one end of battle to the other day after day sun up to sun down, and they who sit bollocks to buttocks in the soil hearing catastrophe in the nearby earth that shakes and shivers loose leaves and branches from tree limbs thirty feet tall, whether or not this and that catastrophe of today, tomorrow or the next tomorrow does not matter to the war's end because, and *because* is always a dangerous thought, the battle will always be the battle to come, and that battle will always be the battle to end all battles, and that battle will always be the battle that ends the war, and that will be the end of the war that ends all war.

Cloudbursts of artillery smoke as black as swarming bees, and below it bloodshed as red as roses wide and far that evokes the abyss of the first god of gods, the eldest ancient abyss so old and deep that it lay below the deepest waters of the deepest sea, the Hebrew *tehom*, so the dying man learnt it to speak it to all who would listen, the vast fathomless beneath of the bottom of all waters everywhere, that *beneath* of agents of doom lurking shameless, scarred and pitted by desuetude and desiccation, those dead inside before dead outside, those whom the dying man said that in the name of the Nazarene revered nothing of the Nazarene, nor any of his angels, those southern slavers and their kin, and their kin's kin whom the commander waged war against, showing to them neither pity nor mercy till they fled, died or groveled in the dust on their bare bellies. He sermoned again and again from the well of Congress, and in public venues where the gathered gathered, and at tables to all and sundry within earshot of doors, walls and windows wherever people might hear of the abyss older than creation, purveyor of destruction.

He sermoned, lectured and hectored—that is the truer word, it for the Trojan prince revealing to his little brother, one Paris, on and on how he will have destroyed Illium for a faithless beauty, so sang old blind Homer, as you know—hectoring till as he lay dying he lay nearly gone, and saw then that all Troy was gone with him, that each leader of each tribe slew a man in his name, as they spoke his name when they dropped the sword deep since he who was the leader of such men deserved the honor to lead the slaughter, even to be slaughtered, who was then larger and taller than any man he led or slew, and as he lay dying that long hard night he saw his body's own ruin, that it so sounded in its fall (arms, chest, head, and all after) his affrighted horse flew off to leave him ground bound for what was his life left at Cold Harbor, that massacre, where thousands of Union wounded hid among thousands of Union dead, those so doomed from the onslaught that each pinned his name to his shirt so as to be known after all that could be lost had been lost.

Those that rushed in close laid sword to the fallen man's shoulder to cut his brawn from his body, driving the sword broad stroke down till the shoulder dropped off and the arm, whole and entire, fell to burning sand that blushed with his blood, and so horrid darkness struck through him, the story says, as soldiers took the spoils, and as he lay dying he could not help but see that blood was shed by the sacred rage of pagan gods one after another, who so ripped his navel at a distance (that would be the javelin) that the wound shut his eyes opened only forever on the ground where he fell (arms, chest, head, and all after) onto sacred soil that poured out his innards there to make the hot soil blush, and he could not help but see, as he lay dying, that above his nipple (that would be the left breast), the sword swore true through his lungs so that from chest to his middest it swiped his belly open till his stomach fell to his feet. And yet all others around him hid among his carcass as among thousands of other carcasses of this martial plain and this martial beach that faced the sky or faced the sea that knew nothing of these acts among those undead who could not reprehend the fight—so many dead and dying strewed the field as far as the eye could see. Strife, battle, bloody things, blood feasts that he saw on and on in his dream after dream while he lay as dying as dying gets.

The children wore nightgowns and slippers and robes while they played with last year's toys for the last time since tomorrow night they would play with next year's toys for the first time. It is the memory of ornamented tree at Christmas that smelt of the nearby woods, of the shine of gifts under ribbon and bow, and the aroma of pastry and cocoa, and then there is this, that on the other side of every window in the consular house the evening sky snew gray and blue so that the fireplace in every room lit to warm walls and floors. Christmas eventide, so Clara's sister remembered, and the governess remembered, and the maid too, that all who heard heard Rathbone walk quickly from his room at the far end of the hallway, out of the shadow that was the farthest room of the consular house, where he had passed days and nights for years speaking to himself or to no one, or addressing the dead, or being addressed by them, and so when he walked swiftly in his riding boots the children silenced since he did not ever walk that way, but instead like a man safe in slippers.

So many did not remember how many stood, or knelt, or paced in vigil near its end, the end of the end, so-called, that when the sky drizzled a dull rain that sounded against the window of the death scene, and so sounded against all windows in all rooms of the rooming house, and the roof too sounded of the rain, that the number thereby increased year after year till the many who would claim to know the vigil knew only the rain so that till those by hundreds died off the numbers who recited or wrote that they were present did not diminish among all who had prayed, or wept, or kept concord in God's name. Yet those who would claim among those there that they placed coins against the lids of the dead man's eyes always grew in number so that, many wrote year after year, while those who died laying claim that they saw the death those who did not yet die lay claim to doing more than they could have done, thereby being more than they could have been that long hard night, whether to lid his eyes forever against them falling open like the mouth fell open or lidding the eyes so as to pay the ferryman for crossing the dead man from life to the true nowhere inside the paganism the lost soul admired, envied and read of the ancient world.

Picture now fields at sunset across the war of atonement year in year out whereby more than a half million died and more than a half million lay maimed in battle after battle named for towns, cities, hills, and valleys that told the geography more south than north without naming battles and skirmishes for generals or soldiers who lived or died in those battles and skirmishes, or who were brave and who were cowards in those battles and skirmishes, and yet it was never not *Lincoln's War* inside this or that newspaper or this or that mind both south and north of the four years year after year that brethren slaughtered brethren. Attending opera thirty times during his tenure, for which he was assaulted in newspapers wide and far, he replied that if he did not do so he would want to hang himself. His favorite opera: *Faust,* by Gounod. When they were not more than a half million dead or more than a half million who lay maimed day in day out year over year they were millions after millions undone by war and grief and despair, and when they were not dead, maimed or desperate they were living soldiers who lay beside one another who lay beside dead and wounded so as to conceal themselves, as a consequence of which they lay listening to the sorrows and pains of the maimed, hearing them call beloveds or call God to save them by any means God might know to do so, even among some, so many said, who hoped to wake up Negro and a slave instead, or to wake up a Chinee in China, or a Latin in papist Rome, and those feigning death saw there then carrion birds eat their neighbors from eyes to entrails till the true fall of darkness that the turkey fowl, crows and ravens slept in. Attending song recitals at the manse each of the four seasons across the four years of his tenure, for which he was assaulted in newspapers wide and far, he replied that if he did not do so he would want to hang himself. His favorite aria: *Casta Diva* from Bellini's *Norma* (forbidden love between Druid and Roman across the battlefields of Gaul—100-50 BC—resolved by suicides in flames).

Of the inmost speech among maimed, wounded and souls under peach, apple and cherry trees trying there not to die, they lay as if at peace, out of the urge to resurrect their bodies, as if overseen therefore by a beloved who knelt beside this and that soldier, her eyes fixed on his face, her eyes to his eyes, kneeling there as calm and cool as stone in succor and compassion, those senses that make grief grief in the end for the terrified soul who can neither move nor feel under this or that tree, but who listens to the sound the breeze makes of it, the sound of childhood therefore, he who will not sleep again, and will not dream again, who would begin in his despair to turn already to dust (that would be mortality), turn to the browning and leavings all about his dying or maimed body, or his fear of death, or of limbless life, who lay wise in the fog of knowledge that for him, and for his beloved kneeling beside him, his war was ended.

Alone or with his wife, the doomed man named author of the war of atonement attended every play by Shakespeare performed there during his tenure, for which he was assaulted in newspapers wide and far, as a consequence of which he remarked again and again that if he did not do so he would want to hang himself, now and then pointing with his longest finger to an elm or oak in the line of everyone's sight. His favorite play: *Macbeth,* since it conflated bloody civil war with a terrible marriage to a scheming woman. His favorite performance of Shakespeare: John Booth's *Richard III,* after which he aspired to shake the actor's hand, but the player fled when he heard of Abraham's intention, flying down the same alley on the same mare he would ride after mortally wounding one of his few fans.

Who knelt at his deathbed?—she was Ann come to him out of true nowhere to say this that he knew already, *Think of me for a moment now and then,* as she had said, so some wrote, as she lay dying on her deathbed in his arms decades before he lay dying on his deathbed with her soul beside him, and so he saw her to remember her lips and eyes before him that death was not death, and saw then her breasts and buttocks, of which he spoke to all who would listen while she lived and loved him, and yet even as she came to him to say that death was not death she died again before his dying eyes, as she had always died again and again in his dreams, and then when he did not dream since he did not sleep she died again and again among his waking thoughts of her that brought him to tears, tears he did not hide from any in the room who would look at them till his long bony fingers concealed his long bony face not with shame or embarrassment, no, but because he saw in the palms of his hands that seeing her of a sudden he knew too private to share with the world external. Ann convulsed and sickened in his hands over and over, shivering in sweat and blood in his arms that held her fast and gentle like the sick birds he held in his large hairy fingers so as to stroke their beaks and heads back to life, holding Ann to his chest to comfort her so as to stop the dying, so as to pass to her his living. His heart died with her heart, so he said to all who would listen, buried thereafter in her coffin with her heart, as you know, as his widow's heart she buried in his coffin with him decades later, so she said to all who would listen, as he had said at Ann's grave decades before, so she said too to all who would listen since he had said it again and again year after year even to his wife, and even to others before his wife, saying that since Ann lay dead it must be paradise to lay dead.

Christmas eventide, so Clara's sister remembered, and the governess remembered, and the maid remembered, that Rathbone walked swiftly and heavily in his riding boots with his pistol in one hand and his dagger in the other till his wife who was his sister met him at the door to their children's playroom, and there she smiled at them before locking the door behind her and urging her husband to their bedroom since intimacy with her calmed him as it had since their adolescence together when as brother and sister Clara consoled him with her touch. Those who saw to remember saw him swiftly and heavily take to their bedroom, striding with determination as if he had thought through a theme to its end, or so her sister would say, after which Clara closed that door too behind her to seal her husband and brother from what was left of the house, or so the governess would say. The children listened at the large Black Forest door of their playroom, pressing their ears and hearing nothing till they heard screams, and there were curses to hear, and cries of pain there were to hear so that the children began to sob without knowing why they sobbed. Soon they saw and heard their aunt and governess enter to embrace them till each in their turn gathered in their fear as they lay in the arms of a weeping aunt and a weeping governess that of the voices filling the house now among strangers not one belonged to their mother.

Fearless of the blows of war, terror to the farthest enemies that he struck down for thousands of miles wide and far, as he lay dying holy and holier in his covenant with a god he believed only as a god of reckoning that made of his a warrior's will to unite his tribes at all cost to whomever must undergo the punishment for dividing them, as he lay dying he heard in his innermost ear the flourish of bugles and trumpets and ancient horns that beckoned battle across thousands of years of war across the blood-built rainbow of human existence. As he lay dying shadows shed his only light, already naked under blankets, already awaiting the shroud that was the country's flag as wide and high as a wall, as you know, and so half in the underworld that he dreaded and dreamt of night after night, and when he did not dream it since he did not sleep he saw it for himself in the beholding of his darker mind, a soul among souls there in the mire and haze where those dead with swords in their hands or muskets at arms across thousands of years of battle won and lost that no longer mattered in the least in the deepest *beneath* of the deepest waters not known even to a map, *dying* of that ilk.

Across the diagonal of the bed there too he saw himself set his sword in the soil to fall on it by his own will, to hurry the rescue that ends existence, that fiasco, and opens nonexistence, that fiasco, after all resolve among the weariest saddest men in the world who acted together and then acted no longer, none but shrouds of eyes too deep set to see into, if eyes at all for wandering, but no rapture to undergo and no Eden to enter (that would be heaven, brethren), none but all things human estranged and sunless. There was no Ann beside him of a sudden, no poisoned mother neither, no two children dead even, those too small in death, no, only the maw *Nothing* as true, ancient and as wide as a whale mouth eating the sea it swims, a sea like that drowning the dying man, sinking him to the beneath as worn as creation, purveyor of destruction. There was no war, there were no slaves, our country was not yet born.

Learn these then that were the dying man's remembrances, good and ill, decade after decade so that he saw them again and again, reciting them over and over, suffering them in his inmost being, dreamt them and their themes year after year till death, those being therefore more than death themes of lamentations and dirges to him and to his inmost being. When not death themes his were love themes, but these always and again emerged as the death of love, or of the beloved, or of the beloved's love, or of the beloved's love on and on beyond the grave, and so of infinite sadness therefore, and of infinite madness therefore, and the despair thereof, that too, and so over and over the desire for death—*love* of that ilk. The dying man lay dying in the sufferance of love's dark dreams, as he suffered the war's dark dreams that were nothing like those of love but by the mood inside and out of eternal loss that covered the landscape as far as the eye could see under grim clouds hard as granite that let a smooth determined rain pervade the city's sky and soil the last moments of the dying dreamer's life.

So there was this as he lay dying, that nothing stood left to be done that he could have done other than he did, and nothing could have been done that would have seen the war not be the war it was, the war fated when the first kidnapped man of color stepped onto the soil, God's soil, from thousands of miles distant, who was thereby deemed the chosen among them that he did not drown or starve or thirst to death inside ships that stormed at sea, God's sea, and was not beaten thereat for an unwilling slave under a star-crossed sky, God's sky, that bent the world between *there* of his birth and *here* of his bondage and death. Two hundred fifty years of slavery grew in the ground like milkweed that had poisoned the dying man's mother, who lay more than one week dying with her son beside her as she screamed, and cried out to God, wept and fouled herself before bleeding her insides out everywhere she could bleed, at the last tearing her scalp and flesh from the pain that the child could not answer. He saw again and again that death diminished him and stank up the world of the living from existence to nonexistence north to south, and then never more than when he made war that he knew would stink up the world worse, but that he knew must happen from the first time he saw slaves chained for auction, three diapered men on a riverboat to St. Louis, moved at whip and gun to sit in the sun by the wealthy white trash of the lower states, or their foremen, or their slavers who brought slaves by thousands along this and that river, caged inside this and that prison wagon, who walked them by hundreds too behind horses that fed and drank first. Abraham sat on a barrel on the boat, so his friend wrote, his smile gone at the sight, his face dark at the sight, his eyes cast down by the sight, and said then the name his friend had never before heard him say: *God must hate us for what we do.*

Now that he lay as dying as dying gets, what was left in him of life had been what lay left to him to see of his mother's life at her deathbed, as days before it had been at his aunt's deathbed by the same poison that was killing his mother, and the same days before at his uncle's deathbed by the same poison that killed his aunt, and was killing his mother, but that neither he nor his father ate to die from since they worked the farm while those who lay dead and dying of poison gathered berries for breakfast that he too had wanted to gather, so that as his father lay dying decades later, and as his half-brother pleaded with him to forgive his father for being his father, the dying man asked if his father lay dying, and when his half-brother affirmed that the old man's death stood imminent, the son said to him, *Then I don't see the point.* What was left of dying at Manassas, and then dying at Shiloh, and then at Antietam dying, on and on when he lay dying, he did as he had been dying at Thermopylae thousands of Greek years before and dying in the valley of salt that was in Syria thousands of Hebrew years before.

At cockcrow rain began that would have been the same simple rain of the day before if it had remained the day before, and so this was a differing rain, yet as soft and assuring as the day before, now that Abraham lay dying once and for all. Now that he lay dying his dying was more even than before since he had no breath to go on doing so, and even with no breath he dreamt he spilt immortal blood again and again wherever whenever blood could spill—the copper smell of it letting whole and entire from the limp body, exsanguinations that left all but the husk gone to ground. Wound or be wounded, he heard the cry, gut or be gutted, he heard the cry, and there was this, that the coward's sword never had edges whereby the honored man rendered lifeless the ends of fingers first, then the fat of cheeks, then what blinded the man to his friends, then what cost the man his speech, these that birthed widows and orphans till the theme of it (that would be spilt blood) darkened the earth, inflamed the body's surround and the air above till the swift terrible sword left limbs and loins embraced by birds and beasts more than by the woman the dead man loved.

Barbed horse, there on the plain, with yawning jaw in the bold charge that swells the hearts of beast and rider, there on the sand, where the army of men hear and feel the ground groan to the animal's beat, its thighs and ribs wadded for battle, and so to the high helm nodding at his horse's run the lance come from the sky strikes with a scream through the metal hiding the soldier's face, strikes then the skull inside it, through to the brain split inside front to back, and so as dead as dead gets the corpse rides on and on inside his armor on the horse flying in terror across the plain and the beach whereat the hot heart of the beast will blow miles away and together they fall (chest, head and all after). Of a Sunday named the afternoon supper, where therefore chicken thighs and turkey wings lay boned in platters, Abraham would survey his audience before narrating one or another gruesome battle or reciting among verses good and ill that impressed his memory at its deepest, those that gave him the solace of companion thought by their themes as constant for him as sun and moon seen or not –mortality, strife, loss, love, and not these only, but the futility of them since here was the tragic ground of all human endeavor: we do not only die, we are born to it as ducks to ponds. *Thus mourned all Troy,* he would recite setting down his napkin. And they did.

Enter Abraham then, by his mortal wound enter, thereby his mortal mind, therein its memory, this mosaic that knows the cold corpses white and black inside it by thousands who are become millions black and white inside it across two hundred fifty years by the moment of his wound, the mortal one, and yet whose mortal body did not disarticulate on battle ground torn limb after limb there by cannonade, saber, sword, or the wilder creatures of God's nature, and did not exsanguinate on battle ground so as to enrich the soil by death till nothing rested but the husk of him, and did not know the pain either of the lost leg, or arm, or hoof, or ear, or hand, or eye gouged (one or another, or both), or nose sliced by half that was not blown off by rifle shot or bomb. None of these did he undergo to die by so that laying him out crooked across the bed too short for his feet, his was the anguish of an already anguished mind that could not sleep ever without dreams, even leaning into death could not live unconscious without dreams, and so instead of knowing nothing his mind knew everything, sometimes all at once, knew of his thought or of his memory the image of his fate, its unfolding in his inmost time, even knowing sounds nearby, those of his grievers grieving what was left of his existence, of the mind fading no less captive for that, dying but did not know he lay dying, or even that he did not only sleep so as to wake to a day of rest, and yet he dreamt with no respite till the gloaming when all of his life the cock wrested him from his dreams by crowing, though this dawn no cock crew (that would be the rain), and he died instead of waking.

Only at the end of the end did his mind stutter, and that would be his children he saw, and his dead beloved, and his dead mother who were farthest from living in his memory, and so nearest to him in dying, those dead already who knew what it was to be dead once for all time, those that he sought at the end of the end for succor or solace, or only in sadness, in this melancholy that gave to him the sad dark will to war, and to be warred against for it even to the deaths of a half million, as you know, and to the maiming of a half million, as you know, and to the plight of millions who fled south and farther south, or west and farther west, as you know, those who died or were maimed fleeing in the face of his sadness, those who knew to fear the sadness that fired his will to war against iniquity as old as the countryside. Dying after an unendurable existence, he endured it since he had not ever across the long dark arc of it hanged himself by that tree yonder to which he would point a long finger wherever trees could be found, assaying them by looking up and down their branches to the topmost height so as to size the sturdiness that their lower limbs might bear his weight at the rope's end. He judged too if he might clamber some of this and that tree to do away with the burden of himself since it was an act better done alone by darkness where most shameful, merciful and pitiful deeds were done, and a strong tree therefore with a handsome wide trunk therefore (that would be always oak or elm), or so he told it to all who would listen as he staged his death in word pictures that he had recited to himself from childhood year after year, never more than during the war of atonement, but before it too—at his mother's death, and at his beloved's death, and at the day he married, and at the day of his election, and at the day he swore in, and at the day his children died, and at the day he caused the first man to die in the first skirmish that reconciled brethren to brethren. Batwing doors of a saloon Abraham peered above, now and always yearning to become drunken once and forever.

Not only did he not hang himself by any tree anywhere, neither did his wife who spoke of her death nearly as often as he spoke of his, and it was she who reminded him that self-hanging was woman's way since he admired Greek theatre, and the Hebrew bible, and the plays of William Shakespeare wherein one after another woman who despaired of life dispatched herself in a noose, and yet she thought poison for herself, a potion like the potions she knew that calmed her or put her to deep dreamless sleep. Between them they knew this as a consequence of living, that beds were made for bearing nightmares and babies and death, and so as he lay dying she confessed that she had demanded to go to the theatre when he preferred the celebration ball where hundreds of officers in dress blues and brass buttons would dance with the women they loved. The last she saw of him before being banished from the room forever he lay naked under a blanket, as you know, crosswise on the daybed, as you know, whereat she threw herself onto his chest, kissed his face again and again, and shouted to all who would listen, *Did I order my husband dead?* And so a decade later her only living immediacy, son Robert, who had declined his mother's invitation to see the famous play, committed her to a mental hospital on behalf of suicidal thoughts and a pernicious capacity for financial ruination.

As I am perfectly sane, she wrote from the asylum, *I do not wish to be driven insane.* Later she wrote from the asylum, *I am chained to a wall like the monster in Frankenstein. God alone knows of my agony,* she wrote from the asylum. Hellcat, she-wolf, schemer, so many wrote of her after her husband's death, and they wrote of her as jealous, spiteful and petty, and they described her poutiness, dowdiness, and her vengeful acts and words. Splenetic and deranged, so many wrote once she became a widow, and once she became a widow, so many wrote, she grew brazen, flirtatious, wanton, and given to wearing low cut dresses exhibiting too much ample bosom. From her room at the asylum the widow wrote, *I am followed everywhere by a wandering Jew.* But as her husband lay dying, she wept bereft to remember her husband's unshakeable sense of fate to him and to his country, and therefore to the long hard life of the world that stretched from ancients he revered among gods he feared at his own downward turn to death, speaking again and again of his belief in the *infernum* of dwelling in death as he had dwelt alive even as the killer of hundreds of thousands, suffering the nonexistence of death as he had existed, *fate* of that ilk, *eternity* of that ilk.

A brief nod of the sun would light the caravan of his dead body out of the rooming house into the public street so that all who saw and stared stared and saw the gathered end not only of his life, but of his body that would traverse the country for weeks on ice by train, that would thereby become a vessel of mourning war and praying to peace among hundreds of thousands who stood in rain and more rain to view it pass, and that at the end of the end would be the object of a failed plot to kidnap for ransom. But for now at gloaming's end it was enough that his corpse lay concealed by a flag as wide and high as a wall, as you know, and that soldiers in dress blue buttoned by brass with epaulets shaping their shoulders led a procession of mourners, friends and family, and of horsemen with sabers at the ready, and of snipers on rooftops, and rifle bearers at each corner of this and that street where the dead man and all after crossed ruts as hard as marble and waters flowing from this end of the city to that, where the manse awaited the cadaver barely beyond the back alleys of bars and brothels that he would walk at sunset bearing the hickory cane of his wife's choice.

The dense darkness left hundreds in exile where they followed the corpse, adding poison to the drizzle and unspeakable sadness to both such as Abraham knew day in day out across decades and decades of grief, madness and despair, in these to such depth that he thought them *sublime* to suffer. Say this then, and hear that too so as to picture whole and entire the iniquity begun in the country before it was such, and see and hear too why it began in the thoughts of them who began it, and so picture those beings and the women that birthed them for hundreds of years of spirit sickness and sin down to their bitter ends on their bellies and breasts in the dust, or strung at their spines to cottonwoods, and then picture too those whose arms and legs spread wide under peach, cherry and apple trees awaiting resurrection men, so-called, who retrieved cadavers and dug up corpses so as to return them to their families, and when to none those who resurrected the dead set them down nowhere for nothing roadside, lakeside, up and down river, or back under this and that peach, cherry and apple tree as if they had succumbed there one by one year after year, or grew there like weeds.

worse than dog we stink dead so that you don't need to see to know they lay by hundreds across a land bed, them that won't be gathered like we gathered, no, so that a body at sunset be gone by sunrise, a stench of supper gone by breakfast, and so we learnt not to mind killing so much as the stink of the dead we kilt till we was men before and after we kilt or got kilt but not men no more doing it, no, but things not of nature or of the nature of men, things we had no name for that we grew into to get ready to die or make somebody else die   to stop the stink of death we that gathered the dead threw corpses down wells of lost farms so that we saw the faces of them that we dropped before we dropped them, nor did we count these dead as dead since we neither buried nor burnt any as it was that we used them to putrefact the water from then on to forever so as to poison enemies or suffer them to die by thirst, and so after the first elephant of the first battle on the first field of it I saw we roped, hauled and tamped down the dead to straight their limbs, by which we rolled one after another body into a holler like mine here this day that I died in, and them we hooked by Bowies melted to hooks whereby we drug one after another across from their death scenes to the same hole or holler of other death scenes like them till we filled it like a sand hill or a slave ship cramped with the living clambering over the dead and dying, and it looked the same as the stories we told of, but for the quake of the sea, but of the same blackness too cause corpses blacken quicker in the wide open sun than them in the shade, but them that we failed to bury by dozens or hundreds one on top of the other we burnt since by dozens or hundreds they split open to the touch till the spilt innards stinked worse than the stink of death of its own self, worse now not only than a dead dog but a dead upright not split by heat or bugs or varmints, by whatever it were that sickened us to smell worse than death, leaving them by hundreds or even thousands to get ate by critters drawn like it were a pig roast to a soldier, a stink we smelt for days

and for miles away caught in our nose hairs like skeeters
and so on into our brains to grow a memory I learnt like
the roof of my hand reminding me of me in this holler—an
elephant of that ilk   that what kept us together till the end
we named unnatural death, as if we could yet hope of old
age to take us home, and yet we was half dead already at
the sight of such ends as we saw day in day out that went
on and on in the minds of us, or what is left of them after
the sight of such ends, and the fear of it, and the dread of
the fear of it that sees you kilt by your own side for dreading
and fearing and seizing up in the limbs, or why them that
tortured men tortured them and why them that took women
by force took them to beat them too, afraid of not feeling
nothing if not rage on the world, as if the killing were not
enough since they too might be kilt so that when we kilt we
thought instead it weren't us lying dead, no, but us walking
amongst hundreds of men like us but dead and so not like
us, them laid out like posing to look dead, but for the stench,
and then to see how each man died that we didn't die that
way, most ways none of us knew heretofore, and there is this
that we never knew to do or to see, and that were to cut the
throats of wounded men near to the last breath of them so
to speed them on their way to the true nowhere and by these
same Bowies afterward to behead mules for meat and then
to paint our faces in the blood of others like red Indians for
bravery—all these doings that were the reckoning we heard
tell of, this we hated till it sickened us, told again and again
by officers that no coloreds sailed the Mayflower, nor one

stepped onto the rocks at Plymouth, as if they and theirs did   when the job was not to kill, it was to die, and if it were to kill it were not to die, and then it were not to die by disease, and I won't, and not to die from the trots, and I won't, nor by snakebite or cutlass either, and I am not to die for a coward or a thief or a raper, nor drowned strapped by spurs to a mount thrashing on a river flow as fast and cold as waterfall, no, so I died a good death God asks, prayerful and manly both, sanguine by it, without war not doing it so soon unless kicked by a horse I groomed a burr of, but since there is war it were better I came to it than not, to be here even in this scrub holler I gather as the last of me since though no birds sing and no dogs bark I hear no more of artillery strewing fields and land bends of horsemen and gun walkers and wagons and ass carts like chariots in the sea Moses left behind, and yet with no pillow under me, and no bed, and none to shut my eyes forever, them to be food for birds, if even such sent by god, and yet I have time to think to my mind of my dying, to say to myself here is where I died, that others who find what of me is left to find can say here is where he died, where and how that are God's deciding, his harrowing my soul, mama would say, if I own one of those since I never rested on it if I did, and do, and will in the everlast even though in the God damn of things as I see them the everlast may be hell, the second death, mama would say, since I kilt and kilt again, muddied up in the face after and whooping like a savage among savages till spent of it we each by each lay quiet in our bedrolls to

think on our misdeeds and on the God who needs to forgive
us them even as I lay undone since but for dying with peace
I know nothing to live for, and so see nothing but Eden out
of this reckoning whereby at sunset the tree limb over me is
haunted and shivers like a soul soldier waiting, the man I
kilt at the one good boot God left to me   mama's fawnskin
slippers I remember when I remember mama, that and by
two fingers snapping the chicken's neck on Sunday, only
two till the neck drooped limp and sleeping—a reckoning
of that ilk I remember when I remember mama in the lord's
God damn of things of this world wherein I coddled no blue
veined bare breasts, and now I expect not to

Looking left, those are Alps, and as far as the eye can see, that is Germany.

In winter only one approach to the village opens whether by train or by tracks bearing the train since the river freezes thick, hard and early. Ravines beside the track narrow and deepen where at its slowest trestles as old as trees tremble below which there is nothing less than nothing to observe, where there is air to observe or there is sky to observe, but at each creaking or crying trestle there is a deeper darker gorge black with coal dust and smoke. Deepest chasms open underfoot that squeeze the hats of knees with gloved fingers after pulling a long dark scarf tighter across this or that face. Every hour of the morning one mountain after another passes the window blue with frost till the engine's plume of steam points to an ancient low stone wall lifting itself from the snow, and so there is something other than nothing, and these are ruins that cleave to stone shards where in summer goats climb. Where ruins lay lay signs that sometime the train's surround was awash in desire, despair and human ill, all that ruins recollect.

Mile after mile of soft white doves fall dead onto fatally flawed earth (that would be the blizzard) so that black maple and leatherleaf viburnum freeze to the Alpenside, and yet the world below thaws so as to exist.

Still hundreds of feet above a sea, if there were a sea nearby to measure, the landscape browns to elicit one birdkin a-wing, and there a quick brown fox disappears into the snow. Tighten the wool scarf so that those black eyes stare from beneath the brim of a fedora blacker than the scarf if not and never blacker than the eyes. Observe shadows emerge behind denuded tree lines ripe for avalanche, as of a glowing moon that leans into afternoon whereat farther on up or down a sky gun metal blue waits instead of this suspicion of perfect nothing and its nowhere. Shadows evoke humanity and humanity thinks as a consequence of which words exist and as a consequence more words exist, and these think till most thoughts are unfit to think, are they not? See morose cudding cows in a pasture that renders them harmless, and yet where are cows are farmers, and where farmers are are farms, and where these are villages erect, and inside these villages villagers reside.

The other side of the window thunders, clouds behind it, cloud bellies pregnant with more snow against the creeping iron-dark thaw where tracks and its train descend to the unfathomable suasion that every exit from a tunnel or trestle or bend in the tracks has primed the entrance to the next of these so that the next entrance, exit or bend begets another, each deriving one from the other on and on, and as metal cries out against metal this is as close to being there without being there as it gets. Seeing ways through, over and down the Alps becomes of a sudden somewhere instead of nowhere that it was, and now more here than there therefore, and more now than later traversing this and that chasm, gorge or crevasse (God's vantage), those words for *abyss* in the books God wrote, if God wrote them, if for God there is anything below other than abyss, *bottom of the waters,* so wrote God in his native language, if that is his native language. *Tehom,* he called all below to see that was not him, if that is his language, or if hers, or if no one's.

Now, there, the surround of small brown farms where hoofed creatures stand or kneel as they remark in indifferent stupor the passing train, its steam, its whistle, its wail. Here snow falls yellow across gas lamps against a suspicious dark sunset the blue of winter. Next, tracks neither continue nor end, but turn and turn again whence they came so as to go along the same crests and valleys sooner rather than later. Scarred suitcase in glove, scarf drawn tightly across the face, wide fedora hiding eyes as black as black gets—assume that the carriage lying on its side in the snow would suffer the same cracked wheel if it had been hired for someone else departing the train, and yet this is not a village to be read by a foreigner. Now skirt the village by an alley beside a stable whose half naked farrier hammers a flaming amber horseshoe till once and for all shop windows pass, their owners and keepers closing for the day, glimpsing before averting their gaze, wary that black are evil eyes to beware the curse thereof.

Boots echo against the walkway, as they do everywhere on earth that is quiet, cobbled or bricked, and these lead or follow without fail to the village square that glows brighter than high noon of a summer and where those black stones remember witches burnt above them to end this or that plague, women first stripped bare and flogged till they spoke in tongues to Satan of God before being violated by the stiff hide of a horse's pizzle or by hot sulphur poured into their birth canals, and then, only then, posted, chained and set afire under heaven's umbrella where each in her turn searched for salvation that did not come but in death, the salvation that comes to all, witches and not, but here see those that succumbed to fire and smoke and torture that lit the square like noon of a summer's day for centuries and centuries.

Let us say that in the village square at this moment St. Nikolas and the baby Christ wait to arrive, and so it is the night that they bestow gifts to the unworthy, and let us say that who is unworthy cleanses at the ringing of bells and the adoration of tall trees with bright ornamentals whose angels perch on the highest thin branch, and that *kinder* sing carols of the season, let us say, *Adeste fidelis*, for instance, that of *lacrimosa, dolorosa—fidelis* of that ilk, let us say. Beyond this festive temper darkness quickly returns since fewer and fewer shivering gas lamps light the way till knees exhaust, and the arm bearing the scarred suitcase exhausts from cold, snow and worry. Only then pause before the iron gates of the monastic ground, such gates that memorize the history of western gods in filigree, and that open to vast bronze doors taller than three men. For centuries travelers would study mosaics of floors and windows in this space, and would study walls in fresco telling of this and that saint tortured unto death for believing what he and she believed, and travelers meanwhile overheard a vast pipe organ built by the Dutch, and in summer inhaled garden fragrances and the hanging fruit of them too—all these the traveler would partake of till screams from the afflicted sounded, and their mad laughter, and then their ravings and their curses because they were cursed. Now only one accursed madman overhears the concussion of his riding boots against the stone floors of his rooms, the two, that for sleeping, that for sitting, where none but one family member ever visited and this was decades before and this was to be assured that the lunacy would remain incurable and that the prisoner did not suffer other than in his mind.

And now say this, that standing before bronze doors beyond the iron gates one lamp lights the way by the Old Testament and one by the New book so that here and now in the dark of winter enter by the door of covenant and obeisance among the divided selves and wounded others whose names that never stop flowing from the mouth would be forever Adam and Eve and Cain and Abel, Abraham and God, Abraham and Isaac,

Isaac and Ishmael, Saul and God, David and Saul, David and God, Job and God, Job and Job—go in by a *way* of that ilk so as to leave behind thoughts of mercy, or pity, or forgiveness, or redemption, or resurrection, to say nothing of seeing the light unless it is seeing the light till blind (*light* of that ilk, brethren). Be in mind that nothing will be known of him by voice, touch or anything other than madness so that he could be just another lunatic in the asylum, another last lunatic since lunatics are more alike than not, happy lunatics happy in the same way, the unhappy each in their own way, rent by guilt, anguished by nightmares and by all that makes madmen mad whether it is summer or winter, whether flowers bloom or wither and die, and whether they reside alone or among other lunatics, and whether they suffer visitors of the flesh or souls only that glide across the floor or glide above it or glide only in the deep well of memory—all no less lunatic, are they not?

Here, so the valet points, the sitting room where a fire blazes, and a wall of books flickers and darkens, and in a corner, look, a wide horned Victrola on a high table, and then there, opposite the library, those are drawings that fill the wall. The window to the world is wide and high, framed into dozens of discrete views so that life outside the madhouse can be seen only as mosaics in the cathedral, though at differing hours of the day and differing times of the year the window reflects nothing other than the viewer of it, each vision as small as a self-portrait. There is a chaise meeting the Victrola on the edge of which the memory of a human head depresses a stained satin pillow while below this a disturbed blanket as spiny as an elephant's ear fits the curve of adult scapulars—here is the scene of nightmares and their days. In front of a pocked wall empty of diverting drawings a writing table as thin in the desk and legs as a small spider awaits the lunatic, and yet a tea table rests below the horizon of drawings hoarding the wall opposite so that an audience can appreciate the artist's work, condemn it or question its themes while sipping something as clear as water from a decanter more empty than full.

Christmas eventide, so her sister remembered, and the governess remembered, and the maid remembered, that Rathbone's shadow emerged and receded only to emerge and recede again and again as he swiftly and heavily crossed the long candlelit corridor from the farthest room in the house to the children's play room. Pistol in one hand and dagger in the other their father met their mother who smiled to the children huddled with terror by the fireplace before locking the door behind her. Those who saw to remember whatever they could remember saw him swiftly and heavily take to the bedroom, striding with determination, as if he had thought through a theme to its end, or so their aunt would say, after which Clara closed that door too, or so their governess would say, and finally their aunt would say this, that when she entered the bedroom at the report of the pistol she found her sister's body bloodied from stab wounds even as she smelt the small dark smoking hole above her nipple. Then Clara whispered to her ear, *at last he's killed me.* And he had.

Enter Rathbone, man in the box, in the worst seat in the theatre, lone living lunatic here, best witness to the crime of his century those damp nights of dread and despair decades and continents and languages ago. Enter Rathbone in dressing gown skirting his ankles below which he wears soft slippers with flower petals stitched on the roof. Enter Rathbone, vested inside his dressing gown and wearing a necktie pinned to his collar by bright red studs. In silence he crosses the room to wind the stem of the Victrola that has fainted during the play of a lone cello, of nothing more than a lone cello because it is evening, and since it is evening voices inside the walls speak at their lowest register of the day. The cello scrapes and cuts while Rathbone's thin soft voice reports that we are listening to the first such music outside of a concert hall. *The walls crepitate and so I play the Victrola with the biggest horn to unhear the voices of interred monks and interred lunatics and of the assassins on the other side of every wall and window.* Enter Rathbone, father, husband, brother, best witness to the crime of the century, last monk in the monastery, last lunatic in the asylum. *I would shake your hand, but mine is redder than the devil's hoof,* he says.

Time and scene—these are night inside the high-arched chamber behind the lowest of two towers at the *Mariendom*, village H, domain H. The stones of the floor smooth and dark where Rathbone has paced day in day out nearly three decades of sleepless memory wherein discordance does not matter in the least, neither memory ill-remembered nor disproven either. The room trembles candlelit among reflecting window panes frosted blue under a moon bathing the garden gray where Rathbone stares it down. Look to the bottom of the grounds among dead, dying and sleeping trees where the small cemetery buries monks and madmen alike, that democracy after existence, existence—that fiasco. Beyond these dead a polished engraved headstone squats in the earth as moonglow white as the deceased's breasts before she deceased, bearing her family name and lines from a poem that she admired (this would be *She Walks in Beauty*). Persuaded that the other side of the window remains deserted, Rathbone soon sits at his desk to write as he has done night after night decade after decade, gently dipping his pen into the mouth of an ink bottle inside a well in the wood, the wood mahogany, the ink blacker than the inside of a boot, the pen as long as a dagger, its point as sharp as a needle so that it scratches the paper it writes against thereby sounding like a cat wanting in for the night. Rathbone blows into his hands and pinches eyeglasses onto the bridge of his nose before retrieving a sheet of paper from a sheaf of them a foot high.

Every other moment, however we measure it, the writing interrupts while the writer glances here and there in the room (the one for sitting) in search of a blur in the cornice of his sight that may have been the shadow of one of his assassins drawing itself across a wall behind his back, the assassin whole and entire approaching from the other side of the vast window framing all that Rathbone knows to be the world external to him. He disturbs the writing in yet another moment, however we measure that, with a severe search of drawings on the wall behind him, persuaded that some have moved so that a dog's muzzle has become the startled eyes of a ferret Rathbone memorized walking the cemetery, or this and that drawing of a lion and a horse and a housecat transported by an illicit draft from the fireplace marking the arrival of an ill-used soul once again into his rooms, and yet there is this, that any and all of his drawings may have transferred themselves only in Rathbone's mind since the worst of his affliction is the knowledge that he suffers it, that things here and there move to become things there and here, that voices and visions nowhere to be found find themselves in his presence day in day out year after year.

Drawn to the world's window by distant sounds from the village square, Rathbone cannot discern whether these celebrate cheer or rage, nor does it matter whether they praise the rebirth of the apocalypt or they praise the immolation of witches stripped of their flesh, penetrated everywhere penetrable into and out of their flayed bodies before set aflame amid cries to a righteous God of atonement. It does not matter if the village gathers again to denounce Rathbone's incarceration, marching with torches held high in the wind again to the monastery where no monks live and to the madhouse where none but one madman subsists, to demand that the prisoner remove to another prison far away or that the village whole and entire retrieve him so as to strip him bare, flay his flesh, penetrate all of him penetrable before setting the remainder aflame amid cries to a righteous God of atonement.

Rathbone glares at the glaring moon that traces a downward path to the polished marble that marks the remains of his sister's skull or that marks the illusion of his sister's skull or that marks its absence since he has overheard the rumor inside the walls that her remains returned to America decades before, during the ghost of night while Rathbone slept or did not sleep, but did or did not sleep nowhere near the retrieved coffin, its contents, their rattle and jag, the cadaver beyond stench. The moonlit stone would grow in a ground of lifeless dirt therefore, a hollow earth so-called as thousands of stones measured the dead across vast orchards empty of bones from the war of atonement, and this would make of his sister Clara the truer last sacrifice of that war. Again and again night in night out Rathbone awaits the rise of his sister from her interment after he sees her again and again claw her living body from its grave because a black dog claws and circles the ground above. Either she rises so as to glide into his sitting room or she fails, but inside either theme of his madness Rathbone cannot conceive his sister's absence. The nonexistence of her nonexistence he cannot conceive for if he conceived it his madness would worsen, darken and widen till he saw no apparition of her and heard no voice of her inside the deepest well of his ears or inside the deepest geography of the walls in his surround. His survival rests in the earth below the name stone above the hollow where Clara has lain for decades and decades now or has not lain though her soul glides to her brother night after night to whisper into his innermost mind, melting with his body to penetrate all that is penetrable. Whether buried or not, there or not, she will not be removed from the madness that binds them forever now, whatever forever measures, as it bound them for decade after decade before he could not save her.

Sight of a tawny mouse brooking his slipper reminds him why he has walked to the window and it is this, that he came to search neither for murderous voices nor for souls on fire, but for a word he could not retrieve from an avalanche of them tumbling off the moonstruck Alps of his surround. In an instant the word he desires arrests the winter before him, but on his return to the desk where he would write it the word tumbles into this or that chasm lost forever till the thinker does not remember even that he lost it, if *thinker* is the word. And so here we return crook backed to the writing table where all the written writes itself by candlelight and where every night the writer writes *What has to happen, happen now,* if *writer* is the word, if *writing* is the word. And when what has to happen neither happens nor does not Rathbone writes such again night after night day in day out year after year, as he has one decade after another while waiting for it to happen, whatever it is that he cannot name that must happen, if *happen* is the word. From oppressive beams overhead and the oppression of dark narrow rooms beset by nightmares and the visions that incite them, gruesome thoughts one after another befall the monastery by the monastery gate and then inside the monastic door smelling of Old Testament where verse after verse regarding dead souls haunts him, consoles him or solicits true and false memory, which no longer matters in the least.

There were ploughboys and farriers and road hounds, and that is those who plied a trade of sorts before the war of atonement, not those hayseed straw chewers, tobacco leeches or corn liquor purveyors of marshes and backwoods, no, and yet all handed muskets, lead and powder to defend of what they themselves knew nothing other than that black folk were not them and that the government far off was not them, them who carried needle and thread to sew their own wounds out of haversacks named *housewives* hung to their ammo belts by string. The death upon death of these comes only to go again and again, his own death the last death among the dead who witnessed the assassin and the assassinated nearly a half century before, death upon death that comes and goes again and again in the sleepless night after night, those dead by rifle, by pistol, by saber, by dagger, by cannon, by fire, and by water too, those he saw drown atop their drowning horses.

He saw again and again innards half-chewed strewn by all shapes and sizes of creatures from one end of the grassy war sea to another, from Sharpsburg to the Potomac therefore, the country bent double and crouching since before it was a country of men speaking one to another in accents to deride and despise, those to speak south from north till those in Mississippi could not hear those in New Jersey, or the Babel that was the bane of the plain speakers, and that is not to say of the slaves themselves, of their sing song slang at either pitch or words, and of their rituals that spoke to elsewhere as if they were praying on the moon. After all that, Rathbone still lives when most of that dread night forty five years before have died so that none who touched the dying man yet lived but the dying man's son and Dr. Leale, and few who heard in the theatre yet lived, and none lived still who saw him carried in the rain of the dirt street awash in mud and dung and blood other than Dr. Leale— these dead come and go night after night season after season year in year out whether Rathbone distinguishes them or not, remembers them or not and wills them or not till whether they existed or not no longer matters in the least. Warm lead and cold steel, brethren.

Hear bells of the village square till Rathbone shuffles skin and bones in dressing gown, slippers and scarf to the window as wide and high as the world will ever be while a capacious winter moon lights all of it everywhere for everyone. Tolling annihilation, bells call to lit faggots and to flaying, to the violation of one after another vacancy in the victim's body, and so at the stake of her penance someone's sister searches the sky for one or another god to save her, for one or another eternity to open to her or to open into her as the horse's or the bull's pizzle opens into her. Rathbone again witnesses Clara's corpse confined to bandages and linens foot to head like an ancient queen put quickly into her coffin and removed for all time from his sight. At the bottom of the garden, beyond the dead and sleeping trees and shrubs, beyond markers of anonymous monks and madmen, even beyond the wrapped and buried sister's remains—beyond all these in the heart of winter stand black yawning gates taller than three men that must be entered before the bronze doors must be entered, these also taller than three men. By these Rathbone would debouch from the monastery of his asylum if he could, by these save himself from madness and the godliness that ensues if he could. They do not know it, but he would not save himself if he could.

Rathbone dreads still worse whatever arrives next that he knows to be the next on and on over and over without relent even if the worst beyond worse that is not his dead sister's visit will always be the hindmost sight of the door that always opens beyond his reach from the far arm of the settee in the box in the theatre a half century before. Rathbone neither hears nor sees the door open towards him, sees neither who opens it nor why they do till in an instant he knows more than anyone anywhere in the world and will always remember more than anyone anywhere in the world of that act, and those acts, and those failings in the surrounding storms of mud, dung and blood that long hard Friday Christians still call Good. Rathbone's derangement of the world as he found it, and of his existence inside his derangement, spares him everything but the memory of all that has been lost to him, and lost by him, maddening battle after battle in the war of his atonement, undergoing battle thrice that he smelt and heard and saw day in day out month after month of the atonement and the rectifications thereby. So many said of him before, during and after across decades and decades that he suffered the seeping into him his secret affliction till he swore a sacred bond between Abraham, the assassin and himself awash in blood from shoulder to elbow and back again. *The first words were given in fire and darkness,* Abraham would say to all who would listen as he exhorted his armies to annihilate those who had caused the land to be accursed, themselves accursed ones therefore, the *golem,* and cursing the rest thereby. *Believe me because of my enemies,* said Abraham lifting an arm above the gathered, *let them be blotted from the book of the living,* said Abraham fisting the hand the arm lifted.

His life whistled out his nose, the hairs inside the last of him to move.

Abraham in his tomb now forty-five years.

As if those moments are not drear enough Rathbone again and again walks with swift deliberate meaning from the lightless room in the consular home to the children's playroom lit by candles and by the ornaments of Christmas on a tree as tall as the ceiling and as fragrant as the forest where the tree is found year in year out that is now found over and over night in night out decades later. He knows Clara's body even in the darkness of the bedroom that she shares with her husband to whom she bares her breast one more time and one last time to nurse him into a deep sleep out of his madness. And now the intruder intrudes from a window beside a tree shining under a moon, setting the stage therefore for another killing, as the intruder intruded decades before while the audience laughed at actors on a stage, laughed at the words they spoke, and laughing at the gestures they invented to exaggerate the words they spoke, laughing too again and again at the broad expressions they invented, as broad and laughable as their costumes since these too invited the audience to laugh.

Talons on chest, chin and thighs—the rest you can see for yourself.

Abraham spoke of the numberless terrible wonders walking the world, but none to match the dark of mankind, so Rathbone remembers night after night year after year, the worst wonder across heaving seas at all compass points being this, that under cold clear skies we destroy the world more than we create it, so Rathbone remembers that Abraham spoke and remembers therefore day in day out decade after decade. The commander of atonement said to all who would listen wherever listeners could be gathered that our land casts out that man who weds depravity so as never to share hearth again, or to think thoughts again, thereby exiling forever from humanity whoever does evil ungodly deeds, so Rathbone again and again remembers night in night out that Abraham spoke, and in his affliction Rathbone does not hear his memory speak, but hears Abraham for the one only time and sees for the one only time Abraham speaking it. Look, see, where the commander points by the finger extending from the fist lifted by the arm, there where the ground gathers to it a bellyful of bodies so that the land empties of any sign of upright life.

Beasts only roam the battlefield where Abraham walks after smoke and cannonade clear, months after the unnamable dead have been gathered by ass cart to bury or to be devoured to the bone by other creatures beloved of God, such varmints and birds who hide and fly from scene after scene of violent death to wait for the still and silent cadaverous nation among woods, hollows and bracken. Look there, where Abraham walks at Gettysburg so many months later, a booted foot under a sheet of snow stopping the ground growing anything but bones. Other than that these men died Abraham knew nothing of them, more than a half million, but he knew that of them. As for the war *qua* war Rathbone killed nobody and nobody killed Rathbone.

Hear this though, that memory remembers their father walking quickly towards them from the far end of the hallway, out of the shadow of the farthest room in the consular house, where he no longer passed only nights, he passed days too for years and years speaking to himself or not speaking to anyone, or speaking to the dead, and then of a sudden he walked swiftly in heavy boots that silenced the children, that caused them to huddle before the fireplace. Among the household of his wife, sister-in-law, governess, maid, none had heard him walk either swiftly or heavily before, but always quietly and with the grace of a dancer, of a man safe in slippers. Moving swiftly and heavily therefore, with deliberation thereby, as of a matter concluded in the man's mind, his war boots sounded the floor louder than the fireplace crackled till Mother appeared in the doorway warning her offspring to remain where they stood no matter what they heard, urging them in a whisper, so the eldest said, that no matter what they might hear through the door they were forbidden to see what there might be to see because of what they heard, so the second eldest said. And so they pressed their ears to the large dark Black Forest door, hearing nothing till there were screams to hear, and curses to hear, and cries of pain to hear again and again so that Rathbone's children began to sob without knowing why they sobbed. Soon they heard the voices of strangers in the house, and soon saw and heard their aunt and their governess enter to console them while they darkly realized each in their turn each in their way lying in the arms of a sobbing aunt and a sobbing governess that they sobbed because of all the voices they heard again and again not once did they hear their mother's.

In the dark and darker memory of his affliction Rathbone would have saved the immovable and irretrievably wounded, those felled again and again by bullet, cannon and saber, and he would if he could have saved the commander in his chair in the box in the theatre, or he should have, or he would have, as he should have and would have saved his sister if he could have, as he would have saved her husband if he could have, as he should have, saving all and sundry in war and peace killed whether by door, window or battle does not matter in the least. Indwell at the deepest trough of the darkest chasm in Rathbone's mind, and here unnamable shapeless beasts prevail day in day out unless it is beset night after night by the soul of the sister he could not save. The dying and then dead commander of the atonement a half century before remains in soul to Rathbone since he would have saved him if he could that dreadful night of rain, mud, dung, and blood, as he would have saved his sister if he could have before she became soul only on that dreadful night of snow, cold, children, and blood, saving them both if he could have, each in their turn in their time, and so they resurrect night in night out only to die again night out night in decade after decade, *resurrection* of that ilk, yet only to vanish in the gloaming of a dawn without a sun to show for it that breaks against the vast window Rathbone watches for mayhem in the nearby—the only window to the world he has learnt from in thirty years.

Rathbone has beheld from the world of the window set before him aeroplanes in skies, balloons above baskets with humanity inside, swollen dirigibles propelled front and rear, armies gathered and grown for the next of the rest of the new century's wars to end all wars once for all, and he has beheld automobiles parked before the monastery while visitors listen to the organ in the cathedral and pray, overhearing footsteps on stone of such visitors when they come and when they go, and their children's footsteps, and their children's children's footsteps—three decades of others who come before they go, as three decades of monks and madmen pray and rave to the last instant of unremembered time.

Life pried Abraham's jaws open so as to leave the mouth (this would be the sigh that all nearby heard).

Abraham in his tomb now forty-five years.

As if these moments are not drear enough, Rathbone paces the length and width of his prison while walls at all compass points watch him do it, as his sister's soul watches him in slippers and gown and scarf because he excavates the lower depth and ghastly splendor of a yearning that has made madness of him. The madness made of him observing his sister's bare breasts night after night for year after year as she speaks to him of the dead husband her brother could not save, appealing thereby to the walls that conspire to poison Rathbone by day, day in day out, whether by food, water or schnapps does not matter in the least. Each night Rathbone remembers so as to write his terrors so as to consign them to flames in the fireplace, and this he does night after night to know what he must forget, what his affliction forgets for him till night after night his memory of this murder and that murder is the first and only memory of it, of deed and misdeed, of the done and undone, of madness and worse madness, of his ill and the ill of others.

His memory suffers ruin over and over, ruin akin to that of Abraham unconscious on the spot slumped in his chair, and who now slumps in his chair one night after another in Rathbone's memory, emerging from the bottom of his derangement to the surface before it is memory lost again and again, and akin to that of the suddenly dying sister sprawled on the bedroom carpet, blood spreading like sunset, her legs and arms as wide as a lover's, her bare breasts draining of blood and muscle and tissue one night after another before it is memory lost again and again, if only to rise again the next night, and the next, each time for the first time year in year out, death after death, murder after murder before his eyes as far as his eyes can see.

Hear then how the soul of Rathbone's sister groans not only for her murder, or for the death to come soon of her brother by half, but for the death of her husband not saved by her brother, the next murder in the family thereby, his dead sister risen from her grave groaning for the affliction of her living brother that he has seen murder again, again and again by failing to forbid murder across decades and decades of living till he is convinced that all would still live but for himself still living. Night after night his sister's husband lies dead beside his dying wife, each in their turn in their time bleeding out their chests where their wounds reek of metal and gunpowder, and smell like food to rats too frightened to leave their corners. And so night after night blood ribbons into puddles on the carpet they share, soaking to cracks and gouges and the grout of the hard dark floor.

Night after night Clara dies in the horror that outlived her, in the agony of repeating beyond mortality the punishment for her desires, as if the purpose of her life has always been to undergo death and death again. *At last he has killed me,* she says over and over on the carpet on the floor from midnight till dawn those dreadful nights that Rathbone fails and fails again to save this victim or that victim. Each victim was the last to know they were the victim, as Rathbone was the first to know each was the victim, to know therefore who was the killer, knowing the victim who slumped in his chair in a box of the theatre, slumping and unconscious unto death as a consequence, a victim nothing like his sister, who lay conscious and dying and talking on the bloody carpet beside her bloody dead husband, leaving now none but Rathbone the living brother to fail to forbid the murder of, whether poisoned by water, food or schnapps would not matter in the least, or by starvation at his own volition, or by thirst at his own volition so as to forbid the voices inside the walls of his rooms—one for sitting, one for sleeping, as you know—from beholding the threats they conspire to triumph night and day year after year decade after decade. All these victims of violent death and as different in their dying as sun and moon, and Rathbone saved neither one nor the other. *If I had saved the first,* Rathbone writes, *I might have saved the second. I saved neither,* writes Rathbone. *I spared none.*

believe not in my cause but in the smoke rising still out of my missing foot, that on the right, where the pointing ends and the boot begins, and as for heroes we knew none till in this wet trench of the last holler of hollers we was all of us heroic in our deaths, this man in that trench heroic, and him in the next holler heroic, them silent now after so much squealing and weeping and outcalling names whose persons never arrived to save anybody from anything so that dying learnt us one by one why God made the other side of things, so much did we dread dying at the end of the end till we owned no mind left to fear by while them of us left here now to die quiet and last and more alone than them who died hearing everybody moan and fret just like them, a gathering of that ilk I am the last of, so I come to fear the mind of me that fears, wanting to be mindless so, not dreaming neither, for that were a dream of death when I had it, and I had it on and on even before dying in my holler in the surround of moles and gophers and other patient vermin to disgrace my being with their teeth where weeds and rats grow lush and fat in my nearby in the Lord's God damn of things   we begun disgraced by lice and jiggers even before the first time we saw the elephant, and we ate these bugs when we drunk the water we washed in that was the only water we knew to hand, and so these hatched gametes in our throats and bellies and bowels till those grew to hatch their own gametes inside of us one and all so to harm our innards that brought to us cramps and shites and head and bone ache laying us out sick for miles long and wide, forever or more chained to each other by sores and disease and the blood thereby, innards that worm bleeders fell out our bungholes by where we marched or sat or sleeped or keeled over, troopers as hapless as wharf rats pissing blood and who shat black ropes as awful as death to smell till we treated our sickness with dogwood bark that we chewed or boiled to a soup, but no less laid away in swamps and bogs, croakers mostly, envying the officers what sat in saddles sidewise for their piles swollen out till one by one these too tipped over or their horses tipped over, all sick, all fevered, but I did not die, not then or there, not among the dirty runners we grew into, them who heard shots to the east so as to let out scampering to the west, men of the crowd that were running to the same safe idea where it were quiet but for bird song and leaf crush and the long breath that hunkers down to wait to die, or not, even me bapsoused by the pastor of the same Sunday the neighbor baby got ate by a scrap fed pig on the road before the houses, and so there be Sunday, church, gizzards and grits smelling the kitchen from the frypan, and then screaming before the grownups came running to see the cur's muzzle near to the leftovers of the child, and so since this thing I remember of my bapsousing I think of pig come to gobble me after my going, what is left of me, to which I reconcile no good end of myself other than it be my end, and only once to do it, and that is the good news, and among them I knew best I am the last to die, the war for me and mine done, but most of the dead I did not know, and that is the good news, and so I be the last that can whistle in the dark of my sinning, either thinking on this or that farm girl I did not touch or *on those soiled doves I knew the pictures of, them whose voices I never heard but saw them naked front to back up to down in all their beckoning   of the whores we named nurses in houses we named hospitals we said of them I seen Venus as of midnight and Mercury in the morning since we was slathered on our privates by mercy angels as old as witchcraft, them that moved along the line of fornicators with our britches down and our soldiers held out for salve on a spoon, each of us holding the sleeping pig in an open palm while this and that mercy ladled her witches brew across the roof of the thing before at the tip every jack of us lifted to see mercy resolve the undershot of it too, where the string drives into the coin purse that makes for the troubles till there's a country of old soldiers forgotten their names and even that they was once human, and so it was from that disgrace before God and my dead mother when I begun to lay sad with my doom, and so sleepless in my bedroll rubbing the whistle not even to fruit but to remember that some of us would live and some would not, ipsating by my busy elbow till I couldn't lift the musket, feeding thereby my homesick and holding back the memory of men branded who cowered or stole, or those eagle spread across the circle of a wagon wheel driving cannon or its balls and shrapnel up and down the ruts of a mud wash dried hard by the sun, that punition I bore witness of for three days a man lived, a deserter not fed or watered or talked to till he died and he were cursed by some for living to start with, or rapers strung up for birds like suet*

For all the hangdogs and underdones who flee as far south as south goes or as far west as west goes, both fleeing as far as far goes, death is the theme, death that they need not know to know it, the last truth of the last instant of unremembered time since it is the arc of their pitiful lives, and this has unchanged since the first shot by the first shooter at Sumter till death is like life, only less so. Every day each ragbag still lives he has not yet died, does not yet lay arms and legs wide spread under peach, apple or cherry tree, and so does not thank God to be alive so much as thank God not to be dead, or not to have left behind a limb somewhere, or not to be dragging guts by the handful into woods and meadows while retrieving from the housewife about his neck the needle and thread to sew the bowel back where it belongs.

Rabbits and birds in bushes the guerrillas prefer to be, but are not, or that these thousands might sting like wasps sting, but do not, so that whether scamper or fly or bite they would be any other than an upright these final days of atonement. This fight and flight one and the same executed by washouts and deadheads in gray gone to ribbons spans from one end of the country that is left to be called such to its other, where the Mexicans gather or Indians gather, and the buffalo among them gather too, marauders who follow and kill them, or bushwhack to rob and rape as if to fire war again, a fag end rebellion of plunder, arson and theft, or bandits who think never of war again or rebellion again, no, but of vengeance so as to kill freed slaves and jayhawkers, and any and all who were not them or reminded them of themselves in this, the marauding. Their names will grow famous for their plunder and robbery till one after one these men that kill are killed by gunfire or hanged from trees or gibbets for as far as the eye can see, and this fate shows mercy for them who have burnt alive so-called proclaimed coloreds, or have strung them face down by their testes from sturdy tree limbs, or have opened their bellies with Bowie knives for rodents to enter and snakes to enter, or buried to their necks in the ground with molasses as black as their faces on their faces so as to draw ants and their ilk. White men they murder they murder suddenly because these are as human as themselves if skin still means anything to anybody, and it would be ungodly to torture a living human being, would it not?

We speak now of this therefore, the last days to atone so as to know redemption, and so too we speak of the irredeemable and tone deaf of the atonement, and so we speak of the ragbag guerrilla bushwhackers, of what remains of the remains of the slave south army, its regulars and irregulars, of murderers and marauders therefore after the all has been said and been done for all still living to see, hear and know so as to remember, guerrillas in and out of grays from the Lower Seaboard theatre and the Gulf Approach theatre westward to the Trans-Mississippi theatre and onward to the Western one till at the last what had been the Pacific Coast theatre of operations, but is no more the farthest west the war gets. There is at the end of the end in space and time ocean and more ocean. For thousands there is Australia.

We speak now therefore the story of the larval innards that fouled the nest of the federate (that would be the written word of 1789) so that even at his deathbed near a century after the country became a country, and two centuries and a half of another after the first diapered slave put a naked heel on the naked soil Abraham lay dying as a sinner against sin among millions of sinners for and against it for as far as the eye could see, this sinner who purged not only the land of its corrupted landsmen, but of the words that corrupted them (that would again be the written word of 1789) when the country not yet a country laid claim to becoming one, if not yet a *nation*, as Abraham would lay claim to it for the first time at Gettysburg, no longer sovereignties joined on a map, no, but the one that could be only the one, the permanent and indissouluble without from this day and that day the right to enslave this and that man or woman, as a gift of God no less (that would again be the written word of 1789, the Constitution that constituted what for whom?).

As he lay dying, at last even inside his mind dying, dying in dreams at last if not yet once for all dying, the captain of captains of the atonement and its godliness, and its tragedy thereby, lifts what is left of his thinking to this that he remarked again and again to all who would listen, *Does Lazarus not die twice thanks to divine intervention,* and in reply to his thought on the consequences of the Christ he would add, so many said to remember, *Do not miracles profane what is holiest in nature?* He would consider his mother's death in this regard, and he would consider Ann's death then, and the deaths of his children, and the deaths of more than a half million then, till inside the manse or outside, in the north and in the south, the theme was death and so it was also not death, and this went on and on for four years after which death and not death grew into the pathology of death that Abraham knew more than most, though not for himself unless by premature burial, but for his beloveds who no less died in spite of his knowledge.

By snakeroot, or milkweed, or richweed, or boneset (one and the same by names wherever such herb or root grew from Kentucky, Indiana, Illinois, for instances), it was poison in milk that cows who ate them issued, and yet in that time in that country the berries thereat were mistook for toxins, not the milk that washed them down, so that as he lay dying, and for all the decades after the age of nine of his living Abraham took the root, herb and berries nearby to have killed his mother, not the freshest milk from the fullest cow, and so there was this, that those same herbs, roots and berries killed too his aunt and his uncle, sparing him and his father only till the boy saw all before him vomitous, unconscious and moaning.

Now there followed this, fearing in the heart of his darkness that his mother would be the first to die, he prayed that she would not, and she did not, and then in the heart of his darkness fearing that his mother would be next to die, he prayed that she would not, and she did not, and this he saw as a sign that she would not die if he prayed that she would not, but after a week of agony that lost her inner workings from head to foot of body and mind she died full of his prayers and nothing else. It was his first upright death and like no other therefore so that others decades later only darkened his heart thicker till all who lay dying in agony he believed he knew more of than most, among these hundreds of thousands whom he confessed died by his hand, thereby making the meaning that by night and by day awake or asleep he knew more than most that thousands lay dying all about him from one end of the war to its other with nobody and nothing anywhere to stop it.

As Abraham lay dying in his cursed unconscious thousands took to the streets amid the sounds of horse hoofs and boot heels, and by the clamber of saber against scabbard, and by the remote report of rifle fire, and so they came to believe that he was not dead since he could not die during rifle fire and saber rattle and horses at the gallop. But as hours went after coming, sounds softened before silencing and horses returned lathered and steaming, these thousands held fast to the one thought till silence and stillness told them that the more they came to believe he could not die the more he must be dead, and then that he had lain dead the while they believed he could not die so that these who stood, prayed and sang pronounced sentence on him, burying him before the actual hour, as he had feared for decades in his dreams, his *fearful trip* not yet as done as done gets, so the poet of his death wrote of his death, his trip a trip of that ilk.

As Abraham lay dying thousands suffered the suasions of silence, stillness and a roof of sky without a sun to show for it, and by these wept persuaded that he had for hours lain dead, dead, dead among the raiders and warriors of pagans and Hebrews he revered, dying as surely as all among Greeks and Hebrews, and as surely as Oedipus who blinded his eyes to save Thebes from the curse of himself and his foul deeds, and as surely as Macbeth and Richard Three Sticks died for their foul deeds that warred on their countrymen. Abraham lay burdened by the long arduous labor of giving up the sensorium whole and entire of the calamity the country birthed before it was a country so that elegant thinking met brute force in the commune between men, their gods and gods' curses at their maddest. He warred against millions of simpletons and slavers, millions among no-hopers and stinkpots who neither shouldered a rifle nor negotiated a saber till then, and yet these by thousands every day year in year out stood to make meaning of the meaningless till by the same thousands who were not yet dead they fled west and south as far as these would take them, as you know, ragasses and washouts fleeing or hiding or dressed in hoop skirts and sun bonnets to save themselves when not bushwhacking any and all who passed unawares. Since glory is fleeting and dishonor endures, learn this, brethren, that the first man who fired the first shot at Sumter by the same pistol shot himself at war's end, cursing the land and all who first crawled on it, and yet these deeds and this weapon rounded his life, did they not?

Here then lies the throughline of the country that ran across not only the story of it, but formed the margins of it from ocean to ocean with in between ideas far flung and far fetched and so as stinking as the greasiest hive of suet hanging from a lynch mob's tree limb for daws to peck at the winter long. Fat and muscle as naked as day, putrescence shaped the currency that we speak of, currency that at its root means the running of, by which there are the slave states running on slaves and the late irregulars of it running for their lives, and the while all the currency they know is death, running from it and causing it to others, and that is all they know, and by the end of the end of the atonement that is all they need to know.

Say so as to remember that at the end of the end

Davis fled south and more south till he lived two years in a dark wet dungeon wherein he refused to die till he went free, and he did, and Lee fled south and more south, even though his south was now nothing but a flat catskin map, fleeing broken in the paracardium and mocked by an army of ragtags who one by one deserted him so that he knew now the mind of King Lear and hoped to write Abraham of it till he rode the same horse as he had always ridden, but finally and for the first time in years rode alone on a dusty road so that he knew the mind of Don Quixote and hoped to write Abraham of it, saying to his wife that he wanted now to share his innermost thoughts on war, slavery and the future of blackness in his country with Abraham, and he did not since he could not after Abraham lay as dead as dead gets. Bedridden, he died of a failed heart years after his heart had already been failing. The war spared no one, not generals and scourges, and neither its poets nor philosophers, all scarred, all deadened, bereft of the morals of it when they told the truth each to each.

At all times on all sides the currency became death at the first shot by the first shooter at Sumter, and so all walked with death, its shadow, that valley of, fearful in it, all scarified by enemies as if of a sudden each was given the strength of gods who knew nothing of good and ill, but of power and the whim of wielding it, power the terrible provocateur of slaughter whose onslaught Abraham embraced in the name of the fiercest warrior kings in history, poems and plays. He named them aloud, read of them aloud, spoke aloud with them, dreamt of them, and decided how they decided. And then it was over. Overhear at the end of the atonement the catalogue of sites where spilt blood seeped into soil and rock bed, and into river and creek, the mournful call of the roll of the dead therein across fields more deserted than not till corpses by hundreds and thousands abided there to make these infamous for forever in the national memory of school children no less even more than their elders who would forget that such geography existed where so many fought and died over so much right and wrong, as if adults outgrew penance and redemption the war engraved on the museum doors of the country's touchable facts and artifacts.

From Sumter to Philippi to Rich Mountain to Big Bethel to Manassas (that would be called Bull Run), and so to Balls Bluff and to Hatteras and Roanoke Island (these would be skirmishes of hundreds only dead), and there would come battles the first and second over Fort Fisher years apart, and years before there would arrive the first Kernstorm Battle and the Battle Front Royal, and the Winchester, that battle, and the Seven Days of the Peninsula campaign, and once again at Bull Run (that would be called Manassas), and so on to Chantilly, that battle while the sky stormed thunder, rain and lightning that nearly killed all and sundry without firing a weapon, on and on till Harper's Ferry where three years before the atonement commenced John Brown rode a wagon seated on his own coffin before being hanged for treason (that would be JW Booth concealed in Yankee dress observing among cadets in kepis), then on and on again till South Mountain, that battle, till Antietam, as you know, whereafter Abraham ended the right to enslave Africans in particular, and so to Fredericksburg, Chancellorsville, Gettysburg, as you know, till these led to New Market and Piedmont, and Lynchburg, and so all that would be the Shenandoah Valley of the atonement, and so too after Monocacy, that battle, Winchester (that would be the third such there), on to Fisher's Hill, Mobile Bay, Cedar Creek, Waynesboro (here now the end is nigh, brethren), and that is not to remember those of Cold Harbor, as you know, or Gaines's Mill, as you do not know, or Seven Pines, or Sailor's Creek, the Wilderness, that battle, Appomattox, that battle, that court house with Lee against there Grant, Sheridan, Meade, Ord, and nearby or on the roads at all compass points one hundred fifty thousand blues for as far as the eye could see till that was the end of the end for all time.

The end would be bloody or it would not be, so said both sides of the bridges down rivers and creeks in the nearby who crossed before burning them, an end of that ilk that led Abraham to say to all who would listen, *Rejoice to have done the grief of battles,* so sang old blind Homer, and he spoke to all who would listen gathered on the grasses and mud before the manse that day of days at the end of the end of the atonement, *that those who would have war again should die so as to live in the inferno,* and to all who gathered in the rain under umbrellas or cover of newsprint after mongers of rumor spoke and scribed of the armistice as a false peace he said this, *the abyss is too good for them, its agony not agony enough, for they brought pandemonium with them, neighbors, till there are no demons left in hell.*

The cities of the widest ways in the atonement the armies of the north sacked utterly, as old blind Homer sang of Illium, and so Abraham recalled to memory to all those there who came to hear him in the rain how hundreds and thousands before hundreds of thousands green men and boys in the ways of war stretched face down in dirt one after another across the belief and disbelief that God intended men to own men. *And now it is done,* Abraham intoned so the crowd could hear his words above the growing storm that blew rain and wind into the eyes and ears of the gathered among those who had been strolling home from work or shopping or collecting school children suddenly to see him stepping from the door to address whoever stopped to listen.

Year in year out all had been killing and being killed, dying and being dead, screaming and bleeding sliced, shot and eviscerated at the gizzard, and at the kidney lacerated and inside the bowels split by knife, saber and even spear according to men who learned best where the organs were placed in the interior till all was mourning and being mourned, all the sky and land appeared to all who looked there to be mournful like the planet had been made by gods to appear mournful the way an ancient vase has the look of being looked at. But then the earth stank of this grief, a stench carried by air from one end of the atonement to its other at all compass points, bodies stinking the ground up and the acrid scent of gunpowder stank it too, whether from cannon, rifle or pistol did not matter in the least, and the odor of burning and burnt corpses that undid the odor of corpses rotting under peach, cherry and apple trees. Stench and smoke and the sight day in day out of a jawbone in a cornfield laid to waste or a wristbone or footbone in a wheatfield laid to waste, sights of this ilk, brethren, that were as common as rain and as the rain that set even buried corpses afloat down the streets of the widest cities of the atonement. And now it was done.

Each year after the other this war grew too vivid for those below and above the battle maps till it was too real not to have been meant to be too real, and so there was to the atonement a pathos akin to heroism on the theatrical stage, thereby causing home folk to seek the word in a dictionary in a library so that at supper or on porches or in church meetings under starlight thousands alluded to the pathos the war incited. Now this pervaded the civic streets of thought till horses at a gallop across the wood of a bridge ran informed by pathos, a crack of unexpected distant thunder or the lowing of a heifer rang pathetic in the night's silence, and the orphan sat pathetic on his rump in the dust, and the gimp on his cripple stick, he too looked ripened by pathos for all to see from end to end of the atonement that incited pathos by abusing abusers.

Baneful manslaying, so sang old blind Homer of bodies strewn across beaches and laid against the walls of the old city overrun by invaders at the end of the end of ten years of bloodshed and foolishness at the hearts of men. So said Abraham to the nearby of remnants of what had been warriors months before. Walking, as you know, he addressed them (bones) and articulated them (bones) into the upright warriors they once were who now lay under his boot heels whether buried, half-buried or unburied did not matter in the least, till some walking in silence nearby overheard him say to nobody upright, *nothing like this has been seen before.* And it had not, by any army of any land ancient or modern that had been accounted or written of since nowhere ever had so many died and so many maimed in so little time. It had been as hot as hot gets and as wet as hog fat, and now it was as cold as cold gets and so the fat was colder still as Abraham walked and spoke of the place as an ossuary till the bones he saw were not like other bones scattered and strewn by animals and climate, no, but gathered by unseen hands for all to see so as to remember. To drum taps and a mournful bugle Abraham walked one death ground after another year after year of the atonement, bridging these dead with those dead and those dead with those living, this to reconnoiter the spread and length and depth of the iniquity to gather to his mind the mend it would take to redeem the corrupt heart in the corpse he came to think of as the body of the country. *Hope is born of sorrow,* he remarked to no one in the nearby before he began to speak so as to be heard and not overheard talking to the dead.

At some turn in the field where there should have been headstones, or tombs, or urns pew by pew to house warrior remnants and ashes, all who walked found bones neither strewn nor forgot for as far as the eye could see, but ossein matter harbored there instead, anchored then by the history of lifting God's curse on the country since before it was a country. Know next the storm of tears that those beside him warned against showing to all and sundry, those who wandered aimless as did he till one by one each mourner chanced on a bone stripped bare or bit through months before, and chanced low to the hard soil on a new swarm of buzzless flies out of a porridge of innards and generations of grubs still there then in adamant November. Wandering greater and lesser men among the nameless unmarked dead, Abraham would remark how many dozen fields David the King oversaw among thousands dead, and the decollated members of those dead, and heard the arithmetic of foreskins put by hand inside sacks of sow bladder by boys younger than ten—this to memorize the truest measure of the vanquished armies accounted in books for all time. He walked where the dead once walked who lay forever after spread limb by limb under peach, cherry and apple trees, cadaverene and putrescent veterans who did not know they lay dead and rendered, or torn asunder, or awaiting the mass grave or the bonfire an acre wide that books would make of them on and on decade after decade.

Suffering has united all, black and white, Abraham said walking the killing grounds with his hands clasped at the back of his black greatcoat whether from respect for the dead or fear of them did not matter in the least. Crows he saw, and ravens, strong birds for winter drawn by the sights and sounds of the living among the dead, all those by hundreds walking in silence across the vast battle scene as if tombs erected and headstones grew with this and that man's name carved into its face. Grackles they all saw to hear screech, if not remembered the name of, but blue, black and shiny as flies on the bare limbs of sturdy trees. And so he foresaw the end of the end of the atonement with the walking memory of death after death strewn before him and before all who walked in the nearby, some wearing against their necks the mourning locket of their dead beloved and some wearing against their necks the living locket of their warring beloved not yet dead, not yet wearing the mourning locket of the face of the beloved who would remain as dead as dead gets, the day in day out knowing in the heart where the locket draped that hundreds of thousands had died and more hundreds of thousands were going to die under the same endless sky, cloudless and white in November, after another day of brutal rain as sharp as razors for as far as the eye could see.

Comes here the last of the last of the memento mori, calling to mind, so many said and wrote from the onslaught of saying and scribing, comes now the rugged cross death, the rough cut instrument of the apocalypt's sacrifice that the captain of captains foresaw in himself— atonement and his children's atonement, and that of a half million dead mourned by name or not, and of more unmourned and unnamed, and millions destitute and displaced into the next century white and black alike. Make no mistake, brethren, this was the death of the heart of the country, the ruptured pericardium, even if by a bullet in the neck (that would be JW Booth in the barn on fire) and by a bullet inside the brain from occiput to dura and the left latter cerebrum come to rest in the anterior striatum (that would be the dying before dead Abraham), and yet even so there lay across the scape of the country thousands of dead to come, and therein millions of vermin burrowed into the bellies of them against the cold, frost and winds of winter, some birthing litters inside this and that human carcass, birthing squirrels, mice and such like, and this is another lesson of war to memorize, so sang old blind Homer thousands and thousands of years of that war fought before this other war got fought. Now that does not speak to the freezing upright who burrowed into the moribund flesh of the new dead, cutting their innards open to warm frostbit fingers and toes till steam rose skyward like smoke from a campfire or from a burning citadel, and of these thousands warming themselves some keeled over dead from gases the dead issued or from blood poison boring into cuts and broke scabs of the living trying to go on doing it no less enrapt than scavenging fowl by the sight of corpses against which they huddled from one end of the battleground to the other end of another. There was suffering, brethren, and the will to inflict it. That is all there is to know and all you need to know.

Seven lifted him by arms and hands till they carried him as high as their belts across the damp cool night toward the lantern light swinging distant while a distant voice called *Bring him here,* and so they did, in silence as if not to disturb the dying man's dying, after which most said to the look of him gathered by his disciples that he was more great dying than living, that he had looked for years as though he waited to be dying, if not dead, just as each soldier who lay dying in this and that cornfield, wheatfield or cottonfield knew more of life dying than living it, those hardly known and unfit to do either, those known only by their deaths. Neighbors mourned them who never spoke to them and mourned anybody anywhere who died for the atonement, a stranger even felled by a bullet to the mouth that they knew only this of, or one who died by saber across the belly who they knew of a sudden for an instant and mourned.

They mourned too those who returned alive without this and that limb so that they remembered seeing him or them with it or them that went missing till he and them spent the rest of life as the legless soldier, the armless soldier, the blind soldier, the man without a hand whom they had known since he and they were born. They mourned that they remembered how boys and men were before they were not anymore, but that was not the same mourning as mourning Abraham on his back brain shot in the arms and hands of seven sliding in mud and pig dung across the darkness to the lantern light that death driven day carrying him to the bed on the second floor no less, the farthest back room no less, that would be his Mt. Nebo to the nearby Jordan that Moses could not cross. Make no mistake, in thousands there that night gods haunted the street scenes that witnessed the rise of spirits as true as rumors of war yet to come, and so mothers, sisters and wives wailed and prayed or sang till all was done, as you know, whereas for the dying man there were no more mothers, sisters and wives writing or pleading or cursing him day in day out over the fate of a corpse unburied or unknown, or a coward doomed for his cowardice, or for the missing presumed dead who was neither, no, but as far west as west went, who knew day in day out where he was, and that was no more at war. He did not know the worry, weeping and dread of annihilation to come now that he lay annihilated, knowing if anything other than attic scenes of carnage and the infernal fate of afterlife that his end had at last been staged, that mercifully he was not Lazarus and he would not have the last word.

If anything, he saw Mt. Nebo in Moab where from a distance (that would be the coma) Abraham could behold but not enter the future of the land redeemed, Canaan of the Jerusalem promised to him and his brethren from the written word that birthed the nation he bled dry. He chased the monstrous boar from one end of the land to the other, from the eastern peninsula of the Carolinas and all besides to west of there at Shiloh, Stone River, Vicksburg, Chickamaugua, and all else besides, on and on so as to remember Pea Ridge, Prairie Grove, Wilson's Creek till he slew the giant once forever, stripping its bristles and tusks for all to see whenever they looked across the face of the New Caledonia.

It was the true end of the end of him that he lay near purple at the head, neck and shoulders, and yet as stiff as marble overwatched by then a half dozen surgeons anxious to decorticate his skull so as to retrieve for memory a killing lead ball the size of a toddler's thumb, as you know, a dull hard node no longer round. Look, there, where the fingers point, that is the cause of death, and there opens the hole that incited the bullet to travel the matter of the brain till it made the victim a sleeper in the forever of words and more words and the images they incite, the true nowhere of all that passes.

I die with no flambeaus nor flowers, no grieving mother or Pap or dog or sister who run off with her Gommorah, with only about me the moles and gophers of my undoing by God and God's nature, dogs none like my dog packed together like a wolf den beside an elm yonder waiting for me or another or another to give them the corpse of us to eat off of, make of my or another's belly and chest a nosebag like I harnessed to a mare's muzzle, and however it comes after I be dead from a flaming splint of rail tie or roof tin hot as a sun, if not hobnails explosive from a shell that cleared treetops a half mile off, if not by any of these that therefore I won't know kilt me, I know this, that my end won't be finding itself remembered by a picture plate posed behind the light of a shop window, no, nor looked at by the resurrection men come to sell my death mask to my beloveds, and yet I do not know but that there ever has been the sacred feel to a body in its death rest, a corpse you believe can be raised at the end of time as surely as you wait to see the lost beloved open her eyes there in the box or against the earth where the box goes for forever so that that is what death means till you're doing the dying, till the quiet of a sudden like the quiet of me and my nearby here now feels like the dead wait for the dead to meet them or that the dead bury the dead, shadow soldiers therefore, or soldier souls carried by the dead themselves from one end of the battlefield to another where there is console among the dead and gone, past bothering the scared monkey in me that kilt who I kilt, orphaned thereby who I orphaned, and widowed who I widowed, left behind a flea afflicted mongrel under a porch waiting to its own death for the dead man laying not two leg lengths yonder me, his boot heels to my one, it that I can still sense, his innard no more bleeding and ripped from the chewing and tearing of what I couldn't see in the dark, eated like kin to me when I listened though he were alive to me the first only time that I shot him dead, estrange and kin both in that one only time of knowing him, like us joined in our misery even after he took up the space nearest me when I had no more of a foot than a fish since it were a foot I couldn't walk by, more a stump like a log than a paw even, none by which God could let me lift up by the flat of to flee here for there, wherever in the gloaming that be, but into the woods deeper, where the horseflies come for you in hundreds, them that now I couldn't run from, no, but still no less coming to the glory of war's end, flight of that ilk, if only in the name of a nameless god not of my making   I be walking out of this holler dead, the ghost of myself drifting the true nowhere where comrades abide, and them I kilt abide, if abide is the word, calm as tombstones I am persuaded, like as corpses in coffins, so I am reconciled, but there is this, that I did not backshoot him, and that is the good news, him, there, where the pointing stops and his boots begun

All that Rathbone scribbles between darkness and dawn in the presence of his dead sister, or in the presence of her disembodied voice in the inmost cavern of his ears, or in the presence only of voices inside the walls of his surround, or in the presence only of the mournful cello's exhale out of the gramophone's great tulip—all these interiors informing his derangement he inscribes over and over on sheet after sheet of soft yellow paper that blots the line of his pen into a ribbon from a sheaf of such a foot high. *I know what holds the world together,* writes Rathbone night in night out year after year before sending the thought into the eternity of an angry fire that burns offerings at the first crow of a morning cock whenever there is a sacred sacrifice to stage, and when is there not? Before he remembers nothing that he wrote, or saw, or heard of the night ending—since here comes light from the window of the world at last—Rathbone thinks the thought's answer as it flashes, waxes blue and vanishes. *I know what holds the world together.* Crossing the room with speed and determination past the bloodied bare breasts of his sister's corpse on the carpet, Rathbone beholds her death staged hour after hour night after night decade after decade till her soul vanishes again and again during a dawn without a sun to show for it. In each recognition of her death and disappearance day after night year in year out till the end of the end Rathbone tears the page by half before sailing it to the flame in the fireplace where the sentence flashes black as it flies with the draft of the chimney, the same flame by which souls go and come, the same flame that burnt them to death in the village square for hundreds of years hundreds of years ago.

Of these days exacted on the other side of Rathbone's window into frames no larger any than a self portrait, he beholds over and over again and again that such battle as this his last waged war most on the inner man (that would be eating victuals) and so the army suffered dysentery and dropsy, man by man by thousands fleeing the city's skirts to hide among sleeping chokeberry shrubs and viburnum bushes, honeysuckle too, as if to unearth something of nature to cure their stomachs or to conceal their sickness where they lay underbrush like dogs as sick as dogs, mouths down and pants down into the mud, sludge and their own wormy dung beyond the trumpet's futile peal or the fruitless drumbeat of the Eastern theatre's nowhere of that time and that place. None among thousands could attend to his inner man, as you know, or those that could found flybone foods that lost them their accounts and so these too fell to hands and to knees, these too like dogs as sick as dogs, ending all for the Blues, all cold coffee, or pegged out whether in songs to heaven or in silence did not matter in the least. Too sick to fight they lay dead or dying from one end of the field to the other. *I survived visibly unharmed,* Rathbone informed his sons when he knew them to be his sons and they were too young to know why he informed them.

Someone said that someone shot a bull—look there, beyond the musket smoke, and all among them looked into the gloaming, the Grays who shot and the starving or ill Blues who witnessed from afar—and that bull shot in the meadow of snow sank by fetlock into it, and then to the brisket it leaned down, and all watched on either side as the dewlap sank, and the poll of the creature, and withers of it dropped to the snow, so recited a butcher among the gathered, and the barrel followed down, he told them, then the stifle followed down, he told them, before hock and claw and hoof followed down to the ground below the snow. After this it was skinned, gutted and quartered till the bull lay sere and headless. The last breakfast for the Union dead to come, it was hardtack Rathbone in dressing gown, slippers and scarf memorizes from the vastness of his window into that gloaming there, where he points one finger, so-called hardtack, or the skin of Jesus put upon the soldier's tongue before dying, but in their rifle pits and shebangs against the cold of frozen greatcoats and tarps the fires drew cats, dogs, rats, and hogs too till all the starving huddled together to share or to be shared and to kill or to be killed. Union dead to come ate rabid rats raw and rabid rats ate Union dead to come there in the coldest days of winter. Here too Rathbone suffered no scratch visible anywhere on his flesh despite battling thrice, as you know, and yet saw no further action in the atonement, commencing rather nightmares, shakes and dizzies of the brain, and then the hypos of limbs and innards, enduring in himself the revolt against war in silence other than to ask of his sister and of his sister's circle, and to ask of his mother and of his mother's circle, *Where is the hill worth dying on?*

Now this other whom you see, where I am pointing, passed his life whole and entire waiting to be killed by a stranger from twenty paces distant on the far side of the fire that burnt the stable wherein he concealed himself, his mare and his red notebook. JWBooth in his grave now forty-six years.

Here in his asylum Rathbone wears about his neck a mourning locket bearing the face of his sister by half, she who became his wife, birthed his children and in his madness after her death became sister only again, became in death mother to his nephews and a niece, and it is the portrait of her dead face that he sees when he opens it, and he opens it to remind himself not only that she is dead, but that he did not save her as he should have, and this reminds him that he could not save her husband either from death, and so he saved neither his sister by half nor her husband anymore than he saved the commander of the atonement from death decades and decades before. With his ravaged arm he exhibits to any who will look the locket, its contents, the wall of drawings from nature, the sturdy Victrola, his crepitating wall of bound volumes, a ladder attached to shelves as tall as the ceiling for retrieving this before that from the highest lane of his literature. Rathbone begs forgiveness therefore, saying to any who will listen, *It isn't that the arm is useless, it just isn't useful.* Since morning has come wherein Clara is interred once more Rathbone listens to violins out of his gramophone because voices inside his walls speak at a high register that elicits sunrise, even though the sun neither rises nor sets, but violin notes and chords becalm the singers inside the walls, a dawn chorus therefore of lilting women's voices on three sides in each of his two rooms—one for sleeping, one for sitting, as you know—each no less for overhearing voices, music and for Rathbone to declaim what he declaims as would an actor on a stage with an audience to attend.

At the bottom of the garden, St. Mary's Cathedral, St. Michael's Church, Benedictine monastery, village H., domain H., before the stone bearing his sister's name, therefore his wife's name, therefore his son's mother's name, and his other son's mother's name, and so his daughter's name, Rathbone opens his palm to invite butterflies of snow into them that melt when they touch his glove. Now there is this, that Clara's grave remains as eventful whether Clara's coffin fills it or does not, since Clara's corpse resides inside whether Clara's corpse does or does not, and when it is an impenetrable crust of nut brown earth impervious to touch that Rathbone lays hands on, there, where her heart should be or would have been the day she died, and would have been beating during her life, it does not matter in the least since day in day out she waits to wake and to rise. Where fingers fail to breach the cold ground, clawing no less for that so as to vigil the coffin and the desiccation inside, yes, to sit beside the corpse even if it be nothing other than bone or nothing other than the marrow of bone, *vigil* of that ilk, Rathbone day after day expects the worst of her. At the tolling of bells in the steeple, Rathbone observes worshippers observe him from thirty yards distant as they enter the steps to the cathedral doors higher than three men, bells ringing them to Mass yet again to celebrate yet again the murder of the host of hosts, yet again the promise of apocalypse that arrives for the Christ and the Christ alone.

He lay driven on his back till breathless rank horses delivered him to a surgeon to sew back into him the muscle and tissues of his killed arm, and so rumbling across bricks and stones and flooded roads of mud and dung he beheld numberless corpses afloat across the city while mothers and crones moaned hymns to heaven from their knees on the earth pointing to that immense storm cloud, there, where God's finger curses them and dooms them to a night so long and dark that each of them might as well be blind, that each of them to each might as well be a stranger among strangers, sightless and sick at heart. Rathbone gathers his scarf closer to his throat to atone for *those who neither save nor don't save those that they should save, and all that they could save.* Rathbone, wrong man in the wrong place, who was not to be Abraham's guest, who was not to be in Abraham's box, who was not to be inside the theatre, who was not born to war, not born to save anybody from anybody, atones day in day out for his failures to save those he should have saved if he could have saved them one after another after another. He saved none.

The victim began to turn his head, as if drawn to a sound or sensed movement behind him so that the soft lead bullet entered his skull behind the left ear, as you know, and his widow said that only before she heard the shot fired her husband had concealed his face either to laugh in the privacy of his hands or to escape the laughter around him since of that time then and there he thought nothing risible. Count this real, that a certain order of memory recurred among those who saw what they saw before the murder, and it remembered Abraham spending much of the play buried inside his hands, neither laughing nor not laughing, but instead neither here nor there, instead elsewhere in his mind, either where he had no right to laugh or even to smile, or that he saw over and over this and that of the war he had waged to save the country from itself and its iniquity. After the end of the end many said and many wrote that for years he met no one's eyes with his own and averted his gaze from those whose gaze met his eyes first so that some said guilt wore in his eyes as it wrote on his face and as it wrote his dreams and his sleeplessness.

Mary in her tomb now twenty-nine years.

And Rathbone wonders *what will happen to my rooms after I am dead, and what will happen to my library, and to my drawings, and to my recordings unless these will be immolated in the village square as I will be immolated there. After my keeper sweeps away dust cows and the bones of rats, and washes on hands and knees the grime of thirty years of boots and slippers, and of cinders crushed under heel and toe—who will replace me? Which of the world's deplorables will come to occupy the cave of my affliction, and whose souls will visit him, and will you, my sister, visit him night after night as you visit me, and will the walls crepitate as my walls crepitate and conspire?*

If he could have saved him he would have saved him, and if he could have seen sooner to save him he would have saved him, and if he had seen the door open sooner than he saw it open he could have saved him, and if the door had opened left instead of right he could have sooner seen and could have saved him because he should have saved him if he could have, and if he would have seen the intruder decades later he would have saved his sister or if he had heard the intruder before seeing him he would have saved her so that if the intruder had not stabbed him six times he might have saved his sister from being stabbed thrice and from being shot once into her breast by a bullet no larger than a toddler's thumb, as he would have saved Abraham from a bullet no larger than a toddler's thumb, and so decades later he should have suspected intruders with their intents and their deadly weapons. If he had saved his sister he might have saved his sister's husband so that it might have been the intruder who lay dead on the bedroom carpet instead of his sister and her husband one beside the other bleeding to death while he, Rathbone, lay on the polished wood floor bleeding to death too, but who instead of becoming dead for once and all wore six scars across his chest and belly the rest of his life (that would be twenty-eight years) as he wore a scar from shoulder to elbow the rest of his life after the first murder he failed to prevent (that would be forty-six years) since twice in his lifetime he was stabbed by madmen. *Who would have thought Clara had so much blood inside her,* Rathbone remarked to the court, its jury and an audience of hundreds at his trial for her murder.

Lift the scarred suitcase so as to leave Rathbone to his dying, wait till the last bell to toll tolls its last before departing, till all the congregants have congregated inside the walls of the cathedral, look before leaving at the madness decades and decades old, and only then ease out of the rooms—one for sitting, one for sleeping—as an organ made by the Dutch incites singers to sing this and that hymn to the apocalypt who year in year out threatens to appear, and yet does not. Flee from here and from now till no voice speaks, where any voice would tremble the ground till rocks fall from high places so that every being in the voice's surround would fall on all fours as a large black, shaggy, frothing dog held to the skin of the earth by sickness and by God's need of its death. *I do not need to believe in God for God to exist,* said Abraham to all who would listen. As if the worst that could befall him has befallen him, Rathbone studies the other side of the vast mosaic of windows, each frame no larger than a self-portrait or a mirror to slice his throat by.

I began to observe that fewer and fewer of the afflicted were running and jumping among flowers and shrubs, fewer each year laughing or slobbering or screaming, and then one day I saw an afflicted sitting beside my sister's grave speaking to the soil, addressing the mushrooms of it. After that, I saw no more madmen here.

Clara in her grave twenty-eight years.

All you sinners, hear you this, that at the end of the end, when he lay as dead as dead gets without yet dead, his body carried by seven among soldiers and doctors, as you know, his body shook from jawbone to foot so that these same seven gripped Abraham's limbs tighter to still the shivers that seized him on and on the length of the drear journey from theatre to deathbed. No strength of hand or arm muscle among them could calm the rattle and shake till his mind descended into the nine-hour sleep of dreams he dreaded night after night decade after decade in and out of war, and then all of him grew still. That is what there was to know at the end of the end till at the end of his end Rathbone remembered all that his madness allowed, and so as he lay dying in his time in his turn he asked his keeper of near five decades—*Why do spirits still visit me?*

Abraham, naked and jagged abed in Rathbone's room, the one for sleeping, twenty-seven years.